DARKNESS
FOR THE BASTARDS
OF PIZZOFALCONE

Maurizio de Giovanni

DARKNESS
FOR THE BASTARDS
OF PIZZOFALCONE

Translated from the Italian
by Antony Shugaar

Europa
editions

Europa Editions
214 West 29th Street
New York, N.Y. 10001
www.europaeditions.com
info@europaeditions.com

Copyright © 2013 Giulio Einaudi Editore SpA, Torino
This edition published in arrangement
with Thesis Contents srl and book @ literary agency
First Publication 2016 by Europa Editions

Translation by Antony Shugaar
Original title: *Buio per i bastardi di Pizzofalcone*
Translation copyright © 2016 by Europa Editions

Library of Congress Cataloging in Publication Data is available
ISBN 978-1-60945-337-4

de Giovanni, Maurizio
Darkness for the Bastards of Pizzofalcone

Book design and cover illustration by Emanuele Ragnisco
www.mekkanografici.com

Prepress by Grafica Punto Print – Rome

Printed in the USA

Paola.
All the light I have

DARKNESS
FOR THE BASTARDS
OF PIZZOFALCONE

I

B atman.
Baaatmaaan
The whisper in the dark, in the dank smell, amidst all the
dust.

Batman.

The whoosh of a cape, slicing through the air in front of
Dodo's face.

Batman.

Dodo can see it because of the darkness. It's darker than the
night, darker than the cubbyhole in his bedroom, the one with the
door that never quite shuts and often swings back open with a creak.

His bedroom, warm. His bedroom, with the Avengers poster,
with his album collections and his action figure collections on a
shelf. Arranged by size and story, so that when the housekeeper
dusts them, he has to put them all back where they belong. At
the thought of his room, of the Avengers and the action figures,
tears well up and Dodo swallows them.

Dark in here. The dark is always full of noises. The dark is
never quiet for long.

Every night, in his faraway room, Dodo waits for Mamma's
door to close and then pulls out the little nightlight from when
he was three. No one knows about his little nightlight, the kind
that you plug right into the wall, that emits just a faint glow, a
glow you can hardly even call light.

How I wish I could be in my room, right now. Even if the
cubbyhole door won't stay closed.

Dodo chokes back his tears and jerks at a rustling from the far corner. He couldn't even say how big this place is. He's certainly not about to go exploring.

Batman, he calls as he tightens his sweaty little hand around the action figure. It's a good thing I brought you with me to school this morning. Even if they scold me, even if they tell me I'm not supposed to bring toys to school because now I'm a big boy, I'm almost ten. You and I know it though, that you're not a toy. You're a hero.

When I talk to Papà about it that's what we always say, right? That you're the greatest superhero of them all. That you're the best there is, the strongest. Papà explained it to me, when I was little and we still lived together, when he'd give me piggyback rides and tell me: You're my little king, see, and I'm your giant, I'll take you wherever you want.

Papà explained to me why you're the best hero of them all: It's because you don't have superpowers.

Everyone's great at beating the bad guys if they know how to fly, or if they have superstrength, or eyes that shoot green rays. It's easy that way.

But you, Batman, you're just an ordinary man. But you're brave and you're smart. Do the others fly? Then you invent rockets that fit into your utility belt, or you shoot ropes up onto the tops of tall buildings and climb right up the side. Can the others run at superspeed? Then you have the Batmobile, which runs even faster. You're a hero among heroes, Batman. Because you have the most superpowerful superpower there is: courage. You're like my papà.

I never told Papà that I pull the nightlight out of my drawer at night. I don't want him to think that I'm not courageous. The problem is that I'm still kind of a little kid, but everyone tells me that I look like my papà, and he's big and strong.

You know, Batman, even if you're a hero and it seems as if you're not afraid of anything, I know that, in this big dark room where they tossed us after taking us, even you are just a little bit afraid. I am, too, a little; but just a little. Still, we don't need to worry, because my papà's going to come get us out of here.

Fly, Batman, fly. You're the dark knight, master of the shadows. You're not afraid of the dark, and I can hold onto you as you fly. Fly.

A fist slams against sheet metal, a terrible echoing crash that deafens, blinds, stops the blood. The action figure falls to the floor, the plastic made slippery by the sweaty hand no longer able to grip.

Dodo shrieks in terror, starts, and recoils; then, desperate, he feels around on the ground with both hands: dust, sharp pebbles, gravel, crumpled paper. He finds the action figure, picks it up, and holds it to his face, his cheek streaked with sudden tears. Outside, a roar reverberates, a command barked in a language he doesn't understand.

He crouches in a corner; his back, under his shirt, scratched by the wall; his heart pounding in his ears as if it wants to run away.

Batman, Batman, don't worry. My papà will come and get us. Because he's my giant, and I'm his little king.

II

The minute he peeked through the door into the communal office, the expression on Corporal Marco Aragona's face changed.

"There, I knew it. It's 8:29 A.M. and you're all here already. Don't any of you have lives? And yet you do have homes and families, at least some of you: How can it be that no matter how early in the morning I get here, I always find you guys?"

It had become something of a running joke, Aragona's all but daily habit of showing up in the office just a couple of minutes before the scheduled start of the day and noting, disappointedly, the presence of every member of the Pizzofalcone precinct house's investigative team, already sitting at their desks.

Deputy Captain Giorgio Pisanelli broke off reading a police report and shot him an amused glance over his bifocals.

"One more minute and you'd have been late for work, Arago'. And we might have been duty-bound to write you up."

The junior officer sat down at his desk and swept off his blue-tinted glasses with a well-rehearsed gesture:

"Mr. President, if I hadn't come in talking you wouldn't have even noticed I was here. Old age is a cruel master . . ." The oldest and the youngest member of the team liked to poke regular fun at each other, the former in the tone of a teacher addressing a dimwitted student, the latter harping on senile dementia. "Plus, what fun do you get out of being in here when it's so beautiful outside? You're going to have to explain that to me one of these days."

Peeking her head out from behind her computer screen, Ottavia Calabrese replied: "But if there's no murder by eight in the morning, that doesn't mean we can all just go have ourselves a good time, don't you agree, Aragona? And stop tormenting Pisanelli with this habit of calling him President . . . That's the last thing his ego needs."

"You listen to me, Ottavia: You're just jealous, pure and simple. You wish someone would call you Madame President. But it'll never happen: You are now and will always be our den mother. And have you taken a good look at Pisanelli? Don't you see the resemblance? Plus his first name is Giorgio too, and they're both about the same age." With a nod, Aragona indicated the framed portrait hanging on the wall of the detectives' bullpen, the only decorative feature amidst the pallid green of that nondescript and desolate room that contained practically their entire lives. Then, scratching the clean-shaven, sunlamped chest on display under his flower-print shirt, the three top buttons of which had been left open, he turned theatrically to Pisanelli. "Go ahead and confess, Mr. President: To better serve your country you've infiltrated the Bastards of Pizzofalcone."

Ottavia relinquished her right of rebuttal and vanished behind her computer. By mentioning the Bastards, Aragona had summoned the spectre of the unpleasant fiasco that had led to that team of lawmen becoming what they were today. Right down to their nicknames. If the city's entire police force referred to them by using a collective insult, they certainly had good cause. Four police detectives in that precinct had been caught redhanded dealing cocaine, and Ottavia, with Pisanelli, had been an eyewitness to the sordid affair. Only the two of them had survived. Internal Affairs had turned their lives inside out as if they'd been a pair of socks, and it had taken the hand of God to persuade those feral beasts that the two of them had had nothing to do with the crooked cops. IA had gone so far as to threaten to shut down the precinct entirely. The four renegade cops, now universally referred to as the Bastards of Pizzofalcone, had been replaced. But the mark of shame remained. And once the investigation had been closed, everyone had continued to use that name for the refurbished precinct and its replacement crew. Ottavia still couldn't quite wrap her head around it.

But the new squad, cobbled together from discards of all shapes and sizes from the four corners of the city, faced with the dilemma of whether to meekly accept the insult or fight back, had chosen to take it as a badge of pride. To the collective nickname they'd started to attach individual ones. Because "remarkable people, the ones who wind up in the spotlight for whatever reason, always have nicknames," as Aragona had ventured one day. Ottavia hadn't been able to stifle a laugh. Yes, she liked that one. And she hadn't minded that freshly coined Den Mother either, in spite of its mocking edge. She'd thought about objecting, but then she'd decided that that's actually what she was, their den mother. She never missed a trick, even tucked away behind her beloved computer, and every time they needed something, they all turned to her. As if to a den mother. And after all, she *was* something of a den mother in real life, what with her son. She was the only woman on the squad who had a child.

"What about the Chinaman, where's he? At least he hasn't come in yet this morning."

This time Marco Aragona had set his sights on Lieutenant Giuseppe Lojacono, the man who'd caught the Crocodile; he'd been dubbed "the Chinaman" because of his Asian features.

"Not only is he already here," Ottavia, ever fastidious, informed him, "he's already on the job. A call came in on a burglary around 7:10 this morning, and he went out."

Aragona was stunned: "At 7:10? What's he doing, sleeping in the office?"

"It wouldn't just be *him* doing the sleeping; if anything, it would be *them*. Alex was here too, they went out together."

Alex Di Nardo, the other woman on the investigative team, looked at first glance like a slender, delicate young woman, but she was a crack shot, capable of picking off a fly at thirty yards. She went to the firing range twice a week: what else could they call her if not Calamity? "That way everyone knows just how afraid of her they need to be," Aragona had said one morning. Just now, Corporal Aragona was making a show of combing his hair, checking the results in a hand mirror. He had an Elvis-style pompadour that added a good inch to his height, which was decidedly not that of a basketball player; the hairdo was also a useful way of concealing a bald spot at the very top of his head that was making good on its threat to grow larger.

"What about our fearless leader, Otta'? No need to say a word, he's already in, too, isn't he?"

As he said that, Aragona had glanced pointedly at the half-closed door of the adjoining room: the office of Commissario Gigi Palma. Then he turned with mocking sarcasm to Francesco Romano, the last resident of the detectives' office, who had been barricaded behind his computer the whole time, in complete silence. He was a huge man, broad-shouldered, with a bull neck and a surly expression that advised against starting down any dangerous lines of inquiry. At least it advised the ordinary questioner; it had no effect on Marco Aragona, who was irrepressible that morning:

"Hey there, Hulk! You got your nickname at your old precinct, didn't you? Look out, now he's going to lose his temper, turn lime green, and rip his shirt to pieces . . ."

Romano grumbled darkly: "What would you say if I ripped your shirt to pieces instead? It is, by the way, a horrible piece of clothing."

"Look I paid more for this shirt than all your raggedy wardrobes are worth put together. It's just that you're an old-fashioned hick who doesn't understand real fashion. And it's precisely because I dress casually that I don't look like a cop, while people can smell you pigs coming from a mile away. By the way, while we're on the subject of nicknames, mine ought to be Serpico, because I'm the spitting image, I mean the exact spitting image, of Al Pacino."

Romano snorted: "Al Cappuccino they ought to call you, with that hairdo. If I were you, I'd try to follow that old saying about how the less you talk, the less bullshit you spout. It's true, you don't look like a cop: You look like a standup comedian, the kind still doing open mics."

Aragona glared at him, offended: "No two ways about it, you're past your sell-by date. You don't understand that the profession is evolving, and cops like you are going to wind up like the dinosaurs: long-extinct fossils. Why, did you know that . . ."

The phone rang.

III

Commissario Luigi Palma looked up from the papers on the desk in front of him and tried to catch the voices that reached him through the door he'd left ajar.

His rule had always been never to shut himself up in his office. He wanted his coworkers to feel free to come in and talk to him whenever they needed to; but here, in Pizzofalcone, one of his two doors gave onto the large room that he had decided to convert from a cafeteria into a shared office for the investigative squad, and he worried that some might think he was trying to keep an eye on them. That would achieve the opposite effect: Instead of a first among equals, a sort of older brother whose job it was to supervise investigative activity, rather than to give orders, he would become a mistrustful warden looking to eavesdrop on their conversations.

Any attitude could easily be misunderstood. He was well aware that this wasn't going to be easy; even the chief of police, in their last conversation before assigning him the post, had all but tried to talk Palma out of taking the job. Palma was on his way up, and sooner or later a cushier, more prestigious position would open up somewhere, and he'd have a chance to make the most of his considerable abilities.

But Palma had never liked things easy and, truth be told, he didn't have a lot to lose. The chief of police, though, had no way of knowing that.

Palma was much less interested in his career than one might have imagined by looking at the absolute commitment he lavished on his work. The truth was simple: He had nothing else in his life.

He'd lost both parents a few years ago, first his mother, shortly thereafter his father. They were elderly; Palma thought of himself as "the son of old parents" since he'd been born when his father was in his fififtes and his mother in her forties. His older brother had Down syndrome and had died at the age of twenty, leaving a crater of calm grief in the hearts of his kin that would stay with them for the rest of their lives. Palma wanted children of his own, but the woman he'd married didn't; she was consumed by her work as a doctor, which left no room for anything else. And so, over time, though neither had wanted it to happen, a deep abyss had carved itself between them, and it had been a relief for them both when they had decided first to separate and, later, to divorce.

At that point, Palma had taken a look around. A gentle, affectionate, effusive man who no longer had a birth family, and hadn't created one of his own. Man proposes, fate disposes.

Since he had a natural gift and inclination for running groups, in the end, his job had become his family. And inevitably that had been recognized, which resulted in his serving as deputy captain in a quiet precinct in a residential district where, after his superior officer had taken seriously ill, he'd had a chance to shine as the youngest and most dynamic official in the city's police department.

When his superior officer, the commissario, had resigned to fight his last battle, Palma expected to be promoted to the now empty office; and that's what his men—many of them his seniors—would have wanted; they all valued his sincerity and modesty. But what's logical and right is so rarely done in this world and a woman with more prestigious credentials and stronger political support in Rome had arrived from another city.

It was neither anger nor envy that had prompted him to

leave after that. Quite simply, he knew it would be impossible to keep the precinct running efficiently. He needed to step aside: If he had stayed on, his men would have defied the authority of their new commanding officer and continued to turn to him for help, since he knew the district, the men, and the balance of power in the precinct.

It was then that the affair of the Bastards of Pizzofalcone had gone down, delivering a true body blow to the public image of the local police. Like so many of his colleagues who battled from dawn till dusk, with hard work and great pain, against the decay of life on the streets and in the *vicoli*, largely at the hands of their own inhabitants, Palma had been disgusted, had felt immense rage. But when he learned that the chief of police intended to shut down the precinct entirely, admitting de facto defeat, he rebelled against the idea.

And he asked to take over command of the precinct himself.

An impulsive gesture, no doubt. And a risky one, for sure. But also a way out of the stagnant pond his career—and his life, in a way—had become. A new place, a new situation. And a new group. Something like a new family.

The human resources that had been assigned to him, at least on paper, didn't leave much hope for success. The four bastards, dismissed for conspiring to run a grim drug-dealing ring, had been replaced by new bastards, stray dogs whose original precincts had been all too eager to get rid of them: the hamfisted Aragona, protected by nepotism, tin-eared and offensive, intrusive and rude; the enigmatic Di Nardo, who'd fired her handgun inside her old station house; the silent Romano, subject to outbursts of rage during which he wrapped his powerful hands around the throats of suspects and colleagues alike. And Lojacono? The Sicilian known as "the Chinaman" for his strange almond-shaped eyes? No, he wasn't a reject, Palma had actually requested him. Not that Di Vincenzo, Lojacono's previous boss, hadn't been delighted to be free of him: the mark of infamy that the Chinaman carried with him, that of a transfer away from his home territory because of allegations made, though never proved, by a Mafia turncoat about Lojacono's collusion with organized crime, was exactly the kind that could never be forgiven in law enforcement circles. But Palma had watched Lojacono in action during the hunt for the Crocodile, a serial killer who had terrorized the city months before, and had clearly recognized Lojacono's talent, his fury, his emotional involvement: Those were qualities he sought in his investigators, the things that were needed to succeed in that profession.

Even the two staff members who had survived the purge carried out by the internal affairs commission had proven to be anything but burdens.

The elderly deputy captain Pisanelli knew everything there was to know about the precinct where he was born and where he'd worked his whole life. He was an honest and empathetic man, a source of solid and extensive information that helped to make up for the fact that nearly all the others were pretty much new to the place. If not for his unfortunate obsession with a series of suspicious suicides, he would have been an ideal assistant.

As for Ottavia, at first he'd wondered whether he ought to deploy her in the field, working investigations; then he'd come to understand just how invaluable she was as support staff. The intelligence she managed to cull from the web was at least as valuable as her colleagues' legwork out in the *vicoli* and streets of the city, if not more so. She saved them hours and hours of work by instantly assembling mountains of information that would otherwise have cost a tremendous effort to obtain.

Certainly, Palma had to admit to himself, as he listened to the woman laughing at Aragona's nonsense, the knowledge that she was right there, in the next room, warmed his heart.

He was far too experienced to fail to sense the danger: Nothing good could come when the simple pleasure of working together transformed itself into something different. He was there to supervise a team of police officers, to save the precinct and make it work efficiently; she was there to perform important tasks. It would be unforgivable for either to assign ulterior motives to the other's appearance in the office each morning. Moreover, while he might be unattached, she was married and had a son, a son who was afflicted with autism.

And after all, he might be fooling himself. Maybe those smiles, that solicitous care, the low tone of voice she used only when she spoke to him, were all just figments of his imagination: He was seeing and hearing what he wanted to see and hear. Maybe it was just his own desire playing tricks on him. Too many nights spent sleeping on his office couch, avoiding the messy studio apartment that he didn't have the heart to call home; too many Sundays spent tossing back beers in front of the television, not even watching the screen; too many memories, by now so faded that he was actually afraid he might have made them up in order to fill a vast emptiness.

It wasn't sex that he was yearning for; he'd always thought sex without feeling was meaningless. When he met up with his few friends, old classmates who stubbornly insisted on getting together every couple of months, he stoically bore their mockery; in their opinion he'd slowly become just like their old Religious Studies professor, preaching the joys of the meditative life to a group of pimply and perennially horny teenagers. But Palma wasn't looking for female company with no strings attached. He wanted to assuage his loneliness; another man's wife or girlfriend, with her own family, her own life, her own problems, could hardly do that.

Those excellent reasons, however, smashed themselves up against the reality of Ottavia's face when she got to the office every morning, before all the others. And he lost the battle, miserably, fracturing himself into a thousand specks of subtle pleasure. What harm is there, his subconscious argued, if, after all, nothing is going to happen? If you don't declare yourself, if you don't go for her, if you don't let her think that your interest is any more than merely professional? He knew that he was lying to himself, but he had no wish to erect excessive defenses around himself; come to think of it, he wouldn't have even known how.

He listened to her voice as she answered the phone, smiling at the warm sounds to which he was quickly becoming accustomed.

Then he stopped smiling.

IV

In the morning, the police go on their rounds of burglaries, Lojacono was thinking to himself as he climbed the steep *vicolo*, surrounded by noisy shop assistants putting out merchandise for sale on the street, feral mopeds in search of unlikely routes, and sleepy kids with backpacks slung over their shoulders. Apartment burglaries float to the surface only when the sun rises, washed up by the night onto the shores of dawning consciousness, when the victim of the burglary discovers his or her new condition, and awakens to a nightmare.

Burglary, Lojacono mused, is a very particular crime. It's a rape of one's sense of security, the brusque revelation that it's not enough to lock the front door to keep out the violence of a world seething with pain and fear. It's the police blotter dumped right at your doorstep, yes, yours, even if you've done nothing wrong, even if you might have believed yourself exempt from such grotesqueries, invulnerable to crime. It's the end of tranquility, the event that gives one last violent shove to the orderly world you've labored to build, to the serenity of an oasis that you had considered inviolable.

It's no fun being a cop responding to a burglary call in somone's home. You feel responsible, as if you've failed to provide the protection someone had every right to expect. In the victim's gaze you can read a mute undertone of reproof. I pay my taxes, that gaze always seemed to say; I work hard and honestly, I lead a tough life, navigating a thousand personal hardships, and part of what I earn winds up in your paycheck. And here's what I get for it: my home turned upside down, criminal hands rummaging through my possessions and robbing me not only of my valuables, but also of my domestic peace of mind. You have to admit that this is your fault, too, Mr. Policeman. Where were you while the thieves were pilfering my sense of safety and security? For all I know, you were sound asleep, digesting the dinner I paid for with my taxes.

Lojacono checked the address that he'd jotted down on a scrap of paper. When the phone call had come in, there'd been no one in the office but him, Ottavia Calabrese, and Di Nardo, who'd just arrived. Early risers, his colleagues at the Pizzofalcone precinct: A good sign, though he suspected that it was more a result of existential lacks than any genuine love for the job. A man had sobbed broken phrases in dialect in a way that had struck him as virtually incomprehensible, and in fact he'd finally been forced to hand the receiver over to Alex.

He turned to look at Di Nardo, tilting his head toward the apartment building's front entrance. She nodded, taking in the usual knot of rubberneckers that always gathered mere seconds after any noteworthy event; a few yards further on, the squad car stood parked with a uniformed cop, arms folded across his chest, leaning against the door. The man nodded in greeting.

Strange girl, Di Nardo was. Not that the others weren't equally strange, and probably the strangest of them all was Lojacono himself. But there was something enigmatic about Alex. Graceful, silent, with finely drawn features, she emanated a sense of restrained force, as if she were ready to transform herself into something else. Lojacono had overheard Aragona, shameless gossip that he was, talking about a gunshot fired inside a station house and the officer who'd narrowly missed being hit, but he'd preferred not to delve deeper: After all, didn't they all have some dark chapter in their pasts, there at Pizzofalcone?

His train of thought betrayed him by bringing him an image of home, of the Sicilian province so full of light and shadows: the sudden smell of salt water on a gust of wind, the branches of the almond trees heavy with blossoms. And the memory of the testimony given by Di Fede, the mafioso he'd gone to school with; the words that had changed his life.

Not all had changed for the worse, he thought as he cut his way through the crowd to reach the courtyard and the broad flight of steps that led upstairs from there. For instance, his wife, Sonia's, true colors had been unveiled; she had dumped him and now she never missed the chance, during their rare phone conversations, to unleash a stream of venom and rancor. He'd met people he never would have otherwise, his new colleagues for example. Even his relationship with his daughter, Marinella, was different. And that was a good thing.

For months he hadn't even been able to talk to her, because of the barrier that Sonia had erected between the two of them. He'd missed his daughter, who wasn't quite fourteen, with a kind of physical pain, one of the sharpest in his life. Then, little by little, they'd begun to talk on the phone again, and just two months ago he'd found her on his doorstep in the rain, fleeing the umpteenth screaming match with her mother, in search of solid ground that she thought she'd lost forever.

No easy matter, Lojacono thought to himself. He'd left behind a tender and emotional little girl who still played at being a grown-up lady with her friends, pretending to make coffee dates and go shopping, who put on her mother's clothes and burst out laughing in front of the mirror; now that little girl had become a silent, pensive young woman who dressed all in black, and whose almond-shaped eyes, so similar to his own, were often lost in indecipherable thought. He didn't know how long she planned to stay, and he was afraid to ask. He didn't want Marinella to have even the hint of a thought that she might be less than welcome. He'd informed Marinella's mother that the girl was with him and that she shouldn't worry, and had been forced to endure an endless series of recriminations. In reality, Lojacono wasn't certain which solution would be best for his daughter: whether she should stay with a father who, because of his job, could spend very little time with her, and deal with a new environment, or whether she should go home to a place where she clearly wasn't happy.

Di Nardo's low voice brought him out of his thoughts: "That's the way in."

On the second floor landing there was only one entrance, whose wooden, single-paneled door stood ajar. The apartment building, originally, like so many others in the neighborhood, an aristocratic palazzo owned and inhabited by a single family, had undergone a centuries-long process of deterioration, while decades of social darkness had settled over the quarter as a whole. In the past ten years, though, the drop in rents combined with the increasing demand for apartments in the city center had reversed the trend, so that buildings in this part of town were slowly regaining their prestige. The graffiti on the outside walls had been scraped off, the plaster had been repaired, the flowerbeds in the ancient courtyards had been restored by skilled gardners to their onetime glory and filled with rosebushes and hydrangeas, flowers that on that warm May day seemed to glow with their own light.

The apartment where the burglary had taken place was on the building's second and main floor, the piano nobile. Unlike the other floors, this one hadn't been subdivided into units with less floor space so that they could be more easily rented or sold; that meant the place must be really big. A security camera had been installed over the door; Di Nardo was looking at the camera, too. The young woman called Lojacono's eye to the front door lock, which showed no signs of forced entry. The landing was illuminated by a large window which seemed locked, with the vertical metal latch lodged securely in the marble windowsill. Lojacono, his hand wrapped in a handker-chief, opened the window and saw that it gave onto the interior courtyard. The brass plaque on the door read "S. Parascandolo," beneath ornamental curlicues.

At the entrance stood a uniformed officer who saluted them, snapping the tips of his fingers to the visor of his cap.

"*Buongiorno*, my name's Rispo. We've been here for twenty minutes or so, we forwarded the call from the operations center."

A large foyer opened onto a hallway, and off to the right was the entrance to what might be a living room. Already in the hallway there were scattered garments, bags, and knickknacks littering the floor. Next to the door stood a suitcase and a leather trolley bag, both shut.

"The luggage belongs to the homeowners," Rispo said. "They came back from Ischia this morning and found the place turned upside down. They're in there, in the living room."

Alex pointed out to Lojacono the discreet security cameras, just like the ones outside, each with sensors connected to the alarm system. You certainly couldn't say that S. Parascandolo, whoever that was, thought safety was of little importance. Even though all that attention didn't seem to have done a lot of good.

From the living room came rhythmic sobbing. Someone was crying.

Lojacono started off, followed by Alex.

V

Not all the calls that come into a precinct house are the same.

The phone rings all the time, and there's always someone who answers it, someone who tries to make themselves heard over the cacophony of so many people all talking at the same time. In a precinct house's bullpen, powerful emotions, passions, and sentiments clash: and so voices are raised, there's confusion, there's agitation. In precinct houses people shout, like in some circle of hell.

When Ottavia Calabrese picked up on the second ring, everyone was talking. Aragona was shouting into his own receiver, asking Guida, the officer on duty at the front door, for a coffee; Romano was asking Pisanelli whether he knew of any one-bedroom apartments for rent near the precinct, and Pisanelli was giving him the name of a real estate agency run by a friend of his; Palma had just stuck his head out of his office to say good morning to everyone.

But as soon as Ottavia, who had put one hand up to her ear to shut out the noise, said: "What? Someone took a child?" the room fell into a frozen silence. Calabrese grabbed a pen and started taking notes, her face taut, her voice cold and efficient. Only her eyes betrayed emotion.

Palma took a step forward and came up to her desk, worried. A child. A child had been taken.

Ottavia hung up. Everyone was looking at her.

"A little boy is missing from a school field trip that was

visiting Villa Rosenberg's art gallery, not far from here. They'd just arrived and he vanished right away. One of the teachers made the call, a nun; it's a private school on Via Petrarca."

She spoke in a low voice, distressed but still professional. She was staring straight at Palma, even though she was talking to the group at large. A child.

Palma asked: "How do they know that he was taken? Couldn't he have just wandered off, or be hiding somewhere, or something like that?"

"One of his classmates was with him. The boy said that he walked off with a woman. A blonde woman."

Silence. Tension, anxiety. Palma heaved a sigh.

"All right, let's not waste time. Romano, Aragona, go straight there: Take the car. Pisanelli, get the name of the child, see what you can find out about the family, and if you can, let them know. Ottavia, call Villa Rosenberg back, tell them not to let anyone move: no one is to enter, no one is to leave. I'll inform the operations center and have them send over a couple of squad cars from headquarters. Let's get busy."

To his usual crazy driving, Aragona had now added an embarrassed silence. He didn't much like Francesco Romano, aka Hulk. Something about his gaze, often lost in space, his expression of vague suffering, frightened him; and his buzz cut, his bull neck, his jutting jaw, gave an impression of power held back, ready to explode at any moment. For that matter, what little he knew about him wasn't especially reassuring: A friend of his, a uniformed police officer, had told Aragona that this Hulk had grabbed a suspect who was mocking him by the neck and sent him to the hospital. "Marcu'," he'd said to him, "I was there, and it took three men to pry that guy loose from his hands; another five seconds and he'd have killed him."

Hurtling straight toward a crowd of Japanese tourists without bothering to slow down, horn blaring, so that they fluttered off like so many pigeons, Aragona thought to himself that it wasn't hard to believe: The man looked violent. And then he had that strange sense of humor so that every time Romano replied to one of his jokes, Aragona came off looking like a idiot. He glanced at him quickly: He was gripping the seat with his left hand and the door handle with his right; a muscle was twitching threateningly in his jaw.

When, brakes screeching, they came to a halt in front of the museum, Romano snarled as if Aragona wasn't there: "Even from the way he drives you can tell he's a dumbass."

They got out of the car just as two squad cars rolled up from different directions. At the entrance to the old eighteenth-century villa that now housed an art gallery, confusion reigned: A small knot of tourists trying to enter the museum was crowding the ticket office's cash register, protesting in a rudimentary, German-accented Italian; a private security guard with both arms raised was shouting over them, doing his best to impose calm; one nun was sobbing while another, older nun upbraided her roughly; a group of kids all about ten years old were standing fearfully in a corner of the large room.

As soon as they saw them come in, the two nuns came over.

"You're from the police, is that right?"

"The name's Romano. This is my partner Aragona. Tell me what happened, Sister."

The woman, about sixty, had a round face and blue eyes that sparkled under the black veil.

"I'm Sister Angela, of the order of the Sisters of Charity of the Blessed Virgin Mary. She," and here she pointed to the younger nun, who was still blowing her nose, "is Sister Beatrice. We already told the person on the phone what happened: A little boy was taken. From here, from this museum, less than an hour ago."

Aragona coughed faintly, removing his sunglasses: "What's the child's name? And exactly how did it happen?"

Sister Angela spoke to him disdainfully: "Aren't you a little young, officer, to be in charge of investigating such a grave offense?"

Before Aragona had time to retort, Romano broke in, his tone firm: "My partner's age is not under discussion; especially because I can assure you that we're both quite qualified. What does seem to me to be under discussion here is the fact that a child, who if I understand correctly was entrusted to your care and to the care of your sister, here, has vanished. Now, would you be so kind as to answer the question, please?"

The woman blinked rapidly; she wasn't used to being contradicted.

"I'm the mother superior of the convent where the school is based, and I wasn't present. The children were with Sister Beatrice, who alerted me the instant that Dodo . . . when the little boy, Edoardo Cerchia, disappeared. I rushed over here and then we called you."

Aragona, rendered cocky by Romano's unexpected rush to his defense, said: "So, you weren't present. And what's more, you failed to call the police immediately; instead you wasted precious time talking amongst yourselves. Congratulations!"

Romano turned to him; the expression on his face promised nothing good. Sister Angela blushed.

"I . . . I . . . Sister Beatrice is very young, and she certainly never imagined she would find herself in such a situation. In all these years, it's never happened that . . ."

Romano addressed the youngest nun.

"Sister, please, tell us how it all happened. It's very important that you do your best to remember precisely. Aragona, perhaps you could take a few notes."

Sister Angela tried to regain lost ground: "Now then, this morning at school . . ."

Romano sliced the air with one hand, brusquely: "Mother

Superior, I think you'd better go and see how the children are doing. Leave us alone with Sister Beatrice, thank you."

Once again blinking rapidly, the older nun took a step back, almost as if Romano had literally pushed her. Then she turned away and, putting on a show of offended dignity, headed off toward the group of children.

Sister Beatrice had folded in on herself; now that she was alone, she lost what little nerve had been left to her, and through her tears she stammered: "I . . . I don't know . . . he was with me, in the hall of watercolors, then . . . with all the, all the other children, I . . . just didn't notice . . ."

Aragona, pen and notepad in hand, stopped her: "Calm down, Sister, calm down. Take a deep breath, and speak calmly, otherwise I won't know what you're saying and how can I write it down?"

The young nun took a deep breath, sniffed loudly, and dried her eyes: "You're right, Dottore. Forgive me. I was just scared, I'm sure you can understand. I could imagine anything, except for this thing happening. But the Lord is merciful, and He'll assist me. Perhaps the best thing would be for you to ask me one thing at a time, that way maybe I won't leave out any details."

Romano nodded, glad to take the suggestion.

"Perfect. All right then, let's start with the little boy. His name is Edoardo Cerchia, you said?"

"Yes, we call him Dodo. Mine is a fifth grade class, those are the oldest kids we have, next year they'll go to middle school. Dodo's been with me since first grade, like almost all the other children you see here; they're his classmates. Dodo is a very sweet boy, no trouble at all, an excellent student with perfect behavior. Perhaps he's still a little childish in one or two ways . . . he's very attached to his toys, and I've had to scold him for bringing them to school. But he's sociable, polite, maybe a little introverted."

Aragona was champing at the bit: "Okay, fine, that's the report card, but, Sister, let's get to the point. What happened this morning?"

Sister Beatrice dropped her eyes, making an effort to get her memories straight while Romano glared grimly at his ill-mannered partner.

"We'd organized this field trip a few months ago. The museum opens early just to let school groups in. Of course, for kids this age it's not the greatest, they'd rather go to a theme park, someplace they can play now that it's springtime and it's warmer out, but the Mother . . . Sister Angela believes all the older kids should get an artistic education, so every year we bring the fifth grade here."

Aragona looked around, baffled.

"Poor guys. They must have been bored out of their damn skulls. Oh well, Sister, let's continue."

Sister Beatrice seemed not to have noticed Aragona's vulgar language.

"We assemble them as a group at 7:45 in the morning, before school would usually start, and then we bring them here with the bus that also takes them to school in the morning and back home again at night. Once we've called roll and made sure everyone's here, we leave."

Romano asked: "Is that the only time you check to make sure they're all there?"

"Oh, no! That's practically all I do all day. The museum's docent tells them all about the paintings while I look after the kids."

"So you realized right away that the little Cerchia boy wasn't there? We were told that one of his classmates saw him leave with a blonde woman: Could you confirm that for us? What's that child's name? And how could the boy have gotten away from you if you're so careful?"

The woman began crying again: "One of his classmates, yes . . .

Christian Datola. He was with Dodo when . . . when they took him, and I . . ."

Sister Angela had come over again, unable to restrain herself when she saw that the two policemen were leaning heavily on Sister Beatrice. She broke in with a harsh voice: "Listen, if you're ready to press charges, just say it clearly and we'll call our lawyer. We're the victims here, certainly not the guilty parties. We have our responsibilities to the families, and as a school we're renowned for the care and attention we give to our students. For that matter, and this may be something you're not aware of, our children come from some of the wealthiest and most prominent families in the city, and . . ."

Aragona took off his glasses: "Are you saying that the reason you take such good care is that the families are well-to-do, and that if instead they were poor, you'd go ahead and let the kids murder each other? Congratulations on your charitable approach."

Sister Angela leaned in menacingly close, her finger in Aragona's face: "Listen here, officer: I'm not about to stand here and take your insults. Now you give me your rank, badge number, and first and last name, and I'm going to . . ."

Sister Beatrice interrupted her, tugging on her sleeve and looking wide-eyed toward the front doors of the museum. A woman was just coming through them at a run, followed by a man.

"Mother Superior, this is Signora Cerchia. Dodo's mother."

VI

The living room too had been thoroughly ransacked: It really was a dispiriting sight.

It was as if someone in the middle of moving had simply forgotten to put things into boxes. The shelves, the countertops, and the side tables all stood empty; the floor, by contrast, was littered with an assortment of items that wouldn't have been out of place in a deluxe bazaar of some kind: centerpieces, books, paintings, dishes, glasses, and fine silver.

To Lojacono something didn't add up, and at first he couldn't say what it was; the jumble of colors, fabrics, and textures distracted him. Then he realized that, somehow, it all had been done very carefully, even tidily. Though objects made of fine crystal and breakable pottery were among those on the floor and carpet, nothing was broken. It was as if the thieves had laid everything out and then been interrupted just before they could make off with their loot.

In the midst of all the chaos, perched on the edge of a sofa also occupied by two paintings and a coffee service arranged, incongruously, in order of cup size, as if on display, sat a couple.

The woman was noteworthy; Alex's first thought was that it was impossible to tell her age. The skin on her bare arms and neck bespoke a fiftieth birthday celebrated some time ago, but the energetic interventions of a plastic surgeon had endowed her face and body, sheathered in a flashy dress a couple of sizes smaller than was advisable, with eternal, if synthetic, youth. She was sobbing wholeheartedly, dabbing with a drenched handkerchief at reddened eyes that had been ble-pharoplastically reconstructed; as she wept, she turned her head this way and that, theatrically, as if she were watching a tennis match.

The man, on the other hand, with his ample triple chin, his bulging gut, and his grim, bulldog-like expression, showed every one of his seventy-plus years. He was upset, his hands clenching and unclenching as if they'd taken on a life of their own, his lips trembling. The scene, however, lost much of its dramatic impact thanks to the red, white, and blue flower-print shirt the man was wearing.

Lojacono introduced himself: "I'm Lieutenant Lojacono, and my partner here is Corporal Di Nardo. We're from the Pizzofalcone station house. Do you own this apartment?"

The man replied without getting up off the sofa. He had a strangely high-pitched voice, completely at odds with the body that produced it: He sounded like a little girl with a sore throat.

"We own what's left, yes. I'm Salvatore Parascandolo."

He made no attempt to introduce the woman sitting beside him.

Alex gave him a blank look and then turned to her: "And you're the lady of the house?"

With a visible effort, the woman forced herself to stop moving her head, briefly interrupting both her sobs and the tennis match: "Yes, Susy Parascandolo. What a tragedy this is, miss. What a tragedy."

Lojacono swept his arm wide to take in the mayhem all around them: "So tell me, when did you realize what had happened?"

Parascandolo replied, gazing out at some vague point in the middle distance: "This morning at eight o'clock, when we got back from Ischia. A person goes away for a pleasant weekend, thinking he'll be able to relax, get some rest, and breathe some fresh salt air. Then he comes home, to the place he's certain is the safest of all havens, and finds . . . and finds this."

The thin high voice that came out of that grim face would have been ridiculous, if not for the intense pain that resonated in the man's words.

Alex looked up at the security camera in the corner of the living room: "What about the surveillance system? It looks to me as if the cameras are off. Did the burglars deactivate them?"

That question prompted strange reactions from husband and wife. The man turned slowly toward the woman, as if she herself had been the burglar: "No. My wife here simply forgot to turn them on. After all, who cares about all the stuff in our home? I'm the one who broke my back paying for it, she never contributed a dime. So why bother to turn on the alarm system when we go out? All she needed to do was type in a code, four stupid little numbers, but she didn't bother."

The woman began sobbing even harder: "You can't expect me to remember everything, you know! It's new, we had it installed less than a year ago, I just didn't think of it. And after all, I was late, so many things to do, the suitcase, the things to bring with us, you were waiting for me down at the harbor, the taxi downstairs was honking its horn because it couldn't stay too long in the middle of the street. I just didn't think of it, that's all."

You didn't have to be an expert reader of facial expressions to sense that the Parascandolos detested each other.

"Do you have any idea how they got in?" Lojacono asked.

"Aren't you the ones who should be telling us how they got in?" the man replied nastily. "I was down at the port, waiting for this moron. How do I know, the damn fool may well have also left the door hanging open. The windows are intact and have shutters, which I shut myself. So, given the fact that there's no sign of the door having been forced open, they must have had a set of keys."

"Oh, now you're a detective," Susy hissed through lips that resembled those of a talking porpoise. "Before you were a judge, and now you're a cop."

Alex tried to bring the conversation back around to the burglary: "Do you have any idea what they might have taken? At least at first glance, can you tell whether there's anything missing?"

The man stood up, and it became clear that he was no taller than 5' 3". "Come with me," he said.

Alex and Lojacono followed him down the hallway, doing their best to avoid treading on the clothing and household objects that were scattered everywhere. They paused at the open bedroom door. Here, too, was the same orderly disorder, with objects of every sort pulled out of armoires and dresser drawers and left in piles on the floor. On the side table, on the side of the bed opposite the window, there was even a red leather wallet, with credit cards and business cards fanned out as if in a shopwindow. On the wall to the right, less than five feet off the floor, there was a safe, wide open and empty. Beneath it, leaning neatly against the wall, a landscape painting. Lojacono went over and saw that the safe door, which was operated both by key and by combination, was blackened and had been cut through in more than one place. Oxyacetylene torch, he thought to himself.

He turned to speak to Parascandolo: "What did you have in the safe?"

The man hesitated.

"Nothing much: a watch, a few worthless personal documents. A little cash, at most a couple thousand euros. Nothing to speak of, in other words."

Alex and Lojacono exchanged a glance. The man was lying, and badly. But why?

"What about the rest of the place?" the female officer asked. "Is there anything missing?"

His wife, who had caught up with him and was still whimpering, replied: "No, luckily there doesn't seem to be. I mean, who knows with all this mess, but I think that everything we had is still here. They didn't even take the silver."

"Shut your mouth, stupid," Parascandolo squeaked. "How do you know that they haven't taken anything? For all the time you spend at home, they could have taken who knows what and you wouldn't even be aware of it."

Alex broke in, point-blank: "Are you insured against theft, Signor Parascandolo?"

"No. I'd simply assumed that with an alarm system like this one, and with the maid at home most of the time, there was no reason to lay out any more money on insurance. If the police did their jobs and made sure that taxpaying citizens were safe in their homes, those bloodsucking insurance companies would all be starving."

Lojacono cut the diatribe short: "Fine. For now, there's nothing we can do. Our colleagues from the forensics team are on their way; for the moment touch nothing, if you don't mind. The policeman at the door will stay here with you. We'll speak again as soon as we have the results of their investigation. Signor Parascandolo, what line of business are you in? Would we be able to get in touch with you at your office, or . . ."

"I own a gym with a fitness center, a café, and a restaurant. We have a little swimming pool too, up on the hill, on Via Mastriani. You can reach me there, if I'm not here."

"And your wife?"

"Her too. In fact, she spends more time there than I do. She's in charge of the fitness center."

On the way back, Lojacono asked Alex: "Well? What do you think of that? Pretty strange, no?"

The young woman walked along, lost in thought: "More than one thing about it was strange. First of all, the fact that they didn't take anything. The paintings are valuable; I know a little something about art because my father's a passionate collector, and all of them were watercolors from the late nineteenth century, small format, easy to sell. The silver, too, heavy items, and then there was her jewelry: I saw the various pieces on the big dresser, lined up as if they'd been considered and rejected."

The lieutenant nodded in agreement: "That's right. And then, the place was so tidy: that strange orderly mess, all the objects arranged on the floor as if someone wanted to put them on display. Never seen anything like it. Leaving aside the fact that the door wasn't forced open and that the alarm system hadn't been activated. Incomprehensible."

Di Nardo pursed her lips before speaking: "You know, I'd almost come to the conclusion that the two of them had staged the whole thing, it was done so badly—which is why I asked about the insurance. But given the facts, that wouldn't make any sense."

"No, no sense at all. And I expect that they would have done a better job faking a burglary, even if the two of them don't strike me as rocket scientists. It's baffling."

By now they were almost back to the precinct house. "The thieves knew what they were looking for," Alex said, "they wanted the safe. But they couldn't have found much of anything, at least according to Parascandolo."

"But he was lying, there's no doubt about it. I wonder what was actually in there and, most of all, why he lied to us. We're going to need Ottavia and the President's help working this one. Maybe they can uncover something."

Alex snickered: "The President . . . so Aragona's infected you, eh? The nicknames of the Bastards of Pizzofalcone. In that case, can I call you the Chinaman?"

"Oh, I'm used to it, that's what they called me even back in school . . . Listen, can you keep tabs on the forensic squad?

The minute they have something, let's go talk to them. I have the disagreeable feeling that our friend Parascandolo with his flower-print shirt has lost much more than he's willing to admit."

Di Nardo sighed: "What an unpleasant couple they were, though. How depressing to see two people who live together and hate each other the way those two do."

The young woman was thinking that, all things considered, it was nice to be back in the communal office where the mood was, more or less, one of good cheer.

That's what she was thinking, until she walked through the door.

VII

The woman who came striding through the museum's atrium seemed more irritated than fearful. She'd stopped at the entrance, allowing her eyes to become accustomed to the dim light, then she'd spotted the knot of people with the two nuns and the policemen and had headed straight for them.

Romano observed her as she approached. She was well-dressed and very sure of herself. A man with a thick head of gray hair and a beard trailed two steps behind.

"Sister Angela, what's this I hear? Where is Dodo?"

The nun flashed her a smile, then shot Aragona a sidelong glare, as if everything that had happened were somehow his fault.

"*Buongiorno*, Signora. Unfortunately, there was an incident this morning, and we thought it best to call in these gentlemen here to give us a hand. Apparently, Dodo . . . wandered off, and we can't seem to find him. I'm quite sure, though, that . . ."

Romano interrupted her and introduced himself, and then added: "My partner Aragona and I just got here. They called us because the boy has been missing for more than an hour. You're the mother, I imagine, Signora Cerchia."

The woman scrutinized him. She was imposing and impeccably groomed; she wore a navy blue jacket over a dress the same light blue color of her eyes. Her features were regular; she had a wide mouth and a nose that had been surgically reduced so that there was too much empty space in her face.

She turned to look at Sister Angela: "You actually called the police? He's probably right outside playing on the grounds with some friend. Did you look carefully? Or maybe he just fell behind, sometimes he gets distracted, he lives in his own little world. Did you check the bathrooms? He might have fallen asleep."

Aragona puffed out his cheeks: "Signora, I'm not sure I'd be so confident that this is a simple matter. My partner told you that more than an hour's gone by. Don't you think these two nuns here would have checked the bathrooms before calling us? Now why don't you tell us whether your husband, or an aunt, or anyone else might have come to get the boy without the nuns' being told. If that's the case, then we'll just make a couple of phone calls, case closed, and we can all go home."

The woman furrowed her brow: "Listen, you, what are you trying to insinuate? That I wouldn't be aware if someone decided to pick up my son before the end of the school day? No, the answer is absolutely not. No one was supposed to come and get him, no one but me or someone I specifically send has permission to pick him up."

"Signora Cerchia . . ."

"And don't call me Signora Cerchia, I haven't been Signora Cerchia in years. My name is Borrelli, Eva Borrelli."

Romano tried to calm things down: "All right, Signora Borrelli. We're all working toward the same objective: we're trying to figure out where the child is and we're trying to get him back here."

"Then do your job, damn it," the woman hissed. "Find him!"

Without getting any closer to her, the man who was with the woman murmured: "Eva, sweetheart, try to calm down, please. It'll all turn out fine, you'll see."

Aragona looked him up and down, his gaze lingering on the man's shapeless corduroy trousers: "Just who would you be?"

The woman replied: "He has nothing to do with what happened. In any case, he's Manuel Scarano, my boyfriend. Manuel, if you don't mind, keep out of this."

Her lapdog, not her boyfriend; that's what Aragona thought as the man stepped back as if he'd just been slapped in the face. To the policeman, it looked as if Manuel were happy just to have been introduced by name.

Romano tried to jump-start the conversation by turning to Sister Beatrice: "Sister, you mentioned a boy who was with Dodo when someone led him away. Could you bring him here, please?"

The nun gave the mother superior a worried glance, as if requesting permission. Reluctantly, the woman nodded, and Sister Beatrice headed off toward the group of students. She came back leading a chubby, red-cheeked little boy by the hand; as they walked, the boy turned happily to look back at his classmates, relishing his moment of glory. Romano greeted him: "Ciao, what's your name?"

Sister Beatrice prompted him to answer with a ferocious glare: "Christian Datola," said the child. His pronunciation of the letter "r" was so slurred that it vanished entirely.

"You were with Dodo, when . . . when he left, isn't that right? Can you tell me what happened?"

Christian nodded and then said to Sister Beatrice: "Teacher, when is Dodo coming back?"

"Why do you ask," Romano queried, "did he say he'd be coming back? Exactly what did he say? Tell me everything, both before and after the moment you lost sight of him. Everything, it's important."

"We were looking at a painting, in the first room. There was a warrior on horseback, and I was telling Dodo that the painting was wrong, because there was no blood on the sword. If you're killing people, and there were lots of dead people on the ground in the painting, then the sword would have to be covered with blood, no? So then Dodo . . ."

Sister Angela broke in sharply: "Datola, don't wander off topic. Answer the question you were asked, and that's it!"

"Listen, Sister What's-Your-Name," Aragona retorted, "why don't you let us ask the questions and let the boy answer however he wants. Any detail could prove useful. In fact, do me a favor, since the kid can't talk freely so long as you're around. Go look after your students and stop interfering with our work."

The nun blushed right up to the hem of her veil, pressed her lips together, and walked away, offended. Romano shot another glare at Aragona for his brusque manners, but deep down he had to give him a few points; the young cop was still at less than zero, but he was rising in Romano's estimation. Datola, immediately relieved by the absence of the nun, whom he clearly feared, continued: "Dodo said that I was right about the painting. By then Sister Beatrice and the rest of our class had moved on into the next room, and we were about to go catch up with them; but Dodo turned toward the entrance and waved hello."

"Did you see who he was waving at?" Romano asked.

The boy sniffed loudly. "Over there, where you get the tickets. There was a lady."

"And then what happened?" asked Aragona.

"I went to Sister Beatrice."

"What about Dodo?" asked the boy's mother.

Christian turned to look at her and shrugged.

"I don't know. I didn't see him after that."

Romano pressed on: "What did she look like, this lady? Do you remember if she said anything, how she was dressed, or . . ."

"She was wearing a sweatshirt with the hood pulled up over her head, and I saw some blonde hair sticking out from under it. She waved to Dodo to come over to her. I didn't even see if he did go, because I left the room right away. If Sister Beatrice called roll and we weren't there, she'd get mad and write it in the logbook."

Romano made sure that Aragona had taken note of the boy's name and, confident that he wasn't going to get any more information out of him, gave him permission to go back to the other kids.

Dodo's mother was beginning to show signs of concern. She kept looking around, as if she expected her son to appear from one minute to the next; every so often she'd confer with her hairy boyfriend. Then she said: "What do you intend to do now? What's next?"

Aragona spread both arms helplessly: "Signora, it's not like we have a script. Do you have any idea who this blonde could be, if in fact she did take your boy?"

The woman stared into space for a moment, thinking hard, then murmured: "No. It could have been anyone, a friend, a chance acquaintance, the mother of another classmate. I have no idea."

Romano broke in: "All right then, give us your information and go home, maybe the boy has already come home with someone. Are you going to let the father know? If you prefer, we could . . ."

"No, he . . . he doesn't live here, he's up north. I'll take care of it, I'll call him myself. After all, that's my responsibility, isn't it? I imagine it is."

"So now what do we do?" Aragona asked Romano after she'd left.

Romano thought it over: "Why don't we go over the museum ourselves with a fine-toothed comb; tell the two uniforms outside what we're doing. And seeing as they have security cameras, let's put in a call to the station house for authorization to requisition the recordings."

Aragona nodded: "And after that?"

"And after that, we keep our fingers crossed."

VIII

Lojacono and Di Nardo found themselves back in a bullpen whose atmosphere was very different from the one they'd expected. Romano and Aragona were gone; Pisanelli and Palma, standing in front of Ottavia's desk, were waiting in silence for their colleague to finish talking on the phone.

Calabrese sat listening ashen-faced, concentrating, every so often muttering an affirmative word or two into the receiver. Even Guida had left his post at the front entrance and climbed upstairs to the second floor where he stood, looking pained, at the door, as if afraid to interrupt.

"What's going on?" Lojacono asked.

Palma gestured for him to wait until Ottavia was done talking. The woman ended the conversation and stared at the commissario: "Nothing. Not a trace on the grounds or in the museum. And none of the staff, not the guard at the door nor the people at the ticket booth and the information desk, remember seeing him go by. Romano says that if the boy had gone out alone, someone would have noticed; there isn't much of a crowd at that time of day. He and Aragona think the kid must really have left with someone."

Palma nodded tensely.

"What about the security cameras?"

"Anyone want to tell us what's happening?" Alex asked, looking at her colleagues.

Ottavia answered Palma: "Two of the four are out of order.

The museum's already called the company that maintains them three times trying to get them fixed; they've been broken since Christmas because of a short circuit. Of the two working cameras, one is in a room that the boy never reached, and the other one's in the atrium; we might get something from that one. I sent an email to the district attorney requesting an order to requisition the tapes, and as soon as I get a response I'll forward it to the museum. Then maybe Romano and Aragona can bring the tapes here. In any case, I told them to wait there."

Pisanelli broke in, calmly: "Excuse me, Otta', did they give you the names of the boy and his parents?"

The question fell into a tense silence. For the first time, thanks to the elderly deputy captain's unmistakable train of thought, the possibility that the child had been kidnapped had been made explicit.

Palma tried to calm everyone down: "It's still too soon to say. Maybe a relative came by and got him, or he went to get something to eat with a friend. Children do that kind of thing. Let's hold on, it hasn't even been three hours . . ."

"You know as well as I do that time is working against us, right?" Pisanelli objected quietly. "It's better to get to work. Then if it all turns out to be a tempest in a teapot, as we hope, we've only done a little bit of unnecessary legwork. All right, then, Ottavia: Who are the parents?"

Calabrese consulted a scrap of paper on which she'd scribbled notes during the phone call: "The little boy is named Edoardo Cerchia, but everyone calls him Dodo. The father, Alberto, lives up north, according to the information we obtained from the mother, Eva Borrelli, who lives with the child at Via Petrarca 51B."

"Fuck," Pisanelli muttered. Though it had been uttered in little more than a whisper, the word echoed throughout the room: The deputy captain never cursed. "Borrelli's daughter. *Mamma mia*, let's just hope that . . . Borrelli's daughter."

"Jesus!" said Guida.

Everyone was looking at the deputy captain with a quizzical expression. Pisanelli realized, and turned to Palma: "Edoardo Borrelli is one of the wealthiest men in the city. Eva is his only daughter, and the boy is his only grandson. Believe me, we'd better get moving. And fast."

Ottavia closed her eyes; Palma ran a hand through his untidy hair, his expression disconsolate.

Alex asked again: "Does anyone want to tell us what's going on, please?"

Sitting across from each other in the commissario's office, Palma and Lojacono were both staring at the desktop piled high with papers.

"As you can see, we don't have anything solid at the moment. If you'd all been here, I would have sent you; but you weren't here. You're the most experienced, you know it and I know it, and even if I still hope it'll all turn out to be a ridiculous misunderstanding, this case threatens to be very, very thorny."

Lojacono was motionless, expressionless. That pose, so typical of him when he was thinking, emphasized his quasi-Asian features.

"Excuse me, boss, but if this really did turn out to be a kidnapping, don't you think police headquarters would take the case for itself? They're not likely to leave something like this in our hands."

Palma made a face: "No, I've already talked to them. They've had the press on their backs for a while now; there must be someone in there who's not only handing out press releases, but also leaking inside information to those jackals. If the investigation was yanked away from us, word would get out to the media right away, and that would be worse for everyone. For now, they'd rather have us work the case and keep them informed about progress. And let's hope we make some."

"I understand. Well then?"

"So I'm thinking that, when Romano and Aragona get back, I'm going to have them give you all the information and let you take over the case. In fact, I might have you work with Romano, that way we won't waste time."

Lojacono thought it over. "Listen, boss, I don't think that's a good idea."

Palma gave him a questioning look. "Why not?"

"As you know, we're a very strange group. We all have our flaws. We all feel as if we're under constant scrutiny, in the crosshairs so to speak. And in a profession like ours, teamwork is fundamental."

Palma intertwined his fingers and rested his chin on them.

Lojacono went on: "If Romano or Aragona, who by the way are both excellent cops, see someone pull the case out from under them, what are they supposed to think? That you, and therefore we, don't have faith in them. That we consider them unsuited to continue their work merely because this case is high-profile. You'd lose them, in other words. And you'd never get them back."

The commissario scratched his head.

"I see what you mean, and you're right. But I can't run the risk of entrusting an investigation like this one to a pair like Romano and Aragona: Romano had and may still have serious personal problems, and Aragona's just playing at being a cop; he's only made it this far thanks to some serious nepotism. You can see the problem, can't you?"

"Romano is a good cop, and I'm sure that he'll be able to keep his personal problems separate from his work; as for Aragona, believe me, he's much better than he seems."

"Not that that's saying much, truth be told."

Lojacono thought about Aragona's fondness for vulgarity and penchant for saying the wrong thing, and in particular the way he drove: "No, not that that's saying much. But, after all, boss, this whole station house is a little bit crazy, isn't it? Listen to me, let's leave things the way they are. If anything, we can all talk things over, and each of us will get the chance to speak his or her own mind. Don't worry, Romano and Aragona won't do or see anything any different from what the rest of us would do or see."

Palma sat silent for a while, then added: "All right. And after all, maybe the kid is already back home."

IX

"Hello?"

"It's me."

"I know. You're half an hour late."

"I wait for him to sleeping."

"Why, wasn't she there?"

"She came back late from working. She must go, if not, Signora looking for her."

"I get it. Tell her to be careful. To make sure she isn't seen by . . . by anyone."

"Yes, told her. All good, anyway. No problem, like telling you."

"Yes, I know. I heard."

"I thinking, if place have video camera and get picture of face . . ."

"No, don't worry. There won't be any trouble. I checked. Tell me how it went."

"I waiting outside in car. She going in, head covered like you saying. Seeing boy from front door, calling him. He coming, he happy. Everything like you say."

"What about him . . . how is he doing, now?"

"He fine. In storeroom, I bringing water and food. You not worrying nothing. Instead, when you calling?"

"Like we agreed: The first phone call will be tomorrow afternoon. Keep it short, just the information. Then another call, twenty-four hours later. Always you calling, that's important."

"Yes, I knowing. And if . . . if some problem with boy?"

"*What kind of problem? There can't be any problems! Remember that the money . . .*"

"*Yes, I knowing: money in advance before, rest of money later. But if boy, for example, not being well, or making noise, or . . .*"

"*How many times do I need to tell you? Just make sure that the boy doesn't make any noise. And make very sure he isn't left in complete darkness. Most important: Either you or she have to be there at all times, never leave him alone. If someone went by and he called out, you'd be in big trouble. Got it?*"

"*Got it, got it. I knowing. But no one pass by here. No one, never. There is gate with chain, I broke and changed padlock with key, and only I and she having key. But money? You promising that we not doing anything difficult, only keep boy, and you giving money quickly.*"

"*You've already been paid the advance, haven't you? When the time is right, you'll get the rest. Stay calm. Now we need to avoid making mistakes: The phone calls are going to be crucial. If you get that wrong, if we get that wrong, there'll be no money for anyone, just lots of trouble. You understand?*"

"*You not worrying, we no mistakes. You no mistakes, too, no? Remember: We making our part, you making yours. And if we making mistakes, everyone in trouble. If you making mistakes, just you in trouble. And boy too.*"

"*I know, I know! I have to go now. You turn off your cell phone, and turn it on every four hours. If you see that I tried to get in touch with you, call me back.*"

"*Okay. I knowing.*"

"*And . . . be careful with the boy. Don't hurt him.*"

"*No. If you not making mistakes.*"

X

Looking out from the balcony, Marinella Lojacono observed with fascination the slice of the city that teemed at her feet. This place was like Palermo, and yet different, even if she couldn't explain how. Certainly they were both different from Agrigento, worlds apart.

She'd lived in Agrigento until she was thirteen: just long enough to finish eighth grade. There were the friends she'd grown up with; one girl in particular, Irene, with whom she shared her life. They were still in touch on Facebook, but they wrote each other less and less; Irene had a boyfriend . . . Angelo this and Angelo that, what a pain in the ass.

After Papà's problems, she and Mamma had moved to Palermo. Now, as she looked down at the crowds, at people running and shoving each other, Marinella remembered her first days in that new city. Neither she nor her mother had been in the best state of mind, and that certainly hadn't made things easier. Plus, Papà's absence had been an intolerable burden. He'd always been the buffer between her and her mother, the only thing that stopped them from pecking each other to death. Marinella was silent, very reserved, and subject to long spells of brooding; her mother, Sonia, was exuberant and intrusive, always eager to stick her nose into Marinella's business.

Not that she had much business, to tell the truth. She'd had a hard time fitting in; her schoolmates were too different from her, and her grades, which had always been outstanding, had dropped precipitously. When, after extreme effort, she'd finally made a friend, her mother had made sure to chase that friend away by bursting rudely into her room and delivering a long, cringe-inducing sermon on the fact that her girlfriend was smoking a cigarette.

That had been the straw that broke the camel's back. With cold determination, Marinella had checked the ferry schedules; three days later she'd completed her last round of exams so that she wouldn't have to repeat the year; she'd packed her few possessions into a backpack, and she'd left.

A scooter went roaring up the street against traffic, and a car stopped to let it go by. The boy on the moped waved his thanks, and the car tapped its horn in response. She felt like laughing: People sure were strange around there. Strange but nice. The Palermitans had struck her as more cautious, less willing to reach out; but maybe she'd just had a bad attitude. Here on the other hand, whenever she went out shopping or for a walk, she got unasked-for smiles, and now and then some kid her age would greet her as if she were a friend.

She liked taking care of the apartment. Lojacono had selected the place practically at random, believing he'd be living there briefly and alone; he was messy and lazy, and Marinella, who was very exacting, had found a place that more or less needed to be rescued. Her father had told her not to worry about it, to enjoy the time she had here as if it were a holiday. But it wasn't a chore for her. For that matter, it might not even be a vacation.

She went back inside, reluctantly leaving the gentle spring air and the pleasant chaos that rose from the street below to the fifth-floor window.

A couple of nights ago, her father had told her that at first he'd hated the city, but that little by little he'd gotten used to it. Unlike him, she had immediately felt comfortable there. But Papà had been catapulted there from a place he'd never left. She hadn't been. Perhaps that's why they'd reacted to it so differently. Because usually Marinella and her father agreed. It had always been that way: They had a special rapport, they understood each other with a glance of those eyes, so strange and so similar, an unmistakable facial feature that united them the way their personalities did. Being torn away from her father had been traumatic, and the fact that her mother only spoke ill of him had just made her miss him more.

So, Marinella thought to herself, the solution was obvious: She'd stay here and live in the place she preferred, with the person she preferred. To take care of him.

As she was neatly folding and placing the linen in the drawers, her thoughts went to the woman that she'd seen coming home with her father the night she'd arrived. Then and there, the flood of her emotions had been so strong—the desire to throw her arms around him; the fear of his reaction to the fact that she'd run away—that she'd barely even noticed her. What's more, the woman had left almost immediately, very discreetly. But it wasn't so hard to figure out: A magistrate, someone her father worked with, going home with a man who lived alone, after midnight. It could only mean one thing.

Of course her father had assured her that they'd just needed to discuss a few loose ends on an investigation they'd just closed, and that he'd needed to give her a document; that it was all strictly professional. But Marinella and Laura, that was the bitch's name, had exchanged a quick glance, and women only need one glance to know everything they need to know. She would have been happy, the bitch, if Marinella had simply gotten out of her way. Sorry to tell you, thought the girl, but I don't intend to.

Still, that woman must never have actually been inside her father's apartment, because she saw not a trace of her presence: not pair of underwear, not a toothbrush, not a box of tampons. Marinella knew well that women marked their territory, that they planted little flags to testify to their presence; and she'd found nothing of the sort. Just in the nick of time, then, she thought wickedly.

Somewhere, someone switched on a radio and turned the volume up; a neomelodic song filled the air. She liked that too, about this city: There was always music. Someone was always playing an instrument, or singing, or listening to a CD, or the radio, or a TV; or else a cart was going by, the vendor calling his wares. There was always music.

Marinella went over to the mirror to get ready. Perhaps she wasn't traditionally beautiful, but she was well on her way to becoming attractive in a special, distinctive way. Her narrow eyes, high cheekbones, and glossy raven hair all came from her father; her long legs, full lips, and lithe physique were from her mother, who could still make men stop and turn in the street.

She'd gotten into the habit of making her face up a little, just enough to "*fare la femmina*," or "play the woman," as her mamma liked to say, but without going overboard. She had another reason now, too, though she wouldn't have admitted it even under torture.

She pressed her lips together to apply the lipstick, concealing a smile. On three separate occasions, on the stairs, she'd run into a guy.

Older than her, he must have been eighteen, maybe twenty; tall, athletic, carrying a bag full of books, and trotting down the stairs, whistling. The first time he'd stopped whistling, as if surprised at the sight of her; the second time he'd given her a long level look; the third time he'd actually breathed a quiet *ciao*. She hadn't replied, she'd lowered her eyes and hurried past; but her heart had done a somersault in her chest.

The time of day was always the same, the bag of books and his apparent age spoke of university classes to be attended, the speed with which he descended the stairs suggested he lived above her, on the sixth floor, say, or at most the seventh; and leaving aside old Signorina Parisi, who lived alone with her cats and dogs, and the Gargiulos, who were an elderly, childless couple, she'd narrowed the list of possibilities down to the D'Amatos and the Rossinis. She was, after all, a policeman's daughter.

And so, sharpening the weapons with which nature had endowed her, she was about to go visit the first of those two families and shamelessly ask if she could borrow two eggs: she'd waited until it was Thursday afternoon, the day that the local grocery stores all closed, for that very reason. She knew that at more or less this time of the day, the mysterious tune-whistler was about to go out; perhaps he would open the door himself.

The spring air carried the notes of the unknown neomelodic song, along with the disorderly racket of the bustling street below. A kid started crying and an exasperated woman began shouting at him. It was almost dinnertime, and the air was beginning to fill with the scent of minced garlic.

God, how she loved that city.

XI

A nyone who entered the large bullpen out of which Pizzofalcone's investigative team worked would have found himself face-to-face with an odd spectacle. All of the officers, plus Commissario Palma, and even Guida, who manned the front desk and had magically chosen just the right moment to be temporarily relieved, were crowded around Ottavia Calabrese's desk, watching the recordings from Villa Rosenberg's security cameras, which she had digitized.

Romano and Aragona had the rumpled appearance of men who had worked hard and come up empty. They'd gone over the art gallery, the grounds, the surrounding area, and even the lobbies of the apartment buildings on the far side of the piazza with a fine-toothed comb, and they'd found nothing. They'd questioned the museum staff, the local shopkeepers, the traffic cops working the streets in the neighborhood, and even a few old men who'd hoped to enjoy a little spring air, but instead were sitting on benches getting lungfuls of smog. Nothing. No one had seen a little boy leave the museum, alone or accompanied, and head off somewhere else. It was as if Dodo—what a terrible nickname, Aragona had thought to himself—had vanished into thin air, had turned to dust and been blown away on the spring breeze all the way down to the sea.

To eliminate any lingering doubts, they'd forced the two nuns to answer about a hundred questions. Did they remember whether the child's behavior had changed in the past few weeks? Had he said anything odd, unusual? Had there been any changes in his academic performance? What about his mood? Nothing, nothing at all. If Dodo had been unhappy, if he'd planned to run away from home, to do something foolish, he'd shown no warning signs. Everything had been perfectly normal, everything had gone just as usual, everything had been calm.

Except for the fact that Dodo had just vanished into thin air.

The original footage, in black and white, was pretty grainy; to be fair, the cameras were meant to catch someone removing paintings from the museum without permission, not people kidnapping children. Ottavia had done a little digital magic and managed to improve the resolution ever so slightly, and now they were all watching video coverage of a sleepy morning at the museum as if it were an adrenaline-charged thriller.

Before putting on his glasses to see from the sideline to which he'd been relegated, Pisanelli had closed the shutters, bringing darkness a little earlier than the impending nightfall would have.

"Guida, make yourself useful," Lojacono had said brusquely, "turn the light off."

It had become a kind of sadistic game to berate Guida, a sloppy, lazy beat cop who'd been kicked off his beat for manifest incompetence and put on front desk duty at the precinct house. On his first day at Pizzofalcone, Lojacono had dressed him down quite sharply for the state of his uniform and the informality of his salute, and since then, Guida had lived in holy terror of the lieutenant and been absolutely determined to reestablish his lost professional standing. With a single, sharp reproof, the Chinaman had achieved the objective that had eluded dozens of senior officers: He'd turned Guida into a perfect, spit-polished policeman, his salute timely and decisive. The metamorphosis had earned Guida the mockery of many of his coworkers and the approval of Palma, Pisanelli, and

Ottavia, who'd all known him for years: Lojacono alone pretended not to notice the change, to Guida's immense chagrin and the others' endless amusement.

At the lieutenant's command, therefore, Guida sprang into action, and then trotted back to his previous location from where, if he craned his neck, he could glimpse the computer screen.

Ottavia hit fast-forward, and for nearly a minute the picture remained unchanged, unruffled by any human presence, until a museum guard appeared and jetted back and forth across the room like a rocket. Calabrese slowed the film back down to normal speed and said: "There. The museum's open now."

The lightning-fast guard turned human again, sleepy and slow. He turned on the light, checked the paintings on the walls, stuck his hand down his pants, and yawned as he scratched himself. "And to think," Aragona said bitterly, "I shook hands with him when we left, that piece of shit."

Guida snickered, but was then instantly silenced by a glare from Pisanelli. The screen emptied out again, then, after another five minutes telescoped into a few seconds by the magic of technology, it was filled by Sister Beatrice and her group of schoolchildren.

The teacher stopped in front of each painting to listen to the docent's explanations. The children trailed after her, looking bored; some of them lagged behind the larger group, trading soccer cards. Just as they were all about to move on into the next room, the silhouette of Christian Datola, Dodo's friend, appeared.

"There, stop it here," said Romano. "This is the little boy who hung back with the child we're interested in. It's been exactly . . ." and here he looked down at the video's time stamp, ". . . seven minutes. The boy, his name is Christian, said that the last time he saw Dodo the child was still waving, from a distance, at this blonde woman we've all heard about. That means that, at this same point in time, the security camera at the front entrance ought to have recorded something."

Ottavia waited for the group of schoolchildren led by Sister Beatrice to leave the room to make sure that no one had entered the camera's field of view in the few minutes that followed; then she started the other video.

The tension became palpable: The small ad hoc audience was about to make the visual acquaintance of the little boy who might have been kidnapped. Almost imperceptibly, everyone moved a few inches closer to the screen, and Ottavia felt her arm come into contact with Palma, who was standing next to her. She felt a shiver, or rather an electric shock. She focused on the video controls.

The security camera offered a partial view of the atrium, from the door that led out to the grounds to the door that gave onto the first hall of the art gallery. But anyone who came in or went out would certainly have been caught in the frame.

There were a number of tourists with cameras around their necks, a young woman eating something, a father bouncing a child on his shoulders. Like the other footage, this was also in black and white and pretty grainy. People came in, people left. Suddenly a figure appeared, dressed in a gray sweatshirt; the hood was pulled over the figure's head.

Aragona snorted: "A hood, in this heat? Who is that?"

Alex, standing beside him, narrowed her eyes to focus better and said: "It's a woman."

"How can you be so sure?"

The female officer pointed at the screen: "You can just see her breasts, look there. And the shoes have a bit of heel too. That's a woman."

They followed her with their eyes as she walked through the atrium and stopped just short of the entrance proper and the clerk taking tickets. She kept her hands in her pockets and peeked into the first hall. She stood there like that, motionless, for almost two minutes; then she raised her right hand and started to wave. The clerk, who was no more than a yard away, was chatting amiably with the young woman who was eating; he was leaning forward from the waist, his body language making it obvious he was hitting on her.

Romano snarled: "Look at that idiot. Just inches away there's some woman waving her head off at a little boy inside the museum and this numbskull's busy flirting with a girl."

Lojacono, fully focused on the video, replied: "Well, he's not a security guard."

The grainy figure waved one last time, as if inviting someone to come over, then put her hand back in her pocket. A moment later, Dodo appeared.

There he is.

A small child, whose diminutive height made him look younger than his years. He wore dark clothing, a pair of long pants, maybe jeans, tennis shoes, and a light jacket. His hair was tousled, and he looked slightly lost. He went over to the figure in the sweatshirt, who patted him lightly on the cheek, took him by the hand, and then headed with him toward the exit.

They slowly crossed the atrium with no trouble at all; they might as well have been invisible. All around them, everyone went on walking and talking, taking pictures and munching food, all absolutely indifferent.

"Stop them, damn it!" whispered Guida, as if that were still possible. Instead the two of them headed off without a hitch. Just before they went through the door and vanished from the frame, the little boy, for no apparent reason, turned to look at the security camera, as if he wanted to say a silent goodbye to his dear friends at the precinct house of Pizzofalcone.

The unexpected glance hit everyone watching like a punch to the gut. Ottavia murmured: "Sweet mother of God!" while Guida took in a sharp, noisy breath and Lojacono clutched his head with both hands.

Dodo's face was expressionless; in that moment, looking into the lens of the security camera, he betrayed neither fear, nor discomfort, nor pain. He seemed fine. Then he vanished from sight.

Aragona asked Ottavia to run the footage back and freeze on the frame in which the two of them were closest to the security camera.

"Can you zoom in on the boy's hand?"

Ottavia made a face: "Sure, but the picture is already very low-resolution. You won't see a thing, just a series of black and white dots."

She tried anyway. Dodo had something in his hand.

"What is that?" asked Aragona.

No one said a word. At last, Alex murmured: "An action figure. It's a plastic action figure."

XII

Nighttime. Now it's nighttime.

Dodo can tell from the chink in the wall.

One of the walls in the place where they've locked him up is made of sheet metal, that wall he knocked his fist against; the noise scares him, so he stays away. But there's a gap, and a little light ought to filter in through it. But there's no light now. So it's nighttime.

Dodo doesn't really understand what's happening to him. He knows that someone took him, and he knows that he'd better keep quiet and not try to run away or call for help, because that man is horrible and enormous, with that big mustache and long hair.

Dodo remembers a movie he used to watch when he was little, a version of Pinocchio in which Stromboli was played by an actor who looked exactly like the man. Dodo was both afraid of and at the same time fascinated by him: He'd play the DVD over and over so he could see him defeated again and again. This time, who knew how it would end.

Lena had come to get him. Dodo loved Lena, he'd been sorry not to see her anymore. When he'd recognized her, waving to him from far away, he'd gone over: What else should he have done? She was smiling at him, she was so nice. Then they'd left the museum grounds and when they got to the car, Stromboli was there. Lena had signaled to Dodo with her eyes, as if to say: Be careful, let's not make him angry. And he spoke that strange language, in a deep, harsh voice.

The two of them had gotten into the car and sat in the back, side by side, him and Lena. Who could say, maybe Stromboli had taken Lena too. And if Lena's afraid, big and strong as she is, then it really would be best to be good, extra special good.

He'd brought him something to eat.

Hot pockets. But cold.

Dodo likes hot pockets; but he doesn't like them cold. He ate one and a half. Now his stomach hurts, he doesn't much feel like eating anymore. Plus now it's nighttime. Too bad, too, because with the passing hours his eyes had grown accustomed, and it hadn't seemed quite so dark.

The sheet metal wall scares him, but the wall that scares him most is the one with the door that Stromboli came through when he brought the water and the cold hot pockets. God, how big he is. He practically didn't fit through the door. He narrowed his eyes in the darkness, he looked around. He shouted: You where?

Dodo, curled up in the far corner, said: Here.

Then Stromboli laid the plate and the water bottle down on the ground and locked the door back up behind him.

Batman, Dodo murmured to the action figure. Batman, don't be afraid. It's just a matter of time. And after all, if he wanted to hurt us, the last thing he'd do is feed us, right? We just need to wait here, be calm and stay quiet.

Let's make believe that it's dark because we're in the Batcave. Let's make believe that we're the masters of the night, that darkness is our home and we're not afraid. Let's make believe that we're close, tight together, and that we're waiting for day to dawn.

Let's make believe that with our brain waves we can send a signal to my papà and that he'll come right away to get us, and he'll defeat Stromboli in a terrible battle, bare-handed. Or, even better, that Papà shows up with policemen who have guns, because Stromboli is strong, so strong.

I wonder where Lena is, Batman. I wonder where Stromboli

threw her. He's clever, that one is, he knows that if he keeps us together we might come up with a way to escape.

Poor Lena, let's hope that he doesn't hurt her. I wish she could be here, I was happy with her. I remember the strange fairy tales she used to tell me when I couldn't fall asleep and Mamma and Papà had gone out to the theater.

You remember how much fun that was, Batman? On Sundays when Papà was home and he'd play with me all day long. And we'd play Avengers, and I was always you, Batman. You're my oldest action figure, you've been with me since then, since when my papà lived with us, since before he and Mamma started fighting. You've been with me since then. And I'll never let you go. Never.

If only we had our nightlight, eh, Batman? If only we had just a little bit of light, in this great big room.

And maybe a pillow too, to sit on and be more comfortable.

But not to sleep, no. Sleeping is impossible. It's too dark to sleep.

In this much darkness, there's no way to keep out the bad dreams.

XIII

The sight of the video footage had lowered an icy pall over the room.

"Excuse me," Aragona had tried to maintain, "but what does it really change? She could still be a friend, the mother of one of his classmates."

"Oh, really?" Romano had murmured, expressing everyone else's point of view—and perhaps Aragona's as well. "And the hoodie, on a warm May morning, how do we explain that? The way she kept close to the wall, walking quickly so no one would stop her? The way she stood right by the door but was careful not to attract the attention of the ticket taker?"

There was a pained silence, which Ottavia shattered: "I think it's time we called his mother, she was waiting for news. Strange that she hasn't called yet herself."

Palma ran his hand through his hair, the way he always did when he was worried: "I talked to her in my office. She's made a round of phone calls, she's called everyone, relatives, friends, and no one knows anything. I told her to be very careful not to give the impression that there's anything wrong. It's important to keep word from getting out about this possible kidnapping."

Alex gave him a level look: "This isn't the first time for you, is it, boss? It seems to me you know just what to do."

A sad expression appeared on Palma's face. "Yes, I've been through this before, it's true. And that's why, at police head-quarters, they've decided to leave us the case for now, not only to keep leaks from getting into the newspapers and on TV.

Years ago I was in charge of investigating the disappearance of a sixteen-year-old girl in Puglia. She'd run away with a boy, then she'd changed her mind and wanted to go back home; but the boy wouldn't let her. She was rich, or at least well-to-do. Her father was in the meat business."

"And how did it end?" asked Pisanelli.

"Well, that depends on how you look at it. We found her twenty days later. He'd raped and tortured her, but she was alive. In a state of shock, but still alive. Everyone sang our praises, but when I think back to the look on her face . . . I wonder sometimes if it wouldn't have been better . . . Anyway, they tossed him in jail, and I hope he's still there."

"Bastard," murmured Alex.

Romano brought the topic of conversation back to Dodo's mother.

"Anyway, we need to call her back. We have to show her this video, you never know whether she might be able to identify the woman, though it seems unlikely since you basically can't see a thing. And then there's nothing distinctive about her."

Aragona nodded thoughtfully, forgetting to remove his glasses with the usual cinematic gesture: "Right. She doesn't have a limp, she's of average height, average build, wearing a shapeless sweatshirt and pants. She could be anyone. How the heck is the mother supposed to identify her?"

Lojacono shrugged: "Who knows, maybe she'll think of something, some detail. You never know."

Ottavia gave voice to the thought that no one else had dared speak: "Even though we'll be causing her intolerable pain. To see her son . . . in someone else's hands. That would break my heart in two."

"I know," Palma said, "but there's nothing else we can do. I'm going to call the magistrate and request authorization to show her the video. Giorgio, perhaps you could make the phone call to the mother. Ask her if she can arrange for transportation here, so maybe we can keep from attracting notice, or whether she'd rather we sent a car to pick her up."

Half an hour later, Laura Piras, the magistrate on duty, entered the precinct house. No one had gone home, even though it was almost ten at night. As she had told Palma on the phone, her presence wasn't actually necessary, but she preferred to be there: a kidnapping, if that's what it turned out to be, was serious business, deadly serious. A crime that lent itself to media manipulation, and the media had become exceedingly aggressive thanks to a mole in police headquarters. Absolute secrecy would need to be maintained. And then she wanted to watch the woman's reactions in person; that might help her to better understand exactly what had happened.

Up to here, it was strictly a professional matter. But she couldn't conceal from herself that she also wanted to see Lojacono again; recently, their only contact had been a few hurried phone calls. She had the impression that his daughter's unexpected arrival had interrupted something that was in the process of evolving, and she wanted to make sure that this interruption didn't become an end.

Though petite in stature, Laura Piras filled a room the minute she walked in. Her even features, her large dark eyes, and, above all, her figure, which her dark skirt suit did nothing to conceal, inevitably attracted the attention of every male and the concern of every woman present: instinctive reactions Piras would gladly have done without, but that she'd learned to ignore.

"Well," she said, taking a seat in the bullpen after greeting the team with a nod of her head, "what do we know about the family?" Her strong Sardinian accent turned even harsher when she was concentrating.

That's just like Laura, thought Lojacono, masking the joy that was spreading over his face in spite of the circumstances: She goes straight to the point and finds out all about the cast of characters even before it's clear that a crime has been committed.

Pisanelli, putting on his reading glasses and rummaging through his notes, replied: "Yes, Dottoressa, I looked into the family. The boy is named Edoardo Cerchia, he's ten years old, and he's an only child. His parents separated four years ago and divorced last year. His father, Alberto Cerchia, originally from around Bergamo, is a businessman. From what I was able to learn, he's more than well-to-do. He works in scrap metal: He supplies raw materials to industry up in northern Italy. After he and the mother separated he went back north. I don't know if he has a new family, but I'm waiting for more information from my colleagues in Lombardy. Eva, the boy's mother, is the daughter of Edoardo Borrelli, and the boy was named after his grandfather. She has a degree in business and economics, and she, too, is an only child. She doesn't work, but then, of course, she's the daughter of Edoardo Borrelli . . ."

Piras stared at him attentively: "Which means?"

"Well, Dottoressa, Borrelli is one of the richest men in this city. He's well over seventy and for the past fifteen years he's led a quiet and private life, but back in the golden years he was one of the biggest real estate developers in the city's hinterland. There are townships he built up alone, from scratch. There are two magistrates, if you'll forgive me, who are still under investigation for having massaged sentences in trials for malfeasance and bribing public officials."

"They're not relatives of mine," Laura stated flatly. "If they've done something wrong, they'll go to jail, same as anyone else. Go on."

Pisanelli flipped to the next page: "Borrelli is a widower and he lives with a Sinhalese caregiver and a secretary he's had on staff since the boom times of his building business; she's still in charge of everything the old man needs. He has a huge duplex on Via Petrarca, and he never leaves it. He continues to pay for his daughter's luxurious lifestyle, but they don't see much of each other because he can't stand her boyfriend, just as he couldn't stand her husband before him."

Aragona was impressed: "Say, President, how on earth do you find out all this stuff?"

"I have my informants. In this case, the concierge in the apartment building where Borrelli lives is the sister of the grocer who sells me my fruit and vegetables. It's all just a matter of having the right connections."

Piras shot Aragona a look that could have killed: "So you're still free and at large? Remind me to have your driver's license revoked one of these days in the interest of public safety."

The policeman swept off his glasses, looking to impress the magistrate: "Dottoressa, you're not being fair to me. It was simply my intention, when we went to perform judicial inspections, to keep you from wasting time getting from point A to point B."

"And I still thank providence and nepotism for sending you here, away from me. All right, then, Pisanelli, it looks like both the child's father and his grandfather have plenty of money. We'll have to act immediately to freeze their assets."

"Certainly," the deputy captain noted, "it would seem that whoever took the kid got the right one. Moreover, though he doesn't get along with his daughter, old Borrelli adores his grandson. The concierge tells me that the boy is the old man's one weakness."

Palma grimaced: "Forgive me, Dottoressa, but I speak from personal experience. Freezing assets is, as they say in Rome, a *fregnaccia*—a fool's errand. It's not against the law to pay a ransom, all they'd need to do is borrow the funds; or maybe they have money stashed in a foreign bank, and they sidestep the restrictions that way. I know that it has to be done, but it's not going to do a lot of good."

Laura was about to reply when Guida appeared in the doorway: "Signora Borrelli is here. Shall I show her up?"

XIV

E va Borrelli entered the room hesitantly. She was accompanied by her boyfriend Manuel, who as usual walked a step or two behind her.

To Romano and Aragona, who had seen her only a few hours before, she looked like a different person. The confidence, aggressiveness, and strength that she'd displayed at the museum were gone now, lost over the course of a day spent in the pits of despair. Her face was creased and her eyes, as she removed her dark glasses, looked swollen and reddened; her hands were twisting a drenched handkerchief and her lips were trembling and quavering incessantly. It was clear to everyone that Eva was now certain her son had been kidnapped.

She was evidently confused by the presence of so many people. Romano approached her: "Signora, let me introduce you to Commissario Palma, our commanding officer."

In a faltering voice, Eva replied: "But . . . why all these people? You haven't . . . haven't found him, have you? He isn't . . . my little boy isn't . . ."

Palma understood that the woman was afraid she was about to hear a tragic announcement: "No, no, Signora. We have no news, or perhaps I should say we're still working, as you can see. All of the officers on duty, including those assigned to other cases, are here to offer their help. Dottoressa Piras, the magistrate who's working the case, is here, too. But let me ask you, do you have any news?"

Eva felt reassured: "No. I called everyone, everyone I know, everyone who knows Dodo. But no one's seen him since this morning, when the driver dropped him off at school. I . . . I don't know what to think. It all strikes me as so absurd: Who could have taken my child?"

The woman blew her nose. Palma stared for a moment at the man accompanying her.

"Signora, I have to ask you . . . we aren't authorized to discuss the matter in the presence of people not directly involved. I'll have to ask the gentleman who's here with you, I'm afraid, to please wait outside."

Eva jerked to attention, and Romano and Aragona recognized the attitude that had been on display that morning.

"The gentleman who's here with me, Commissario, is my partner. He lives with me and Dodo, he knows the boy very well and loves him deeply. His name is Manuel Scarano, and he's an artist, not a criminal. I beg you to refrain from offending us both by sending him away."

Palma exchanged a glance with Piras, who nodded almost imperceptibly.

"As you wish . . . though I'll have to ask you to sign a release form authorizing Signor Scarano to view the material."

"Material? What material?"

Palma gestured for her to step over to Ottavia's monitor, and then asked Ottavia to start the video.

The video began to run, and frame by frame, a whirlwind of emotions appeared on Dodo's mother's face. When they pointed out the woman in the hoodie she furrowed her brow; when she saw her son appear she lifted her hand to her mouth, eyes wide, and held her breath. And when, just before leaving the frame, the child looked up into the security camera, she heaved in shock, turned pale, and flopped down onto a chair, supported by Manuel, who seemed almost as upset as she was. The silence that ensued, broken only by the woman's sobs, was excruciating for everyone.

Piras stood up and went over to her: "Signora, I understand how you must feel, and I assure you that we're horrified by what has happened, but this is not the time to give in to pain. Every single minute is crucial. Please, do your best to answer a few questions."

Eva seemed to appreciate the magistrate's little speech. She brushed her trembling fingers over her face and said: "Of course, Dottoressa. Go right ahead."

Piras nodded in Palma's direction, and he asked: "Do you recognize the person that took Dodo? Think it over carefully. A detail, some feature: Could it remind you of someone? Keep in mind that your son's friend, Christian, spoke of a blonde woman. From his vantage point, which would have been the same as Dodo's, he must have gotten a better look than we did, so his description of the hair color might well be correct."

The woman thought it over, doing her best to choke down the powerful emotion that was clutching at her throat. She coughed, then said: "No, Dottore. I don't recognize her, she's all covered up, you can't see a thing. But who is she? And why did she take Dodo? My God, oh my God, it's a nightmare. It's a nightmare."

Standing behind her, Scarano rested a hand on her shoulder, caressing it lightly. Palma turned to him: "What about you, Signor Scarano? You didn't recognize anyone in that figure, did you?"

The man looked up. His head of thick salt-and-pepper hair, the beard of the same color, and his massive build all made him look like an aging gorilla, but the watery eyes behind the thick lenses and his low voice were sharply at odds with that image.

"No, Commissario. She's not familiar to me at all. But there's one thing I'm certain of: Dodo, even though he's a very sweet child, would not have gone so willingly with a person he'd never seen before. He would have asked Sister Beatrice for permission, at the very least. So it seems likely that he knew whoever it was, and well."

Though he'd whispered the words, they landed like a bombshell. Eva turned to look at him and said: "You're right, Manuel. You're right! Dodo wouldn't have just walked off with some stranger without a word to anyone. So we need to search among our own . . . among . . ."

Lojacono broke in: "I'm afraid it's not that simple. This woman might very well have told him that you were waiting outside in the car. Or that she had something to give him and that he could come back in right away. We don't have any footage of what happened outside, we don't know how your son was taken."

Aragona confirmed that point: "Precisely. There are no security cameras on that stretch of road. No banks, no jewelry stores. Only a broken-down old bar, a newsstand, and a flower shop, and no one saw anything. They must have moved quickly; they probably had a car waiting. They threw him in and took off."

Eva began to sob again, while Alex, Ottavia, and Piras looked daggers at Aragona.

The magistrate reclaimed control of the situation: "Signora, have you notified the boy's father? It's his right to know about . . . about what's happened."

Eva looked up, some of her lost pride recovered.

"Dottoressa, I waited to be sure about what is sadly turning out to be the truth. It's not easy to say something like this to a man you haven't talked to for years, except to discuss practical matters."

Piras, who wasn't renowned for her diplomacy, replied brusquely: "If you don't think you're up to it, we'll inform him ourselves."

"No, no need. I imagine that's my job. I'll call him from home. What else should I do, in the meantime?"

It was Palma who spoke next, in a gentle voice: "You should try to get some rest, though I know that's probably too much to ask. I can imagine your state of mind. But do make sure your phone lines are open, and that your phones—both your landline and your cell phone—are in working order. And warn all those who might be contacted by whoever the kidnappers turn out to be, which means not only your ex-husband, but also your father."

"Why my father?"

"Because from what we understand he's very fond of the boy, and he's a prominent man. They might assume he'd be most responsive to any eventual demand."

"My God, you're already thinking of . . . of a ransom, is that it?"

"We have to take every possibility into consideration, Signora. And make sure we're ready for whatever happens. I'm going to give you a card with my personal number; please call, no matter what time. And I ask you to think about who Dodo might trust so completely that they could easily lead him away. And here, too, if you happen to come up with any ideas . . ."

"I'll let you know right away, of course. And I'll let my father know, too, tomorrow morning: he'll be asleep by now. He's a sick man, wheelchair-bound."

After Eva and Scarano left, no one dared speak in the communal office.

Piras addressed them all: "What impression did you get? It doesn't seem to me that she has the slightest idea who it could have been."

Palma agreed: "I'm with you on that. But what her boyfriend said strikes me as important: Unless Dodo is especially sociable—and he's not a boy with a tendency to play pranks—it's quite unlikely he would have gone away like that."

Piras sighed.

"All right. I'll give orders to monitor closely both Borrelli's phones and Dodo's grandfather's. In the meantime, Palma, keep me informed. It certainly does seem that this precinct, in its new incarnation, is being put to quite the test. We'll talk tomorrow morning."

After a quick glance at Lojacono, she briskly exited the office.

XV

There are nights.

Nights you arrive at as if to the top of a mountain, your eyes leaden with exhaustion.

Nights full of nothing, when all you want is to sleep face-down, surrounded by the familiar, stale smells of home.

Nights when you need to shut the rest of the world out, nights heavy with a tremendous weight that won't let you breathe while you try your best to keep the fingers of darkness from getting in through the cracks in the windows and tunneling all the way to your soul.

There are nights.

Private Giovanni Guida, before going to bed, performs a careful inspection.

That's what he likes to do, to make sure that everything is shipshape: doors locked, windows open just a crack if what's wanted is a breeze, gas turned off, water too. He usually does it after his wife's gone down for the night, when he turns off the television set after surfing one last time through channels 1 to 6 to see whether anything big has just happened.

Private Giovanni Guida is a cop. He might have remembered the fact late, that's true, and it's true that for too long he'd believed himself no more than a pencil pusher, for better or worse, a pencil pusher who could therefore afford to leave a button undone, or complain about the pain from his sciatica. And he'd put on a bit of belly, too, Private Giovanni Guida, just to underline his professional status, or lack thereof. As for his hair, that's long gone, so it's a good thing he now shaves his head completely, which makes a man look strong, refined, and ageless.

Then a lieutenant shows up from Sicily, and later Private Giovanni Guida hears the gossip about him, about how a gangster back home turned state's witness and accused him of passing information to the Mafia, serious charges, and anyway this guy shows up, and he looks at him, Guida, with those Chinese eyes of his, and in fact that's what they call him, the Chinaman, and with just a few sharp words this guy reminds him that he, Private Giovanni Guida, sent to Pizzofalcone because no one else wants to go there, to the place where that mess with the Bastards took place, is a cop.

And from that day forth the private turns back into a cop, and starts studying the regulations, starts working hard because, even if he's just standing guard at the front door and answering the phone, and talking to the people who come in to file complaints and ask for information, that, too, is a job for a cop.

As he walks down the dark hall, enjoying the silence of a safe and secure apartment, Private Giovanni Guida nears his children's bedroom.

He has three children, Guida does: a young lady age thirteen, another girl just seven, and a little rascal four years old. The girls sleep in a bunk bed, the young delinquent in a trundle bed, against the far wall. The oldest girl sleeps curled up, her face to the wall: She always sleeps that way. The second-oldest sleeps on her back, mouth open, and he tucks the sheets up to her neck: She always kicks the covers off, and ends up with a sore throat. The tiny criminal sleeps on his belly, arms thrown wide: He takes up twice as much room even when he's sleeping, the way he does in his father's heart. He looks down at him, Private Guida does. How quickly a little devil becomes an angel, he thinks: Just let him fall asleep.

Out of his memory, a grainy black-and-white face leaps before Private Giovanni Guida's sleepy eyes. Where were you going, Dodo? Where was that devil with the hoodie over her head taking you? Why aren't you in your little trundle bed, turning from a devil into an angel like the other boys?

Private Giovanni Guida silently gets the chair from the little homework table, brings it over to the little devil's bed, and sits down.

He wants to gaze his fill, while two tears slip slowly and unexpectedly from his eyes.

There are nights.

Nights that betray you, that come in seeming peace and turn out to be full of war and pain.

Nights that enchant you with a false joy, that lure you in with an embrace, and then treacherously stab you in the heart like assassins in the dark, for no good reason.

Despairing nights that seem placid, that might carry a fresh, illusory air about them, that might come with a faint music that you fail to recognize until it's too late, and by then you're already in, and all hope is lost.

There are nights.

Ottavia had been kicked in the face.

That was what the video of the boy in the museum had done to her.

Kicked her in the face.

Because Ottavia, standing out on the balcony of her apartment watching the night roll past in the street below, has no doubts: The boy on the screen turned to look at her.

And anyway, why should he have turned to look up at that camera, the only working camera in the whole run-down security system? Why turn around if there was nothing to see, if he was walking briskly toward the exit, perfectly content, heading toward who knows what fate, hand in hand with his kidnapper? Why, if not to remind her, Ottavia, what a shitty mother she really was, what a shitty wife she was, what a shitty woman she was?

Those tiny, grainy eyes in black and white, those two tiny dots fluttering among the other dots, barely recognizable, stared in mute reproach right at her, Deputy Sergeant Ottavia Calabrese, warning her not to kid herself: It was perfectly clear what she had in her mind and her heart. So she could just cut out pretending to be perfect, loving, and maternal, because he, the boy on the screen, knew exactly who she really was.

The residential street, seven stories below, sat deserted, waiting for dawn so it could begin pulsating once again. Her husband, Gaetano, slept peacefully, lulled by his uncompromising conscience, by the purity of his feelings and by his complete unawareness of the things she felt. Damn you. You and your perfection. You and your infallible respect for positions and prerogatives. You and your incontrovertible certainties, the certainties of an engineer who supervises a team of fifteen. Damn you. And damn me, for not loving you enough, and maybe for never having loved you at all.

With a shiver, Ottavia clutches the collar of her jacket around her neck; she'd thrown on a light coat over her pajamas when she stepped out onto the balcony, suddenly hungry for fresh air.

You know, boy on the screen, more and more often these days I feel as if I'm being suffocated. Who knows, maybe I have a heart problem, I read on the Internet that this could be one of the warning signs. But maybe it's just my sense of guilt.

How old are you, boy on the screen? Ten, or perhaps a hundred. Maybe you know everything, maybe you know that you can climb straight into my heart by sneaking through a computer monitor. Maybe you're three years younger than Riccardo.

Riccardo, who's sleeping like a rock in his bed, taller, stockier, stronger than other boys his age. Riccardo, developmentally disabled, with the mind of a three-year-old child. Riccardo, who may never say anything but that one, blunt word: *mamma, mamma, mamma.* Over and over, endlessly.

Mamma.

What kind of a mamma are you, Ottavia Calabrese? What the hell kind of mother are you really, with all the sorrowful praise you get for washing him, dressing him, taking him to the pool and looking on during his lessons, feeding him and wiping his mouth, the mouth of your son who sits on the floor outside the bathroom when you lock yourself in so you can cry in secret. What kind of mother are you, surrounded by all this praise, you who'd rather be anywhere but in the clutches of a family that is your prison, that is your life sentence?

Ottavia's mind travels through the night to Palma, the commissario she can't even speak to on a first-name basis. That off-kilter smile, his unkempt hair. A man, nothing more and nothing less. A man like any man.

Or perhaps like no man.

Or perhaps a lifeboat in a stormy sea.

Or perhaps the last train, at the end of the night.

Go ahead and look, boy on the screen. Go ahead and look deep down inside me. Uncover my most hidden thoughts, and help me to bring them up to the surface. Help me to see, help me to understand who I am. Who I was and who I've become.

With a last glance out into the darkness, Ottavia goes back inside.

There are nights.

Nights full of luminous threads like headlights on the highway that travel strange paths on their way to intersecting.

Nights suspended between one day and the next, unaware of what came before and of what will follow.

Nights capable of knocking down memories and building new dreams, with bastard flavors that nevertheless have new meanings.

Nights that make you think you can bring the past into the future, that the past might be a load that, instead of crushing you, becomes a driving force.

There are nights.

Lojacono, his fingers knit together behind his head, lies looking up at the ceiling while through the half-open casement window comes the sound of someone playing the piano.

He doesn't know why the hell it is but in that city, one way or another, there's always music playing. Good or bad, poorly recorded or tinny, coming from a radio under the cacophony of shouts and traffic—if you listen, you can always hear music.

At first, when he'd been catapulted into that city from the smoking rubble of his old life, he'd hated this fact. To tell the truth, he'd hated everything about the place. Now he was used to it, and from time to time, he'd seek it out, the music, and he was happy when he found it, concealed under some other noise, folded beneath the sound of a moped motor backfiring or a marital squabble. This time it was some guy practicing the piano in the middle of the night; anywhere else, he'd be risking his life, would have been ripped limb from limb by some exhausted neighbor, but not here. You could say anything you wanted about that city, but it wasn't intolerant.

From the sofa bed in the living room, he could hear Marinella breathing heavily. It still seemed incredible that she was here with him. After all the time he'd spent wishing he could hear her voice, even if only for a quick hello on the phone, now he actually had her close enough to hug, to kiss.

As a father his heart was, as usual, caught midway between happiness and worry. It was wonderful to rediscover their rapport, wonderful not to be afraid he'd never see her again, not to have to wonder how she was, where she was, not to have to think of her locked in eternal combat with her mother. Not to feel anxiety over his uncertainty about what choices she would make.

He knew Marinella as well as he knew himself; he knew how resolute she could be, that she possessed the equilibrium and mental clarity of a very young little old lady, and that she'd make the right decision. He might as well go along and do what he could to make the process easier for her.

Even though they'd never discussed it explicitly, Lojacono had already figured out that Marinella never wanted to go back to Palermo. Every day, she co-opted a few more household linens; a book here and a book there, her makeup, a dresser from Ikea, like an ant she was building herself a new life. He'd checked into it: In spite of the classes she'd missed, her school year had ended successfully; they had all summer to decide what to do next.

While a weary but perfectly solid blues piece pounded out from the unknown piano, the lieutenant thought that he'd have to find a new apartment, with an extra bedroom and a real bed for his daughter. Sonia would no doubt cause trouble, but even she knew that, when confronted with their daughter's determination, there was nothing to be done.

Marinella liked that city. Not that she'd told him so; the two of them spoke in glances, no need to talk. The occasional fleeting laugh, a tilt of the head, the sighs at the sudden sight of panoramic views beyond a curve in the road: They all told him everything he needed to know. She was doing fine. She was happy. Even thinking about how best to take care of him helped.

He and Marinella added up to two, and Marinella and her mother added up to two; but for some odd reason, the first pair was a family, and the second wasn't. Perhaps it was because Sonia, unlike him, was self-sufficient, or at least seemed to be to her daughter; or perhaps it was because they had such similar personalities and tastes, and because of the remarkable physical resemblance that delighted people when they saw them together.

Certainly, Lojacono told himself, watching as car lights streaked by on the ceiling, it wouldn't be easy. But what ever was? Following a devious path, his mind went to Laura and the glance she'd shot him that night as she'd exited the communal office with her usual brisk gait. Laura and her finely drawn silhouette against the rain-speckled car window. Laura and the swelling outline of her breasts. Laura and the quivering heat of her hand in his as they ran toward the front door of his apartment building.

Laura and Marinella.

He wanted to keep things going with Laura. He didn't want to lose this sensation—of something at once different and familiar. He wanted her, wanted a woman who was *his* woman. He wanted to uncover her mysteries, savor her taste, and see if he could still build something.

But he didn't want to lose Marinella; he didn't want to miss seeing her grow up, watching her become a woman, talking to her without really talking, in the afternoon in the fresh sunshine, sharing a pizza by the sea.

Perhaps, he reflected in the night that crept little by little toward the dawn, the two things weren't incompatible. Perhaps each woman could have what she wanted without invading the other's territory. Perhaps for him, there was still a hope of life. And family. Who would have ever thought.

His thoughts, clouded by dreams and exhaustion, slipped away toward that small face in black and white, looking up at the security camera.

I wonder where you are, child. I wonder if you're afraid, tonight. I wonder if you're dreaming, or quaking with fear. I wonder if you're thinking of someone. I wonder if that someone is your papà.

As he finally closed his eyes, Lojacono heard in the waves of music coming from the piano all the anguish of a father whose son had been hacked away from him, all the terror of a son reaching out for help in the darkness. There are nights, he thought, as he slipped into a short, agitated sleep, that should never come.

There are nights.

XVI

T he next morning, even Aragona looked the worse for wear. He flopped down in his chair and said: "Guys, I was up every other hour last night. This thing with the kid is really getting to me; and you know what I've been thinking about most of all? His face when he looked up into the camera. It was almost as if he knew that we'd be watching it later. If you ask me, I'm just too sensitive for this work . . . But hey, is there any news?"

Romano, who was standing over by the window holding a plastic cup, shook his head: "Nothing. The mother called at 7:30; Ottavia answered and told her only that, as of that moment, there was nothing new."

Alex was pouring herself a cup of coffee: "Apparently she informed the boy's father. She called him last night and told him only that their son was missing. And this morning she was going to tell Dodo's grandfather, too, but she was going to wait until it got a bit later, when he was less likely to have a heart attack at the news. That's what she said."

Aragona sighed: "At 7:30 in the morning, and Ottavia answered? And you already know all these things? But it's only 8:15 now! I can understand the President being here, since old people don't need much sleep, but why were you all already here in the office so early?"

Pisanelli remained unruffled: "Look, let me tell you from personal experience: you'll be the last one in even when you're an old man. You spend too much time in front of the mirror, trying to look like somebody else."

Aragona took off his blue-tinted sunglasses: "What do you mean, somebody else? I'm authentic, one hundred percent!"

Lojacono raised his eyes from the screen where he'd been watching the video of the boy for the hundredth time: "Sure you are, cowboy. Come on, get yourself some coffee, seeing that that's at least one thing good old Guida knows how to get right."

Just then a man walked into the room and asked: "Is this where you're working on the missing child? I'm Alberto Cerchia, the father."

They had him sit down at Ottavia's desk, which had the least wobbly chair in the office, and then went to summon Palma, who was on the phone with police headquarters for the first briefing of the day.

Alberto Cerchia was a good-looking man, just over forty, fairly tall, tan, and with a lean physique. Wrinkles around his eyes and a slight graying at his temples betrayed his age, but otherwise, anyone would have thought him ten years younger. He wore a casual navy blue suit and a light-blue shirt open at the neck. He was shaken up and obviously tired; a shadow of stubble just visible on his face and a number of creases in the fabric of his jacket stood in sharp contrast to the general impression of a habitually well-cared-for appearance.

"I only got the news last night," he said, as if to explain the timing of his arrival, "and I got on the road immediately; I was at the Swiss border. There was lots of rain on the highway . . . but of course I couldn't stop. She told me . . . I asked who was in charge of the investigation. So I came here first. Tell me, exactly what happened?"

His voice, with its northern accent, betrayed a pragmatic, impatient personality that preferred to be in charge.

Palma answered for the group by introducing himself: "I'm Commissario Palma, and we took the initial call. Your son was on a school field trip to a museum, the Villa Rosenberg, and he left with a person who hasn't been identified. Since then, yesterday morning at 8:30, we've heard nothing more about him."

The man listened attentively, his brow furrowed, his lips tight.

"So you're telling me that my son Dodo has been kidnapped? Is that what you're telling me?"

Palma coughed uneasily: "We're not certain of that yet. We do know he wasn't taken by force, he went with this person willingly, so . . ."

Cerchia interrupted him, raising one hand; he seemed unable to believe what he was hearing.

"Wait a minute, how could you know that?"

Ottavia broke in, her voice gentle; she understood what that man was going through and did her best to calm him down.

"We have a video from the museum's security camera. It's just a short clip, no more than a few seconds, but . . ."

The man leapt out of his chair: "A video? A video of my son? And you can see the person who took him? Then it's possible to tell . . ."

Palma gestured for him to sit back down: "No, unfortunately it's not possible to see the person clearly, and he or she is wearing a hood over his or her head, plus the video quality isn't very good; in any case, we'll show it to you soon. In the meantime, tell me, when were you informed?"

Cerchia ran his hand through his hair; he seemed disoriented, as if he wasn't entirely sure what he was supposed to be doing there.

"It must have been one in the morning. I was traveling for business, and I was in a hotel. It was . . . was Dodo's mother. The minute I saw her number on the screen, it scared me. If she was calling me at that hour . . . actually, if she was calling me at all, it meant that something serious must have happened.

Something very serious. You see, this woman and I no longer have any relationship at all. The law, which in this country is unfortunately blind, gave her custody of my little boy, though he would actually have chosen to stay with me, which is what I would have wanted with all my heart because he . . . he . . ."

He made a visible effort to keep from being overwhelmed by his emotions. Lojacono, ill at ease, turned to take in the view from the window; witnessing such pain was too much, even for a hardened cop like him. He well remembered how upset he had been about being far away from Marinella, and that had been no kidnapping. Quickly, in his mind, he thanked his lucky stars that his daughter was with him now.

Cerchia continued: "He's my entire life. Nothing, no amount of money, no creature comfort, no luxury, no woman could ever be worth so much as a second of the time we spend together. And she doesn't even give a damn about him; she's too consumed by that ridiculous lover of hers, by her girl-friends, by her club, and by everything else in her worthless life. And now no one knows where the boy is. I understand why she wouldn't have had the nerve to tell me immediately."

Palma broke in: "To be perfectly honest, we were the ones who suggested that she might not want to sound what might turn out to be a false alarm. I want to stress that the child seems to have left the museum of his own free will. It could have been a perfectly ordinary chance encounter, I don't know, some woman who was a family friend, or . . ."

Cerchia leaned forward: "Some woman? Then it was a woman?"

Palma shrugged: "The quality of the images isn't very good, as I told you. But yes, it appears to be a woman."

Cerchia slapped his hand on his thigh: "I knew it; it's her fault, that goddamn slut. It must be some woman who decided to take revenge on her by playing a nasty trick—maybe the wife of one of the men she screwed. And now we'll see, when

I find him—because I'm going to find my son, I promise you that—whether the judge decides to grant her custody again. That whore, that damn whore."

"I should tell you," Alex said, her tone cold, "that your wife was here until late last night. And early this morning, when she called, it was clear she hadn't slept a wink. I assure you that she's every bit as worried as you are. I wouldn't be quite so hard on her, if I were you."

Romano nodded: "I'm Romano, Dottore, and I'm working on your son's case. Let me confirm what my partner here just said: Your wife doesn't have the slightest idea who might have taken the child."

"She's not my wife," Cerchia hissed angrily. "Not anymore. And if she doesn't know who it was, that's just because there are too many suspects to choose from. She and that old bastard of a father of hers manage to generate more hatred than you'd ever believe possible. Now I'd like to see the video, if you don't mind."

Palma helped him around the desk and over to Ottavia's monitor.

Cerchia watched the footage very attentively. When he saw his son enter the frame, cross the room and, just before leaving, look up at the video camera, his reaction was heartbreaking. His expression crumbled as all the muscles in his face contracted; tears poured forth; with his hands, he clutched at his throat, raked through his hair, and covered his mouth. He started sobbing, his shoulders shaking uncontrollably.

Romano and Aragona stared at the floor, wishing they could be any place else but there. Ottavia, deeply moved, gripped his arm to comfort him. Pisanelli coughed.

Palma said: "Dottor Cerchia, please. This won't do anything to help your son, that is, if he does need our help. You saw it yourself: He went with that person perfectly happily. Perhaps he knew he had nothing to fear."

Alberto Cerchia covered his face with his hands and waited a few seconds: "You're right, Commissario. We need to find out where Dodo is and get him back. And as God is my witness, I swear that when we find him, I'm going to keep him close and make sure nothing bad ever happens to him again." His voice, made hoarse by grief, was a barely audible croak; nonetheless, it throbbed with enormous determination. "That's a woman, yes. It seems obvious from the way she moves and by her build. What other evidence do we have?"

Aragona gestured vaguely: "One of his classmates, the boy who was with him when he left, said that she was blond. But he was fairly far away, and after all, he's just a kid."

"A blonde. Well, that's something, isn't it? Did she see the video, the boy's mother?"

"Yes, of course," Palma replied. "But she didn't recognize anyone she knew."

Cerchia made a face: "That idiot wouldn't recognize herself in a mirror. What about the old bastard, what did he say?"

"If you're referring to the boy's grandfather, the signora said that she'd tell him this morning."

"Sure, of course," Cerchia muttered bitterly to himself, "she handles him with kid gloves. But she doesn't think twice about calling me up in the middle of the night and almost getting me killed on a rainy highway. Typical." Then he turned to speak to Palma again: "I have a place here, near where they live. I took it so Dodo could stay with me when I see him every other week. I'll give you the address and my phone number, so you can get in touch with me whenever you need to. I'm going to go see her now; we need to try to figure out just what happened. I'm going to find him, my son. I'll find him."

Lojacono spoke up: "Cerchia, if I could offer a little advice, not as a cop but as a father: Right now you're all in the same boat—your ex-wife, your ex-father-in-law, and everyone else who cares about the child. If you don't want to make our job even harder, don't put Signora Borrelli on the defensive; do your best to cooperate with her, and with us. If the boy has been kidnapped, and like the commissario told you, we still can't be sure of that, the first few times the kidnappers make contact will be crucial to the investigation. So please: help us help you."

Cerchia listened in silence. Then he nodded: "Yes, right now the only thing that matters is that Dodo come home safe and sound. We can discuss the rest afterward."

Palma reiterated the point: "Can you promise me, Dottor Cerchia, that you'll keep calm and let us know about anything new that comes up? We've asked your ex-wife to do the same. Lieutenant Lojacono put it very well: This is no time for grudges, we're all in the same boat."

Cerchia stood up from his chair: "Thank you, Commissario, but no, we're not all in the same boat. I'm his father. His father. And when something happens to a son, believe me, the father is all alone in the boat of pain. Have a good day."

And he left.

XVII

Giorgio Pisanelli was leaning against a pillar at a street corner, a newspaper in hand. He was trying to keep the need to urinate under control.

He'd gone to the bathroom immediately before leaving the office, hoping that would win him at least an hour or so of peace, but nature had decided otherwise.

He'd become a fatalist, Pisanelli, but only as far as nature was concerned. Against the rest of the world he was used to fighting, and indeed he was still fighting, in his silent, gentlemanly way, refusing to resign himself. It was possible to fight against practically everything—cruelty, stupidity, ignorance—and sometimes it was even possible to win; but when it came to nature, there really wasn't much one could do.

Nature had decided to give him prostate cancer.

Who knows for how long nature had been laying the groundwork. It had conspired for years, in the shadows, perhaps since the long-ago day on which some great-great-grandfather had met a great-great-grandmother, to ensure that he'd get to enjoy that stabbing need to pee, even right after he'd gone to the bathroom. A ticking time bomb embedded in his genes that would go off decades, perhaps even centuries, later, with absolute precision. How can anyone fight against that?

Palma had told them all to break ranks and go home; after all, without a phone call from the alleged kidnappers, there wasn't much for them to do. And perhaps, eventually, as they kept telling each other, it was still possible that some aunt would materialize and say to the mother: What on earth, had you forgotten? We'd agreed that we were taking Dodo with us to Disneyland Paris for the weekend. We agreed, the other night at the club, while you were on your fourth cocktail.

In any case, aside from digging deeper into the Borrelli family, there wasn't anything else for Pisanelli to do. So he'd asked for permission to leave the office and, after his third bathroom break in two hours, he'd gone out. After all, his colleagues, too, had things to take care of: Lojacono and Di Nardo had gone to pay a call on the forensic squad about their burglary, Romano and Aragona were going first to the school, and then to see the little boy's mother at home.

Pretending to read his newspaper without taking his eyes off the door across the way, he thought back with a stab of pain to Dodo, and the way he'd looked up at the video camera just before vanishing. He'd reminded Pisanelli of his son Lorenzo as a kid: the same seriousness, the same deep clarity in the dark eyes. How long had it been since they'd spoken? A week, more or less. He should call him. Carmen would have been angry if she'd known that he'd let so much time pass between one phone call and the next.

He looked around for a shadowy corner where he could pee without being seen: after all, it would just be a couple of drops at the most. Like always. Sure, he could go into a café, pay for an espresso he'd barely touch, and ask to use the restroom; but what if she came out at that exact moment? He didn't want to run that risk.

Carmen was Pisanelli's wife. She was sweet, kind, and beautiful. He'd met her twenty years ago, a lifetime really, and he'd fallen in love with her while politely shaking her hand, saying hello after a mutual acquaintance had hastily introduced them. He'd fallen in love when she'd given him a level look with those dark eyes of hers, tilting her head to one side; it's what she did whenever her curiosity was aroused. He'd fallen in love when he heard her voice, as deep and broad as a chord played on a pipe organ. He'd fallen in love. And since falling in love he'd never stopped talking to her; he still talked to her constantly, and she answered back.

Even though she was dead.

Her time bomb had been set to go off almost three years before the one ticking away inside of him, and it had worked perfectly. Not that Giorgio had given up the fight, even then, but through tears he'd promised his wife that he wouldn't let her die engulfed by the agonizing torments the disease could bring, torments she was so afraid of. It hadn't occurred to him that it would be Carmen herself who would crumble before the prospect of that pain.

Leonardo, the monk who had become Pisanelli's best friend, said that it was something that happened; facing an abyss of suffering, human beings display either strength or weakness, and sometimes they choose to end things ahead of schedule. They choose to leapfrog past the evil that's consuming them, and go into the light before their time. That's what Leonardo would tell him, when they sat and reminisced about Carmen without sorrow: Giorgio because he still saw her every second of the day and in his dreams; the monk because he'd helped and comforted her, sustaining her faith to the very end. Giorgio and Leonardo had met at his wife's deathbed, and forged a bond of friendship that bound them still: the last gift that his wife had bestowed upon him before downing an entire bottle of painkillers and going to sleep forever.

Leonardo was right: Grief can cause so much fear that it robs you of your desire to go on breathing, even if you're surrounded by the love of a husband and a son. He himself would have put an end to Carmen's life, if her pain had become too much to handle. He'd been ready. But she'd beat him to it.

He noticed some movement in the atrium of the building

and perked up; but it was a false alarm—just the butcher's boy talking to the doorman.

That was exactly why he was here right now, because he knew how tempting it could be to try to escape when confronted with pain. And he, Giorgio Pisanelli, deputy captain of the state police, fought every day against the temptation to wipe himself from the face of the earth instead of waiting around for the date prescribed by Nefarious Nature. But he couldn't. Not yet. First there was a case to close. First he had a killer to track down.

In the aftermath of Carmen's death, when he'd been left alone in a huge apartment still echoing with her voice, still filled with her scent, when he had turned down Lorenzo's suggestion that he go into retirement and join him up north, he'd asked himself: How does a person decide to kill himself? Where does one find the strength?

He knew the precinct he worked in like the back of his own hands. He'd been born there and he'd lived there all his life, like his parents and his grandparents before him. He knew all the abnormal norms, the usual oddities that characterized it: nothing could surprise him, because he knew how the neighborhood breathed as if it were a beloved, familiar animal, an immense beast that occasionally woke up, but for the most part lay sleeping, now and then shaken by unconscious spasms. And that's how he knew that those suicides were something different.

He'd discovered them one sleepy morning, before that drug-dealing ugliness his four idiot colleagues had gotten tangled up in, four colleagues he still couldn't help but think of with a hint of fondness. With Carmen and her death, still fresh at the time, weighing on his heart and mind, he'd started rummaging through the files and had noticed that over the past ten years, there'd been too many of these cases in the neighborhood. They'd all been handled professionally, no question, each subjected to a careful investigation and properly archived. Suicide notes, different means of death, motives, always good ones, underlying the deed: all within the norm.

And yet he'd never had a moment's doubt. Those weren't suicides.

He'd tried to explain it to the commissario, an old functionary, pragmatic and hardened, tested by years of policework and largely indifferent to wild theories, what with all the work that there was to do. Then, on top of everything else, there'd been the scandal of the Bastards, and so of course the last thing anyone wanted to pay attention to were the fantasies of an old man. Even his new boss, Palma, who really did strike him as a good guy, didn't seem to give his ideas a lot of credence, though out of respect and courtesy, he left him free to investigate whatever he liked. But he was certain, absolutely certain, that those people had been murdered. And he was certain precisely because of Carmen.

Here's how he saw it: in order to want to die you have to be afraid. Depression, the slow falling back into the arms of a life that is no longer life, loneliness, poverty, a tiny pension, none of these things can easily become motives for suicide. To be so afraid that you're willing to die, you need courage. Immense courage.

When Giorgio had confided in Leonardo, he'd seen infinite pity in the monk's clear, light-blue eyes. He'd told him that unfortunately that wasn't how it was, that in fact loneliness was life's chief enemy, that many poor souls choose to end their lives because they can no longer tolerate the silence that surrounds them. That the years go by fast, too fast, but that days spent alone never seem to pass, and can cause intolerable anguish. Leonardo would tell him that he hoped that God, in his infinite so on and so forth, would forgive those benighted souls and so on and so forth, and that He'd welcome them into paradise, etc. But Giorgio was quite certain that someone else's hand had done more than a little to help usher them into the Almighty's presence.

And so he'd started putting the pieces of the puzzle together, with the scrupulous attention to detail that he'd developed over the course of a long career as a cop, collecting statements, eyewitness accounts, stories of shops forced into bankruptcy by the recession, accidental glances, apparently insignificant details. He'd wallpapered his apartment with newspaper clippings, letters, photocopies of scrawled notes, photographs of corpses. And he'd done the same in the office, attracting pity and sarcasm. He'd dug deep, disassembled and reassembled, with stubborn precision. He knew that his colleagues assumed he was losing his marbles, but that was fine by him: At least they left him alone. Aside from Aragona, of course.

His young colleague was the very picture of a bad cop, oafish and egotistical, arrogant and politically incorrect: And yet Giorgio found that it was precisely Aragona, with his obsession with nicknames and TV series, of whom he was fondest. Under his fake tan and those intolerable aviators, he sensed a kind of crude talent, an ungoverned intelligence that could turn him into a first-rate investigator—provided he gave up on trying to look like Serpico.

There she was. She came out of the front door and stopped, squinting into the sun. God, she looked like an elderly woman, but records indicated she was less than sixty. Dirty hair, shapeless sweater, shabby purse. The doorman gave her a brisk glance and didn't bother to say hello. She headed off toward the piazza, dragging her feet.

This was a new development in Pisanelli's investigation. After years spent working on the dead, reconstructing their misguided lives, their chain of misfortunes and, in the end, their incongruous demises, he had decided to break with procedure and identify potential future victims. In the last few months, he'd devoted himself to mapping out the locations of the suicides, in search of some common thread that might link them; in other words, he'd tried to narrow the field. Then he'd gone over the local pharmacies with a fine-toothed comb to find out who was taking psychotropic drugs, and who had recently increased his or her dose. It was hardly an orthodox method, sure, but it was still a method.

And eventually his research had brought him to her, Maria Musella, fifty-eight years old, who lived, barely, off a pitiful surviving spouse's pension, in a tiny apartment she'd inherited from her husband, who'd died ten years earlier. Maria Musella, who begged her doctor to prescribe her something that would help her sleep. Maria Musella, who didn't have a friend, who never went to play bingo, who tried to save money by buying her groceries twice a week from the local market. Today was market day, and Pisanelli was waiting for her to go out so he could get a glimpse of her up close. Maria Musella, who was traveling into a solitary old age filled with nothing and no one.

Maria Musella, the perfect victim.

Pisanelli waited a moment, then he folded his newspaper, put it under his arm, and set off in the same direction the woman was going, carefully moderating his pace to keep the proper distance, even if he suspected that Maria Musella wouldn't have noticed him if he'd stepped on her foot.

The policeman was waiting for someone to approach her. If you want to kill someone, he thought, you need to approach him. And since Maria Musella never saw anyone, if someone did approach her, that person might turn out to be the killer. Of course there would still be plenty of investigating to do, in-depth research to complete, evidence to sift through, but it was a starting point, wasn't it? A starting point. He could go from there.

He'd pee in a bar when the woman came home after doing her shopping. Right now, he needed to follow her. Nature and his ticking time bomb could wait.

He was already anticipating the pleasure of telling Leonardo about these latest developments. Maybe later he'd go see him at the parish church, unless there was news about the boy; he'd asked Ottavia to call him immediately on his cell phone if there was. And if so, he'd put that visit off. After all, there was no rush. Leonardo was always available for a quick chat. And anyway, in a couple days they'd have their weekly lunch at the trattoria Il Gobbo.

Maria Musella stopped in front of a fruit vendor's brightly colored wares. The May sunshine, brazen and indiscreet, beat down on the display, transforming it into a dazzling kaleidoscope that could not but inspire joy. Four boys in tank tops chased after a soccer ball inside a makeshift playing field bounded by shops, crates of vegetables, dumpsters, parked mopeds, and moving scooters. A fat woman sat shelling fresh peas outside of a ground-floor apartment, from whose interior burst the notes of a neomelodic song on the radio. Life—violent, colorful, and smelly—pulsated in every corner of the piazza.

You don't want to die, Maria Musella. If you go out shopping for groceries, if you cook, if you eat, if you wake up in the morning, you don't want to die. Maybe you don't want to keep living, sometimes, but you don't want to die. And that's the crucial difference.

For no particular reason, Pisanelli's thoughts went to Dodo. I wonder where you are, he thought. Let's hope nothing happens to you.

It's May, and the world is too lovely a place just now.

XVIII

Don't trust the month of May.

May will deceive you in the blink of an eye. All it takes is a moment's distraction, a change in plans, an extra laugh, and May will trick you.

Because in this city, May knows how to sneak up behind you. It tiptoes along and in a flash it makes you think you're somewhere else, or in some other time.

Its soft tentacles will embrace you and make you think that everything's fine, that everything's just as it was.

But it's not.

Tiziana's running late this morning. Yesterday night, like an idiot, she stayed up watching a pointless movie on TV, and she got to sleep an hour later than usual.

The people at the office where she works have been waiting for this moment, guns loaded, no doubt about it; she's the last one to be hired, and they don't let anything slide. That's how it is for newcomers: the hardest, most boring jobs, and no respect.

But Tiziana needs her job. That bastard hasn't paid his alimony for at least a year and he won't even answer the phone, he's even figured out how to tell when she calls from a blocked number, the sly son of a bitch. And Francesca always needs something; her feet grow a whole size every three months and every season she has to have a new wardrobe. She's four years old, after all. At that age, it's normal.

She hurries past Francesca's bed, patting her on the head as *she goes by. A rapid, motherly thought: For the past few days her daughter has seemed quiet and preoccupied. Maybe she's just coming down with the flu.*

She goes into the kitchen. She has just a few seconds for her coffee, if Papà made it. From the aroma, she guesses he has. Her father is there, attentive: Good morning, sweetheart, have a biscuit, get something in your stomach, otherwise you'll get a headache. Tiziana nods. It's a good thing you're around, Papà, Francesca and I are lucky that we have you at least, that you took us in, that you're helping me out.

Sweetheart, he says, this will be your home, a home for you and for my little darling. You know that ever since your mother . . . Tiziana goes over and kisses his whiskery cheek; every time that the memory of Mamma passes lightly between them, his eyes glisten.

Don't think about it, Papà. Now we're all together. You see, the weather's starting to get nice: Pretty soon we'll be able to go to the beach, all three of us. And we'll have a few hours of fun, we deserve it, don't we? Now I'm sorry, I've got to fly to the office. I ironed a playsuit for her, so if the weather doesn't change, you can take her to the park if you feel like it.

She blows him another kiss and then Tiziana is out the door and into the street; her father watches her turn the corner, her coat flapping behind. He sighs, shakes his head. Poor daughter, he thinks. What a life, he says. It's a good thing I'm here to take care of them.

Careful not to make noise, he goes to see if Francesca's still sleeping. Sweetheart? Are you asleep? You're just pretending, aren't you? Because now you want to play.

And, walking over to the bed, he unzips his trousers.

You can't trust May.

It's a month that knows how to pretend, suspended between the tail end of winter and the tip of summer's nose. It knows how to mask itself, perhaps behind a thought or a false desire, and it plunges the blade of a hopeless fantasy into your back.

It envelops you in a faint perfume, so light you don't even notice you're smiling until it's too late.

May is a razor-sharp threat that penetrates so deeply, you can't draw even a single breath.

Ciro is a good boy. But the neighborhood where he lives is a tough one.

Still, he's steered clear of the bad crowd, doing his best to keep from being dragged into things. His father is a streetcar operator and to bring home a little extra money, he takes on ridiculous shifts. Ciro wouldn't be able to live with himself if he paid him back by giving him something else to worry about. His father has always told him—in very few words, because he's not the kind who does a lot of talking—that people like them have no one to defend them; if they get mixed up in something, they'll wind up behind bars and they won't make it out again. Better to stick to the straight and narrow, better to work hard, even if only for a pittance.

Ciro knows, he can see how easy it would be to steal what he'd need to be able to go around on a motorcycle, wearing expensive shoes and nice clothing. But he also knows that guys who choose that path don't last. It's safer to work in a café, like he does, waking up at dawn and running up and down the stairs in office buildings delivering trays full of coffee, hoping it's the key to a longer life. That's what Papà says, though not in so many words, and he has to agree.

Ciro is a good boy.

He met a girl, Ciro did. She works as a salesclerk at a women's clothing store, downtown, along the main thoroughfare where he often goes to deliver trays of espressos and cappuccinos. At first, they smiled at each other every time he went past the plate-glass window. Then, one time, he was so busy smiling that *he dropped his tray and everything—coffee, mineral water, and check—went up in the air: a tragedy. She hurried out to help him collect the cups and glasses from under the feet of passersby. It was May. A year ago. It's a nice thing to meet in May. The world is beautiful in May.*

They've been going out for one year exactly, and Ciro wants to do something to celebrate. His friends give their girls lots of things: jewelry, nice clothes. Easy to do, when you have easy money. But Ciro is a good boy; he's never had much money and he never will.

But he doesn't want to let May go by without giving her a gift that'll take her breath away. May is their month, you know, and she's the most beautiful thing on earth, the only good thing that's ever happened to him, to Ciro, the only good luck that's come his way.

It's easy, they told him last night at the pub. The jewelry boutique is tucked away, right by the vicolo *that leads to our neighborhood, get fifty feet away and no one would ever catch you, even if you're on foot. In the last year, we knocked the place over five times, it's like an ATM, little kids rob the place, twelve-year-olds. And after all, it's not like you're trying to ransack the place, just take a thing or two and then you're out of there, those guys won't even come after you, the guy who runs the place is a chump, he's the owner's son, our age: He always gets scared and hides behind the display counter.*

Ciro is a good boy, and he wants a special smile from her this month, this May. May is their month, and he'll never have the money to buy her a ring. Once, just this once. He's not afraid, not running any risks; five minutes and he'll make her happy. It'll last for the rest of his life, her smile. Five minutes.

Marco is a good boy. He's not especially brave, it's true, but he's a jeweler, not a cop or a lion tamer. It doesn't take courage to be a jeweler. Or at least, it's not supposed to. He doesn't even especially like the job, it's just that his father has cancer and he can't come down to run the shop anymore. So it's up to Marco.

Marco is a good boy, and maybe even the robbers understand that he'd just as soon be somewhere else. So he's been robbed five times in less than a year. Once they came in with sledge-hammers and smashed the display cases, once they were armed with a straight razor, and three times they had handguns, which might have been fake, but I'd like to see you face down a guy in a ski mask brandishing something black right under your nose. He throws himself to the floor just like they tell him, that way at least he saves his skin. Be careful, Marco, his father told him, those kids are all hopped up on drugs. One time he even thinks he heard them laugh, those sons of bitches.

Marco is a good boy, but this time he's ready. As soon as the guy bursts into the shop and shouts, Look out, don't do anything stupid, this is a stickup, and grabs a ring off the counter—and the guy has to be a fool, because with all the valuables in there, he grabs a ring with a microscopic two-bit diamond, and the weapon he brought with him is a kitchen knife, unbelievable—Marco hits the floor behind the counter, the way he always does. Only this time there's a rifle behind the counter, legally bought and licensed, fully loaded, a bullet in the chamber, and Marco, who's a good boy but now he's had enough, levels the rifle and shoots the fucking robber in the chest, and Ciro, who's a good boy but, because it's May, just wanted a special smile, flies backward through the plate-glass window, his belly split open like a watermelon.

Ciro and Marco are both good boys. But in the month of May, in this city, anything is possible.

May is a traitor.

A charming bastard of a traitor, with a roguish face that casts a spell and makes you fall in love. A damn slithering serpent, so beautiful to behold that it makes you wish it could last forever.

May echoes with sweet songs; it winds you in its coils with an unfamiliar music that seems brand-new, even though it's actually just that same old tune.

May lets you slip slowly into the abyss.

Peppe's sleepy.

He's always sleepy. There are some who get used to it—actually, almost everyone gets used to it, everyone who takes the night shift to make a little extra cash. These days, with the recession galloping along like a horse across the prairie, people will fight over a few extra euros, and there's a line out the boss's door: Please, let me work the night shift.

Peppe stands in line, just like the others. He needs those euros too, there's never enough money at home. But he can't get used to it; he just can't somehow. And after working the night shift, he walks around like a zombie all the next day, a headache in the background of every thought.

He never even wanted this job, never wanted to be a security guard. With all the risks that they run. He could have made it, going to night school, could have become an accountant, and he would have gotten a job in his uncle's company, working during the day and sleeping at night like everyone else. But his pretty wife, Lucia—though everyone calls her Lucy—who wasn't even his wife at the time, just his girlfriend, thought she'd miscount the days of her cycle and wound up pregnant. With twins, actually. And so goodbye dreams of glory—well, hardly glory; just dreams of a job as an accountant for a company that's not even doing particularly well.

Peppe should be happy to have found that job. The work is hard, but when he goes home he finds two little demons who love him and a wife, Lucia, called Lucy, so pretty and so shapely that she literally turns heads. Even men's heads—in fact especially men's heads, and they think that Peppe doesn't notice. Feast your eyes, feast your eyes and dream on, because I'm the one taking her to bed tonight, this God-given bounty.

Maybe not every night, because of the shifts he works. In fact, it happens pretty rarely, truth be told. But at least he makes a *little extra cash so he can take her out for a pizza, or to the movies, if grandma will keep the twins. Man does not live by bread alone, no? And neither does woman.*

But then May comes along. And May, on certain nights, has this spectacular smell that blows in from the sea and mingles with the odors wafting out from the countryside, and it sweeps the smog and the vast mountains of garbage right out of the air and slips a yearning under your flesh for which there's no relief.

So Peppe asks Salvatore to do him a favor and take over his shift for a couple of hours, just long enough to go home and have a quickie with Lucia, called Lucy, because it's been a week since he's had a chance to see her in that flimsy negligee that drives him crazy. Sure, he'll have to slip Salvatore a few euros for standing in for him, of course he will, but Salvatore has a son at university and he's always after a few spare pennies. But on a May night, with the flowers and the love songs courting each other in the mild spring air as if it hasn't been a century since the last serenades, it's worth the money.

Peppe enters the apartment on tiptoe because he knows that if he wakes up the twins, so long, surprise, it'll take all night to get them back to sleep, and then no more fun with Lucia, called Lucy, in their nice bedroom, wallpapered in pink just the way she wanted it; just a couple more months and they'll have paid off the furniture, too, at last. Peppe hopes that Lucia, called Lucy, is still awake, because if she isn't she'll be startled to see him so unexpectedly.

Yes, Lucia called Lucy is awake. And she's sitting right on top of Luigi's tool, Luigi, the accountant who lives downstairs, who's divorced and works days so he has his nights free. As he pulls out his pistol, Peppe thinks that sure enough, he was right about night school, it had been an excellent idea, because accountants don't have to work the night shift, which means they have all the time to cultivate rewarding relationships with their neighbors.

It's just too bad about the negligee. That beautiful lace negligee that cost a small fortune and looked so good on Lucia, called Lucy. But now, riddled with holes and smeared with blood as it is, it's no good anymore. Just like Luigi's head: I'd love to see how you account for that, Mr. Accountant, with a nice big bullet hole in your forehead.

Suddenly Peppe is terribly sleepy. Mamma mia, how sleepy. It must be the May air.

Look out for May.

Especially because you don't see it coming, accustomed as you are to winter's toxic residue, its last stubborn chills. Don't fall for it, because that sweet warm air does far worse damage.

Silvana is fifteen years old, and she's just had her hair done. It's Friday, she's going out tonight, and all the girls have to be gorgeous.

She's blonde, Silvana is, and her hair is a beautiful color, with copper highlights that emphasize her green eyes. Only her hair is ever so slightly curly, and taming the curls is a mess, especially when it's humid: after three seconds, her hair's wavy again. But these days straight is the look, and the boys look at her so happily when she has this mass of golden hair cascading down past her waist.

Silvana leaves the beauty parlor, waving goodbye to the girls who work there, ciao ciao, I'll let you know how it goes. Between a manicure and a shampoo, she told them all about this guy who's been hanging around, and how she really likes him; so do my hair extra nice today, girls, I'm on the hunt, if he doesn't introduce himself, that's it, I'll get a girlfriend of mine to introduce me to him, I'm not letting him get away.

May doesn't offer any do-overs: May is the perfect time to start something or end it.

Silvana gets on her moped, her helmet hanging off her arm; no way is she going to ruin her hairdo and anyway just feel that air, how wonderful. After all, home's not far. It's late, thinks Silvana: I'll get dressed and go out.

I need to look stunning tonight.

Matteo rolls down his car windows, both windows: Let's get some air in here, just smell that, how glorious. You can say whatever you want about this city, but you can't say that May here isn't spectacular.

Matteo wants a little music to keep him company as he drives to the beach house where he's meeting up with his friends. Even if it's just a short distance, he's really in the mood for some music.

As he drives, he hunts in his car's glove compartment, where he keeps all his music, for a good CD. Not that one, this one's old, this one's not right for this May breeze. There, this one.

This one's perfect.

Matteo's driving downhill, Silvana's driving uphill. Matteo veers toward the center line, reading the CD's label; Silvana veers toward the center line, her hair blowing in the wind, avoiding a pothole.

Matteo and Silvana.

Because you shouldn't trust May, you know.
Not even a little.

XIX

The prospect of having to go to the forensic squad's inter-regional office wasn't an agreeable one to Lojacono. His previous experience hadn't left him with a pleasant memory: The hostility of certain of his colleagues there, as soon as they'd heard where he and Aragona, who had accompanied him, came from, had been palpable.

The Pizzofalcone name, for members of that city's police force, was a mark of infamy difficult to erase. The blow that the scandal had dealt to entire corps' image had been a heavy one, and for quite a while those who never missed a chance to run down law enforcement had had an ideal subject to slap onto the front page and lead off with on the evening news. So it was only natural that even those who, through no fault of their own, had been sent to replace those who had caused the whole mess should be looked on with distaste and suspicion.

When he'd had this trouble with the forensic squad, Lojacono, in order to get some leverage, had been forced to ask Piras to throw her weight around; he didn't like to make use of his friendship with the magistrate, but if it meant getting results on the job, he set aside those scruples. And the doors had opened wide. In any case, the lieutenant was pretty sure that the forensics chief, Rosaria Martone, was a serious, competent person, and that Piras's intervention had served not to influence her, but simply to bring the matter to Martone's attention.

On their way over, he told Alex the story; they were both

happy to have a case to work that would help take their minds off the thought of the missing boy.

The young woman listened attentively and then said: "You know, this whole Bastards of Pizzofalcone thing is a real pain in the neck. And come to think of it, Ottavia and Giorgio, who worked there when it happened, can't bring themselves to speak ill of their four colleagues, have you noticed? They always say that each of the four, for one reason or another, was more or less forced to start selling drugs. As if there's any way to justify what they did. I think they're disgusting. Period."

Lojacono was driving slowly, the window open, enjoying the spring air: "I don't know. I mean, if you look at individual cases, each of us, one way and another, is a little bit of a bastard. Take me, for instance: I'm supposed to be a Mafia informant, you know. And then there's Romano: a cop who beats up suspects. It's only if you look at things from the outside that they seem different. That's all."

"I appreciate the fact that you made no mention of the shot fired in the station house from which I was transferred. That was nice of you. And maybe you're right: Nothing is ever quite what it seems, or at least not everything is. Take this burglary: there's something strange about that couple, and he's not telling us the whole story. If there really was nothing of value in that safe, then you tell me why that's all the thieves stole and why he was so upset about it."

"Yes, those two are strange. And maybe they'd have been strange even without the burglary, who can say. Now let's hear what our colleagues in forensics have to say; and let's hope that Martone agrees to see us, and that we don't wind up with the same bastard as last time."

They'd arrived at the old barracks that served as headquarters for the forensic team. They parked in one of the reserved spaces, staring defiantly at the man at the gate before ostentatiously placing their police insignia on the dashboard.

As usual, the place exuded a sense of efficiency. Men and women in plainclothes, in uniforms, or in white lab coats exited and entered the rooms that gave onto the broad hallway, all carrying documents, evidence in folders, or test tubes; no one was engaging in idle chitchat or drinking coffee or wandering aimlessly, hands in pockets, as would have been normal in any other office. This was a place where people worked, and took their jobs seriously.

Lojacono went over to a fellow officer standing behind a counter and identified himself; once the man had found his name on a checklist, he said: "Lieutenant, please go right ahead, Dottoressa Martone is expecting you. Down this hallway, the last door."

The lesson Piras had administered was proving useful. They'd be meeting with the chief administrator right away.

Lojacono, who already knew the way, strode down the hallway until he reached an office whose door stood ajar; he knocked, calling out as he did so. A woman's voice invited them to come in.

Later, Alex would often look back on that day, and every time she did, a phrase would come to mind, something she'd read in some book: The important encounters of one's life are always unexpected, and generally go unnoticed. From that day forward, she'd have something to say about that.

In her memories, she'd watch Lojacono open the door and take a few steps inside; she'd see him, from behind, duck his head in a gesture of greeting, and she'd hear him say, *Buongiorno*, Dottoressa. Then she'd see him step to one side in order to let her walk past him, introducing her as he did so: This is my partner, Di Nardo; we're here about the burglary at the Parascandolo residence.

She'd remember a large white room, with a large window overlooking the internal courtyard. She'd recall the way her eyes had glanced over the sofa, the coffee table, and the two armchairs arranged in a corner, like a cunning little living room that clashed sharply with the martial ambiance. She'd remember that, once she'd surveyed the space, her eyes had alighted on the person sitting behind the big desk, a pen in her hand and a notebook in front of her, and how her heartbeat had begun to race, contradicting the notion that we cannot clearly perceive the most important meetings in our lives.

Because Alex Di Nardo knew immediately that Rosaria Martone, chief administrator of the inter-regional division of the police forensic squad, the leading authority in her field from Rome to Sicily, would always play an important role in her life. Even if she never saw her again.

As Alex came to an awkward halt behind Lojacono in the doorway, her heart pounding, Martone looked up from her notes and removed her eyeglasses with a graceful gesture that froze in midair when she glimpsed her.

Rosaria was young for her rank, and she looked even younger because of her finely drawn features, her petite frame, and the thick head of dark blond hair that went well with her complexion, which was tan thanks to her natural enthusiasm for fresh air. Her girlish appearance had taken in more than one person, and all had paid dearly for judging that book by its cover: The chief was in fact quite tough, and this toughness was reinforced by a razor-sharp intelligence and a propensity to sarcasm that made her both widely feared and not particularly well liked.

The two women's eyes met and locked. Rosaria, as if lunging toward Alex, stood up from her desk. Lojacono sensed the tension: "Do you know each other?"

Martone approached, curious: "Not in person, but I know the name. It's not every day that we do ballistics tests on a gunshot fired inside the Decumano station house. So you're the girl with the gun."

Alex blushed, and hated herself for it. But her retort was cutting: "There can be many reasons for firing a gun, Dottoressa.

It's hard to understand if you're a cop who works in a laboratory."

The sharp rejoinder must have confirmed an impression that Martone had already formed. She held out her hand: "Right. In that case, let's just say that we're two halves of one whole. I'm Rosaria."

"Alessandra Di Nardo, private first class."

Lojacono was taken aback by the intimacy of her tone; usually Martone was fairly formal.

Rosaria held onto Alex's hand for a fraction of a second too long; the girl felt warm, dry flesh, and the delicate strength of the fingers, and a shiver went down the nape of her neck. Rosaria gestured to the sofa and armchairs: "Please, make yourselves comfortable. I'll get the reports. Parascandolo, you said, right?" Both Lojacono and Alex slid their eyes over Martone's taut and well-rounded derriere, which twitched under the lab coat as she walked. "The weird burglary. That's what we've been calling it here, with the technicians who worked on it. Really odd."

"Oh, yeah?" Lojacono asked. "Why is that?"

Martone sat down in one of the armchairs, a stack of documents in her hands.

"Well, now. Front entrance and concierge's booth: no signs of forced entry. That's reasonable enough. Second-floor apartment. If someone had been walking downstairs, which many did since the elevator has been out of order for the past month and a half, as documented by the dated sign, he or she would have noted one or more strangers fiddling with the lock. No sign of forced entry there either. According to the Parascandolos' statements, the door was found open: for a burglary in which the thieves had keys and there was no forced entry, that's very rare."

Alex was struggling to fight a dry throat. She coughed, then asked: "What if their arms were full of loot?"

"Sure, but what loot? Because the really interesting thing is that the burglar, or burglars, turned the apartment upside down, carefully emptying closets, sideboards, and dressers and laying everything out on the floor, and yet, according to the provisional inventory drawn up by the husband and wife, nothing was taken except for the contents of the safe, which is quite small."

As usual, Lojacono was concentrating in his own way, projecting to the outside world the image of a sleeping Tibetan. Not that it mattered: Martone's eyes never left Alex's face.

"So no valuables were taken. That's the impression we got during our preliminary examination."

"That's right. And according to what I've been told by my colleagues who examined the scene, and as can also be seen from the photographic report, the funny thing is that the armoires and other pieces of furniture were emptied but not ransacked. It makes you think that they weren't looking for something, but that they clumsily tried to make it seem as though they had been. You must have noticed, for example, the wallet lying open on the nightstand: It looked as if it had been laid out just to display its contents. These days, what with online fraud, credit cards like those are worth many times their weight in gold."

Lojacono nodded. "And what do we know about the safe?"

"A Mottura 50cm x 50cm, with a double key-and-mechanical-combination locking system. A good safe, not the very latest model, but solid and well built. The anchoring system was robust, with cemented brackets: difficult to extract and carry away—and in fact, they opened it using oxy-fuel cutting."

"Oxy-fuel cutting?" asked Alex.

"An oxyacetylene torch," Lojacono explained. "That takes time, to open a safe with an oxyacetylene torch."

Martone nodded in confirmation. "That's right. The thief or thieves knew that they could count on no one bothering them."

"Fingerprints, organic residue?"

"Nothing whatsoever. We found only the fingerprints of the husband and wife, and the housekeeper. What's more, the housekeeper's fingerprints all date back to before the burglary. The most recent ones belong to the wife."

The chief fell silent, and for a while there was a thoughtful lull. Nothing about this burglary added up.

Rosaria went on: "If I were you, I'd try to learn more about the couple. It strikes me as a show staged in order to defraud an insurance company."

Lojacono had to disagree: "We thought about that ourselves, but they're not insured. They have a hi-tech alarm system that they forgot to turn on."

Martone made a face: "Well, just think of that. I'll say it again: I'd investigate the two of them. I wouldn't want there to be something else going on here."

Lojacono stood up. "*Grazie*, Dottoressa. You've been very kind, and let me thank you for working so quickly."

Rosaria stood up as well: "And I thank you. Di Nardo, why don't you leave me your phone number?" Alex and Lojacono exchanged a glance. "We're doing further tests," Martone explained, "and I may send the boys over for another inspection. I might have something urgent to communicate, and I believe you, Lieutenant, have other matters to worry about. I wouldn't want to bother you. It's standard for us to get in touch with the lower-ranking partner in cases like this."

Blushing, Alex murmured her phone number, which Martone jotted down on the burglary file.

"*Grazie.* I assure you I'll make good use of it."

XX

A black housekeeper, whose face betrayed keen grief, ushered Romano and Aragona into the living room where Eva awaited them. No attempt to adopt an appropriate facial expression, no special greeting; the woman, who wore a cap and apron, as was standard practice in this, the city's most exclusive neighborhood, was fully absorbed in the atmosphere of grief enveloping the apartment.

Though the household staff, each of whom had certainly been sworn to silence, were nothing but discreet, the officers had still been able to glimpse the same concern for Dodo's safety in the eyes of the concierge and the security guard manning the front gate outside the grounds. Bad news travels like a strong odor, and there's no getting rid of it.

The Borrelli family, formerly the Cerchia family, lived in an apartment whose location made it hard to get to. From the street they went through a narrow gate then along a lane surrounded by greenery that wound halfway up a hill before opening out into a plaza lined with maritime pines, which three buildings, each three stories tall, overlooked: Dodo's apartment was on the third floor of the building in the middle.

The two policemen had walked the entire distance without speaking.

Their visit to the school had added nothing to what little they knew. An increasingly sour Sister Angela and an ever-more heartbroken Sister Beatrice had led them on a tour of the building, an attractive apartment building from the sixties, recently renovated, with a courtyard, gymnasium, and refectory. The student body, some two hundred children ranging in age from five to ten, seemed well disciplined and under the complete control of the teachers: a normal private school for wealthy children in a wealthy neighborhood, as Aragona had remarked acidly in a whispered aside to his partner. The kids' contacts with the outside world were carefully and strictly monitored. The students who weren't taken home on the school's bus waited in a room until their parents or drivers came to pick them up, under the supervision of an alert, powerfully built nun who also served as receptionist. In effect, Romano thought to himself, if someone wanted to kidnap one of the children, this certainly wasn't the place to do it. Better to wait for the right opportunity, like a field trip to a museum.

They'd questioned the teachers of the other classes, the hall monitor, the administrative staff: no one remembered Dodo coming into contact with anyone who wasn't a member of his family, and certainly no one had noticed anything unusual about his behavior. Sister Beatrice had reported certain childish habits—bringing toys to school, for example, especially action figures from the comic books he was so crazy about. Otherwise, Dodo was a normal ten-year-old boy.

Even Sister Angela began to express a certain concern about the persistent lack of news, though this concern was masked by a latent hostility; Romano had noticed that her hands were shaking, and at times she seemed incapable of looking him in the eye. If word got out that one of the students had gone missing, it would be a serious problem for the school. The mere presence of two policemen in the building embarrassed and annoyed her, and it had been with palpable relief that she'd walked them back to their car. The request with which she'd bid them farewell, in a voice just over a whisper, hadn't been to keep her informed about Dodo's fate, but to keep what had happened absolutely secret.

Whereupon Aragona had been unable to resist the temptation to make her sweat just a little: "To the extent that we're able, Sister. To the extent that we're able."

There was a very different atmosphere in the living room of the Borrelli home. Eva's metamorphosis was complete by now, and the confident, irritated woman they'd met at the museum the day before had been transformed into a grief-stricken mother. She seemed to have aged suddenly; her puffy eyes and wrinkled face offered mute testimony to a sleepless night spent waiting for any scrap of news that might attenuate her immense anguish. She met them as they entered, clutching a handkerchief.

"Have you found anything, any clues? You've been over to the school, haven't you? Did the nuns have anything to tell you? Damn them, when this is all over, I'll make them wish they'd never met us, I promise you that. I'll have that shit-hole shut down. You think your child is safe, and then look what happens, those damn incompetents, with all the money they steal every month, in spite of their so-called vow of poverty."

Romano had no good news to offer: "I'm afraid not, Signora. Nothing new emerged from our visit to the school. The boy was happy, he showed no signs of being upset or restless. No one noticed anything. Any news here?"

A look of misery crossed Eva's face: "No, of course not. I'd have called you immediately. And like I told the commissario, none of my girlfriends, none of the mothers of Dodo's classmates, saw him yesterday. I can't tell you how excruciating it was to carry on these conversations, as if nothing at all had happened."

Aragona had walked over to the large wall of windows that offered an incredible vista of the bay; in the distance, sharp and splendid in the clear spring air, the silhouette of the island rose into the blue sky.

The policeman said, without turning around: "*Mamma mia.*

I've never seen a view like this. If you live here, I bet you never feel like going anywhere else on vacation."

Romano sighed: His partner truly was incorrigible.

"Does this strike you," Eva hissed, venomously, "as the right time to make that sort of comment? Why don't you focus on my son instead, and on trying to find out where he is!"

Aragona looked at her: "My dear woman, your son is in fact exactly what I'm focusing on, and by the way, if you'd focused on him just a little more, I wouldn't have to be doing it now. My inopportune comment springs from the thought that if I wanted to get a lot of money in exchange for a kidnapped child, I'd make sure I took one that belonged to a family who lived in a place just like this one. Tell me something: do you have a lot of money? You, personally, I mean."

At the young officer's words, a chill promptly descended. Romano was mortified: The question was a reasonable one, but his partner had hardly chosen the best way of framing it. Eva stood openmouthed, frozen to the spot. Then she exploded: "Get out of my house this instant and don't you dare show your face here ever again. My friends are more highly placed than you can even begin to imagine; I can have you kicked off the police force before you draw your next breath."

Aragona didn't seem particularly impressed. He went into his old glasses-removal routine: "Do as you think best. But listen closely: Anyone who replaces me would have to ask you the exact same question, perhaps with more courtesy, certainly after having wasted a lot more time—and time has never been as precious as it is now. When the moment to get moving comes, we need to be ready, and we don't want to waste essential hours running in the wrong direction. So I'm going to ask you one more time, and by all means, feel free to refuse to answer me, toss me out of your home, or even have me expelled from the country: Does the money belong to you? And if not, whose is it?"

In spite of himself, Romano had to admit he was amused by Aragona's tenacity. Eva let herself fall into the armchair and then said: "I continue to find your manners deeply offensive, officer. And I continue to have an intense desire to kick you out of my home—literally. But lest anyone think that I'm trying to hinder your investigation, I'll answer your question. No, the money isn't mine, and it doesn't belong to my partner Manuel, either; right now Manuel has gone over to my father's house to give him the news, because my father and I aren't on speaking terms. This apartment belongs to my father, the money we live on is money my father gives me and, in part, money from Dodo's father. Now those two, yes, they're both filthy rich. My father built this city in the sixties and seventies. My ex-husband is an industrialist from northern Italy. Is that what you want to know? Satisfied?"

Aragona put his glasses back on.

"Still, living in a place like this makes you look very wealthy indeed. How much is this apartment worth: two million euros? Three? The condominium fees and domestic staff alone must cost you every a month what an average family earns in six."

"Listen, officer, are you here to find my son or do an audit?"

Romano came to his partner's aid: "Signora, we need to figure out what happened and, if possible, foresee the moves that whoever took the boy is going to make. He might be speaking a bit too directly, but Officer Aragona is just trying to gather useful information. By the way, have you seen Dodo's father?"

The woman ran her hand over her eyes.

"Yes, he was here a couple of hours ago. It wasn't easy. But luckily, if nothing else, he didn't start up again with the usual litany of my countless shortcomings. He's so worried he's going to pieces, same as I am for that matter. Now he's at his place, waiting for news. He lives close by."

Romano nodded, relieved that Cerchia had managed to keep

a lid on his temper. He knew very well how difficult it was not to blow your top when you were under stress.

"And Signor Scarano went to inform your father. Why didn't you just call him yourself? You said that the two of you aren't on speaking terms, but in a situation like this one . . ."

"You see, officer, my father is a very . . . unusual person. He tends to become truly intolerable; perhaps our personalities are too similar for us ever to get along. When my mother was alive, she acted as a buffer between us, but now each of us is barricaded behind castle walls, and we're incapable of communicating. He's never happy with anything I do, none of my choices. He couldn't stand Alberto and he made no mystery of the fact; now he can't stand Manuel, who luckily has a lovely character: he's too intelligent a man to let my father yank his chain."

Aragona was astonished: "And that's who you sent to give your father the news?"

"Someone had to do it. If I'd gone, it would have turned into World War Three, and I'm in no condition to listen to a tirade about what a failure I've been as a mother. Manuel will listen to the cavalcade of insults without batting an eye, the way he always does. He has an inner equilibrium that saves him, whatever the situation."

"In any case," Romano said, "we'll have to talk to him ourselves, unless there are new developments."

Just then, as if in response to his words, the phone rang.

XXI

A ssistant district attorney Laura Piras sat contemplating the file folders on her document-strewn desk with satisfaction; she had to congratulate herself. Her decision to order wiretaps on all phone lines registered to the Cerchia and Borrelli families had been timely. This was going to prove useful.

She ought to have waited, theoretically, until it had been confirmed that they really were dealing with a kidnapping—intercepting communications between individual citizens when it wasn't strictly necessary represented both an invasion of privacy and a significant cost to society at large—but the face of that child when he turned to look into the video camera had prompted a mixture of emotions that had caught her entirely by surprise.

She got out of her chair and went over to the window. Ten floors below lay the city's pathetic, half-kilometer-long attempt to build itself a modern business district; the effort had been aborted twenty years earlier in a series of skyscrapers, avenues, and patches of greenery that remained disconnected from the metropolis, linked neither structurally, nor culturally, nor even by train to the rest of the neighborhood. The ideal sort of place from which to cultivate diffidence and keep at bay the passions inspired by beauty. As well as to avoid becoming too reflective, thought Laura; it was perfect only for those who wanted to do nothing but work.

She'd never felt much of a maternal instinct. Not even when

she and Carlo, her first and only boyfriend, killed in a car crash, had talked about sharing a home and spending their lives together; even then she hadn't given much serious thought to the idea of having children. There were too many other things to think about: moving away from Sardinia, her career, the world and how she planned to change it. Back then, the last thing she'd wanted was a distraction.

But the image of Dodo, his expressionless face as he walked blithely out to who knows what fate, had stirred something deep inside her. She felt a stabbing, physical yearning; like a hunger for something, though she couldn't say what.

Her mind, guided by emotions more than by any conscious thought, went to Lojacono. The man who had reawakened her senses, something she'd long ago assumed would never happen again.

She'd taken men to bed over the years; she was a sensuous woman, with a physicality that attracted men's attention. But they'd been fleeting, sporadic relationships that she'd never wanted to pursue or build on.

This time, instead, she found herself dreaming, occasionally, of an end to her solitary life. They weren't really thoughts, strictly speaking: they were pictures, scenes that she imagined. A Sunday dinner. A hike in the mountains. A day at the beach.

How she hated having a biological clock in her body. What's more, even if she managed to overcome her own countless qualms about coupled life, winning that man over might prove to be a challenge.

She knew he liked her, there was no doubt about it: She could read his glances; she could interpret his tone of voice. And that night, when she'd driven him home, the night they'd solved the murder of the notary's wife, if there hadn't been someone waiting for him in the lobby of his apartment building, whatever would have happened would have put their relationship on the right path.

But when they got there, there had indeed been a person waiting for him in the lobby of his building.

His daughter, Marinella. She was only a girl, but in a glance they'd understood each other clearly. Women, Laura thought to herself, understand certain things. She knew how much Lojacono cared about the girl, she'd listened to him talk about Marinella during his long period of separation from her. If she wanted that man, she'd have to breach the wall that Marinella, she was certain, would try to erect between them. It didn't require her deductive skills to see that, since that rainy night, Giuseppe had stopped trying to see her outside of their professional encounters and had been very evasive about his own free time.

Even though they talked on an almost daily basis, sometimes on the flimsiest of excuses. But then she was his contact in the district attorney's office; it was normal for them to be in close touch. Moreover, the successful outcome of his posting to the reconstituted Pizzofalcone precinct would no doubt prove decisive for Lojacono's future career.

Nonsense. She liked him and she wanted him. And he wanted her. The little girl would just have to deal with it. Anyway, she'd have to go home to her mamma sooner or later, wouldn't she?

A light tap at the door.

"Yes?"

Her assistant stuck her head in, a young woman who'd just finished college, with a solemn, perennially terrified look on her face: "Dottoressa, the wiretap team reports that they've picked up an interesting phone call on the Borrelli line. What would you like to do, go and listen, or shall I have them send you an electronic file?"

Laura was already on her way out the door: "Have them send it by email to the Pizzofalcone precinct house, to Chief Officer Palma's address, and while they're doing that, call

Palma and tell him to wait for me. I'm heading over; I want to listen to it with them."

She got there just as Romano and Aragona were returning from their call on Eva Borrelli. The younger officer seemed as giddy as little kid on Christmas: "Dottoressa, you see? The call came in, we're all set, it's a kidnapping."

Laura, climbing the stairs, shot him a glare: "Aragona, I still really can't make up my mind. Are you insane or just stupid? Sometimes it seems like the one thing, but then I start to think it's the other. And anyway, I can't see why you should be so overjoyed."

Aragona, huffing and puffing his way up the stairs, put on his most contrite expression: "Dottoressa, you always try to embarrass me. I'm not overjoyed, how could you think such a thing? I was just saying that now the situation is clear and we can finally start to work on it for real."

Laura threw open the door to the communal office, waving a hand in the direction of Palma, who stood waiting, ready to play the recording.

They were all here now, the show could begin.

XXII

Ottavia's computer speakers broadcast the sound of static throughout the communal office.

This time there was nothing to see, but still Palma was standing next to his colleague, facing the monitor. Laura was sitting at Lojacono's desk, while the lieutenant was leaning against the wall behind her, arms folded, face expressionless. Pisanelli had taken off his reading glasses; he seemed intensely concentrated, as if he were listening to a symphony. Alex was cracking her knuckles one by one, apparently calm. Aragona and Romano were standing in the doorway, as if they were ready to head out in pursuit of someone on a moment's notice.

The background noise was broken by Eva's housekeeper: "Hello, Borrelli residence."

Silence. Then a man's voice, deep and hoarse: "Signora, please."

A brusque, precise tone. A foreign accent was immediately audible. Aragona took off his glasses; no one else made a move.

After a few seconds, there was Eva: "Yes, hello, this is Signora Borrelli. Who's speaking?"

Every word she spoke throbbed with emotion and worry. A distinct rustling sound could be heard. Then, once again, the man with the foreign accent: "Your son is with us. Don't be afraid, if everything goes the way it should, nothing will happen to him. Right now he's fine, he's safe. Wait for the next phone call."

Short, terse sentences, fired off like so many bullets. Eva, in a louder voice, said: "But who are you? Where's Dodo? What have you done to him?"

The sound of static ceased. The conversation had turned into a monologue with Eva repeating, over and over, increasingly distraught: "Hello? Hello?" Until finally, with the phone line still open and the recording under way, she burst into despairing tears.

Then Romano's voice could be heard, asking: "Was that them?"

"Forty-two seconds in all," Ottavia said, her voice mournful. "From the beginning to when the call was ended."

No one felt like talking. Along with the mild spring air, the sound of a car horn came in through the window, followed by a shouted insult.

Romano broke the embarrassed silence: "You heard it, we were there too. I was hoping that there was already a wiretap on the phone, because afterward Borrelli was in no condition to tell us anything: She practically passed out, she hasn't slept in thirty hours by this point."

Aragona put on his glasses and, in a satisfied tone of voice, declared: "He's a foreigner, no doubt about it. You heard the accent, didn't you? He must be a gypsy or something like that. At least now we have something to go on, though I thought right from the beginning it was likely to be one of their kind."

Alex shot him a harsh look: "Of course, because whenever something happens, we always know who to blame, don't we? Just look in the usual places and round up the usual suspects. God, you're so predictable, Aragona."

Her colleague looked around for support from the others: "Well, you heard him yourselves, didn't you? Didn't you hear from the way he talked that he was a foreigner?"

Palma waved a hand in the air: "This isn't the time to start engaging in hack sociology. Yes, I thought the accent sounded foreign, but that doesn't mean much. Leaving aside the fact that you can fake an accent, maybe they just pulled someone off the street and asked him to make the phone call, or it could even be prerecorded, who can say?"

Pisanelli, who was leaning back in his chair as if trying to relax, said: "I don't think it was a recording. The timing of his responses to the housekeeper and the mother was too precise, and the voice was the same from start to finish. No, that wasn't a recording."

Laura nodded: "I agree, and I also agree that this was a foreigner. Slavic, from the sound of it, but I'll get an expert to listen to it. But there's another thing: Didn't you all get the impression that he was reading a text?"

Lojacono, standing behind her, replied: "Yes. You could hear the sound of the page being unfolded, and the slow, flat pace of someone reading."

Romano added: "What's more, when the housekeeper answered the phone, he said: 'Signora, please,' without the article, but after that he spoke in perfect Italian. He was reading, no doubt."

Aragona brushed his hair back: "She was horrified. And that was no act, believe me. She was horrified and afraid."

Palma stared into space and said: "That was just a call made for effect, to create anxiety and fear. That's what they usually do. Now we're certain that this really is a kidnapping and in all likelihood there's going to be a demand for ransom. So we should expect another call about that."

Ottavia continued to stare at her computer, almost as if she expected it to start talking again: "This is the worst part for the family. Now they know that their child is in the hands of strangers, and that they could hurt him at any moment. Every minute will be an eternity."

Piras stood up, as if to shake off her anxiety. "We all have work to do, I imagine. I'm going to get busy freezing assets: the father's, the mother's, and the grandfather's. By the way, I think this would be a good time to swing by and pay a call on old man Borrelli."

Lojacono, still motionless in the position he'd assumed when he started listening, broke in: "I'd take a look at some of the background characters, the housekeeper for example, and the mother's boyfriend: Whoever took the child did it at the only possible moment, and it strikes me as a little much in terms of pure luck. If you ask me, it's possible that they knew his schedule and routine in detail."

"Then there's the other matter," Alex murmured.

"Which?" asked Aragona.

"If the man was reading a text, then we need to figure out who wrote it. And why."

Di Nardo's voice was little more than a whisper, but her words resounded like a gunshot. An electric shock of determination ran through the communal office. Romano agreed, determinedly: "Then let's get busy. The countdown has started, I believe."

"We'll need to inform the father, too," Ottavia said, "or at least make sure that Borrelli does. We have to make sure they put their differences aside: we can't run the risk of having some valuable piece of information slip through the cracks just because those two won't speak to each other."

"True," admitted Palma, "maybe I should call the father. Romano and Aragona can go call on old man Borrelli. You, Giorgio, make some calls to your friends at the banks, see if you can find out the actual financial situation of Eva Borrelli and her boyfriend, what's his name . . . Manuel Scarano. Ottavia, you coordinate and help Pisanelli with his research online. Di Nardo and Lojacono, if you can get free of your burglary case, maybe you can help us out."

Laura liked the way the commissario intervened directly, entrusting each member of his staff with a specific task. A proactive approach, ideal for encouraging teamwork and, at the same time, the kind of thing that could speed up the investigation. She'd do the same, to the extent that she was able. Because in the last hour, everything had changed.

Now it was a kidnapping.

XXIII

He wanders around his home like a lion in a cage. And really, to call it a home is an exaggeration. It's nice, of course. It looks out onto every possible shade of blue: the sea, the sky, the silhouette of the island and the peninsula in the distance. But an apartment becomes a home when you live in it. Not just because it has hardwood floors and all the modern conveniences.

Alberto can't seem to read, or listen to music, or even channel surf. He's tried, but he just can't do it.

Dodo.

He thinks of him all the time, he's like a sound track, like background noise, like the background in a painting. Dodo sneaks into his thoughts even during the confused and agitated sleep he only managed to achieve in the very early hours of the morning, as the night that seemed to have gone on forever was dissolving into dawn.

His little boy.

He walks back into the little room he set up for him, in that impersonal apartment he comes back to every fifteen days, the place that remains, despite his efforts, stubbornly anonymous, where he feels out of place, as if he were in a hotel. Dodo's room too is anonymous. The bed, almost never used because when he stays over he sleeps in his papà's bed, of course. The desk, where Dodo never sits because they do his homework in there, at the living room table. The shelves full of new toys because the ones that Dodo really cares about are *there*.

There. In the other home. And that really *was* a home.

No thanks to her, to be clear, because she never gave a damn about having a home. But that was where he and Dodo lived together.

He goes to the balcony, leans out to smoke a cigarette and think. The city streams by far away, the river of cars along the waterfront visible but silent at that distance. A city that—with its incomprehensible chaos, its sudden madnesses, its incessant noise—has always been alien to him.

But it's also the only place he ever even had the illusion of happiness.

His little boy.

A million snapshots, holidays at the beach and in the mountains, first days of school, adoring eyes on him: I'm your giant, you're my little king.

He runs his hand over his eyes, fogged with grief and exhaustion. A useless giant. He couldn't stop someone from hurting his little king.

But I'll fix everything, my little one, he murmurs to the city that streams past indifferently. I'll fix everything, and we'll soon forget all about this. We'll be together forever, I'll never leave you again. Because we know it, you and I, that we need to stay together. The principle is a simple one: You're my son, and once you're free, you'll come live with me.

He looks out the window toward the apartment where she lives with her boyfriend, that asshole, that useless creature. And then he looks up, where the old son of a bitch is holed up. You see, old man, what useless creatures your daughter and her lover are? You see that they couldn't even keep someone from taking your grandson, my son, while you sat there helpless in your goddamned wheelchair? Impressive, aren't they?

He lights another cigarette, barely noticing the way his hands are trembling. He still can't imagine how he kept from throttling them both the night before, when he went to ask for an explanation of what had happened. He remembers her face, bathed in tears and grief, as she told him the nothing that she knew. He'd have said, You're crying now, you whore?, and he'd have said it gladly. What are you crying about, now that my son has been taken by strangers? And the boyfriend, that solemn dickhead, standing behind her like a butler, nodding his head. If he'd yelled, "Boo," the sheep would have screamed and hidden behind the sofa. Coward.

But he'd promised the police that he wouldn't lose his cool, and he hadn't.

Those useless cops. They couldn't find their own noses in the fog.

Oh, how they'll laugh, he and Dodo, when they talk about him, about Manuel. The big old sheep, they call him, with that head of hair that looks like wool and his complete lack of courage. He's not like you, Papà, says Dodo. You're strong, like Batman. He couldn't even be Batman's nemesis, because even that takes courage.

I'm going to free you, Dodo, he says to the city. He says it aloud, and a startled pigeon takes to the air with a rustle of flapping wings, setting back down on another balcony thirty feet away. I'll free you soon, very soon. And when you're free we can go on vacation together, alone, someplace beautiful, the most beautiful place there is.

Because while it's true that right now I'm your useless giant, it's also true that I'll be your courageous giant again. You'll see.

His cell phone rings. And his heart leaps into his mouth.

XXIV

Y es, hello."
     "This is me. Did phone call."
     "I know. How's it going there?"
"He all right. Not eating much, not crying though."
"And what's he doing?"
"Talking. Whispering, like prayer. I hearing him talking."
"He's talking? But who is he talking to?"
"I think toy. He have toy, little action figure. I think he talking to that."
"Ah, okay, well, leave him alone."
"He bothering me a little, seem like praying. I banging fist, then he shut up."
"No, I'm telling you: Leave him alone. He has to do something, doesn't he? Tell him he has to eat, though. He shouldn't lose weight, we don't want him to get sick. Remember, we can't do him any harm."
"Yes, but I need to scaring him. If I not scaring him, he calling for help or running away."
"Yes, of course. But do it without laying a hand on him. He can't be hurt, we can't leave marks. That's important."
"You not be worrying. And now?"
"Now you know what to do, I wrote everything down for you very clearly. You need to wait until the time I told you and then make the other phone call. You still have the sheet of paper, right?"
"Yes, I have."

"*Check and make sure, please.*"

"*I have paper, fuck! If I saying I have, I have!*"

"*Listen, listen very carefully: don't you ever dare speak to me like that again. Never again, have I made myself clear? Remember that you're nothing but a stupid animal, that you're no good to anyone, and that you've had a stroke of luck that you're never going to have again. Do you understand me, animal?*"

"*I . . . sorry, you right, I . . .*"

"*Yes, I'm right. I'm so right that, if I feel like it, I can have you thrown in jail, you and your whore. You have no evidence to tie me to this, and I can prove that you did it all on your own, the two of you, understood? I've got you in hand, not the other way around.*"

"*Sorry, you right, fuck, I making mistake. You not worry, I do like we agree.*"

"*There, that's better. Behave like the obedient animal that you are. You don't have much to do, but you can't make any mistakes. All right, go on.*"

"*I making another phone call, tonight. And I saying things written on paper. Today Lena go to boy, she talking to him, she telling him she afraid of me. Then tomorrow we talking, and after that, every six hours.*"

"*Very good. Very good, my well-trained animal.*"

"*I no like when you saying I animal. I no animal.*"

"*No, eh? All right then, I won't say it again. But don't make mistakes.*"

"*I not make mistakes. But you not forget: all the money promised, and plus two plane tickets to America.*"

"*Or by ship, if the plane seems too dangerous. That's our agreement.*"

"*Yes, or ship. But I like better plane, faster. Okay?*"

"*There, now you're even talking like an American. We'll see; in any case, yes, you'll get to leave, the two of you. It's also in my own best interest to get you out of here. You just make sure that everything goes off smoothly, and that nothing bad happens to him."*

"No, nothing bad happening to him. And when Lena going, she convincing him to eat. He fine, no rats in there, I having checked, no cold at night, I giving him blanket, too. Plus he have his action figure, no?"

"Yes. At least he has his action figure. You let him play. He saw you, didn't he?"

"Yes, he saw. He afraid of me, I shouting, banging fist, making ugly, ugly face."

"It must not have taken much effort."

"You joking. But it not last much longer, eh? You promised."

"No. It won't last much longer, if we don't make any mistakes."

"We no making mistakes. But you remembering your promise."

"I remember. And you remember that nothing bad must happen to him."

"No, no one harming him."

"Good. No one is to harm him."

XXV

Romano and Aragona had called Dodo's father and asked him to join them at Eva's place. Now that the situation was, unfortunately, clear, they wanted to come to an agreement about what course of action to take in response to the various eventualities that might present themselves.

When they reached the apartment building, they found Alberto Cerchia waiting for them outside the downstairs door.

"Excuse me, I preferred to wait for you to arrive before going up. I'm not sure I'm ready to . . . I mean, I'd just rather we all go up together, if you don't mind. Is there any news?"

"You've spoken to the commissario, I believe," Romano replied.

"Yes, he told me about the phone call. When can I hear the recording?"

Aragona brandished his cell phone: "I had them put it on here. But first let's go see the signora."

Eva met them at the door. She seemed to be in even worse shape than she'd been that morning. She extended a lukewarm greeting to her ex-husband, then turned to the two policemen: "Please, come in."

Sitting in the living room in an armchair was Manuel. Alberto reacted with a surge of annoyance: "Does he really need to be here? If you ask me, this doesn't concern him."

"This is my home," Eva responded icily, "and I decide who stays and who goes. Let me remind you that Manuel spends much more time with Dodo than you do, so I think his presence is useful."

Scarano broke in: "I don't want to be a source of tension, Eva. If you think it's best, I'm glad to wait in the other room. The insults I took from your father were enough for today."

"I said that I wanted you here, Manuel. And that's that."

The woman's peremptory tone put an end to the discussion.

Aragona started the recording; everyone listened in silence. Eva shook her head: "I don't remember any of this, it's as if that's someone else speaking to this criminal. Good God. I don't remember a thing."

"That's normal, Signora," Romano said. "You're very tired and you're experiencing extreme emotional tension. But I have to ask you, and I mean all of you, whether you think you might recognize this voice."

Alberto and Manuel, practically in unison, shook their heads no. Eva said: "No, I'm sure I don't. Now that I hear it again, there seems to be a foreign accent."

"Yes, we had the same impression, Signora. And clearly we're pursuing that lead. What we're most interested in, in this phase . . ."

Alberto leapt to his feet, his face twisted in anger: "In this phase? What are you saying, that in a situation like this one there are phases? What the fuck are you talking about? This is my son who's been kidnapped, do you understand that? My son!"

Romano and Aragona were both surprised by Cerchia's reaction.

"I certainly didn't mean to give the impression that we're taking this lightly, Dottore. We're trying to gather every possible piece of evidence we can to . . ."

"And we're the ones who are supposed to provide you with that evidence? Haven't you seen the state the boy's mother is in? We're here, our son has been missing for almost two days, and you're talking to us about evidence? Do you have any idea how to do your fucking job?"

Aragona had noticed his partner do something that worried him: Romano had unclenched and clenched his fist. Then he saw him slip his right hand into his trouser pocket and wait a moment before answering: "Dottore, I understand that you're in a state. But believe me, we know how to do our job and we're following procedure."

Cerchia's eyes, wide open and ringed in red, his mouth, twisted in a sardonic grimace, and his horrified expression, all spoke volumes about his state of mind.

"Ah, procedure. As if I were applying for a passport. As if this were just some fucking bureaucratic detail, a form to fill out. You know what you can do with your procedure, officer? You can stuff it up . . ."

Aragona saw the muscles in Romano's arm flexing. He leapt forward, placing himself between his partner and Dodo's father.

"Can you quit being such a pain in the ass? We're here to end your son's suffering and also end your own, and you start shouting like an idiot. If you like, we can leave and let you take care of things all by yourself, and then we'll see how you do. Enough is enough, fuck."

The tanned little policeman's reaction caught everyone off guard. Cerchia opened and shut his mouth a couple of times, as if gasping for air. Aragona, seeing his partner's face relax, heaved a sigh of relief. Romano inhaled, exhaled, and said: "All right, now let's all calm down a little, please. We're only playing into the kidnappers' hands. We need to keep our minds clear. My partner Aragona and I are working on this case nonstop with the support of all the officers in the precinct as well as the magistrate in charge. You can be sure of that. I should let you know that all your phone lines have been tapped, and in the next few hours, as required by law, your bank accounts are going to be frozen."

Cerchia stammered: "But . . . but how can you do that? I need my bank accounts for work. I have suppliers to pay, salaries . . ."

Aragona blew out his cheeks in exasperation: "As you yourself pointed out earlier, Dottore, the situation is serious. And if it's serious, it needs to be faced head-on. That means that your suppliers will have to wait for a few days. For truly urgent transactions you can always contact the magistrate, Dottoressa Piras; she has the power to authorize specific payments. Debit and credit cards will still work, so your day-to-day needs should be taken care of."

In a broken voice, Eva asked: "Do you think that before long we're going to receive a demand for . . . that they're going to want money to free Dodo? And what happens, if we don't pay? Because if our accounts are frozen . . ."

Manuel spoke to her in a gentle voice: "Don't worry, sweetheart. Dodo will come back home, and soon. I promise."

"You promise?" Cerchia replied venomously. "And exactly what do you promise, since you don't have a penny to your name and you've been sponging off this family for years? Or maybe you think you're going to rescue Dodo yourself, with your brains and your brawn?"

Scarano eyed him ironically: "Oh, right, because you on the other hand were right here with him to stop them from taking him, weren't you? The brave and powerful daddykins, who happens to live a thousand kilometers away. You don't even remember what he looks like, your son, that's how little you see of him."

Alberto lunged forward with a roar. Romano stretched out an arm and stopped him with no apparent effort.

"I would advise you not to fly off the handle like that again, Dottore. I really would."

Eva burst into tears: "Don't you realize that Dodo's in the hands of some complete stranger right this very instant? And the two of you, instead of trying to figure out how to help him, are butting heads like a couple of teenagers."

Scarano nodded: "You're right, sweetheart, I apologize. To you, not to him."

Cerchia, massaging the place where Romano had grabbed him, said through clenched teeth: "Right. What matters now is freeing Dodo. But I swear to you that as soon as this thing is over, we're going to come back to this discussion. And we're going to review the whole situation, because it's not at all clear to me that my son is better off living with you here than with me. I'll hire the best lawyers in the country, and we'll see how it turns out."

"What you do afterward," Aragona said, "if you don't mind my saying so, is of little interest to us. What's important now is to avoid making mistakes. My partner Romano and I will need to have a talk with Dodo's grandfather. For that matter, it seems clear that it's his money they want."

Eva blinked rapidly: "Why would you say that?"

Aragona went into his glasses-removal routine and replied in a tone that mimicked—or so he thought—that of the Italian actor who dubs Al Pacino: "Because you, Signora, don't have any cash on hand, as you told us, but the kidnappers still called you, not Dottor Cerchia, who does. And so, if the kidnappers are familiar with the family's finances, then by contacting you they're reaching out to Dodo's grandfather."

Romano stopped him: "Or else they just called the one number they found in the phone book. Let's not speculate wildly, à la Columbo, Arago', at least not while we have so little evidence. Now we need to go. Dottor Cerchia, why don't you come downstairs with us, I think that would be best."

"All right, but I have no intention of standing idly by while my son is being held who knows where."

Aragona eyed him coldly: "We can't stop you from doing what you want. But if you screw up and the child suffers the consequences, you'll have to sort that out with your conscience. My advice to you is to keep cool and wait for news. Maybe, if you think it might help, you could even try praying."

XXVI

I f it had been possible to see Brother Leonardo Calisi, parish priest of the church of the Santissima Annunziata and abbot of the adjoining Franciscan monastery, through the confessional, the sight might have provoked a few sarcastic comments; the chair he'd clambered onto, struggling with the tails of his habit and his sacred vestments, was too tall for his feet to reach the floor.

In fact, it would have been more accurate to call him five feet short instead of five feet tall—not including his church-issued sandals, which anyway added little to his diminutive stature. Little. That's the word that came to the minds of those who crossed paths with him in the aisles of the church, or saw him struggling up the streets of the neighborhood, invariably at a trot, forever working to bring succor to the poor and the needy.

But any aesthetic considerations were quickly set aside because it was immediately clear that there was nothing little about his character. A second glance revealed the clear blue eyes, the curly, snow-white hair, and the captivating, clever face that made Brother Leonardo a figure beloved to young and old. A few years ago, the Catholic curia had expressed their intention to transfer him to another parish, a routine rotation, but such had been the clamor among the faithful that the proposal was immediately discarded.

Brother Leonardo was a good man. Generosity and altruism were the rules, set in stone, guiding his life, a life devoted to compassion and mercy. And yet he never lost the ironic streak that made him excellent company even to those who weren't especially familiar with religion.

While a teenage girl with too strong a sex drive told him about her torments, the Franciscan monk dangled his feet in the air and thought about his best friend, Giorgio Pisanelli. Brother Leonardo suspected himself guilty of a sin, albeit a very venial one, because no man of the cloth, much less a parish priest, and even less than that the abbot of a monastery, ought to have a best friend; he ought to devote the same degree of affection to every parishioner, every fellow brother, every human being. But perhaps it was the Lord's will that Giorgio, in the immense loneliness that had come in the wake of his wife, Carmen's, death, should have found in him of all people the comfort he could not draw from his faith. Leonardo, moreover, took authentic intellectual pleasure from his conversations with the policeman, those over lunch at the trattoria Il Gobbo as well as the more hurried talks they had at the parish church. The conversation was always sparkling and intelligent, and the anecdotes that they exchanged about the neighborhood they both knew like the backs of their own hands were practically endless.

Recently, however, the obsession his friend had developed with the suicides was becoming dangerous. Convinced that someone else's hand—always the same one—was behind the deaths, Giorgio never tired of gathering evidence that could help him to reconstruct the moment in which each poor person had committed his or her last act. Leonardo felt conflicting emotions about his friend's fixation: On the one hand, he would have preferred to see him at peace, but, on the other, he realized that it was this very fixation that allowed him to maintain his grip on life, that gave him a reason to get up in the morning, go to the office, get through the day.

That was the matter he was pondering, even as he did his

best to explain to the young lady on the other side of the confessional grate that regularly and devotedly servicing three classmates sexually was not a behavior exactly encouraged by the Catholic church; a reason to live, he mused, however wrongheaded, was still an important thing.

For many years, twelve to be exact, Leonardo had been, day after day, running up against the disease that was raging like an epidemic through large cities everywhere: loneliness. There was no place on earth, he always said, as deserted and empty as a major western metropolis, where invisible men and women carried on lives not dissimilar from those of old, sick animals, exiled from the herd and easy prey for prowling carnivores.

Every day, from dawn to dusk, in the cool shade of the confessional, redolent of incense, in the cozy warmth of the sacristy, out on the streets and in the narrow and intricate *vicoli* of the neighborhood, in dismal living rooms furnished with threadbare sofas that once bubbled with laughter, Leonardo was brought face-to-face with the desire to end one's own life.

And he worked tirelessly to rekindle the flame of bygone happiness, the memory of love or the dream of a future; but far too often his efforts, before the bottomless abyss of drab despair, proved useless.

There were always those who managed to muster the immense courage required to commit the supreme act of existential cowardice. They were few in number, however. Most of them were afraid, or else lacked even the energy needed to swallow a bottle of sleeping pills or throw themselves down the stairs.

What should a spiritual father do? A guide, a brother in faith? These were the questions Brother Leonardo kept asking himself. Should he impart a hasty benediction and go on his way, abandoning these people to their fate? It was easy to help children, tied as they were to the desire for and prospect of the future; or young women who, after overcoming the impasse of a terrible moment, could resume lives of joy; even drug addicts, once freed from their dependencies, possessed a force that allowed them to surmount every obstacle in their paths. In those cases, Leonardo could see the concrete results of his work; it was easy to feel proud in the sight of the Lord.

What was true Holiness? Where did the greatness of a Higher Spirit find its fulfillment? When did the true and complete Imitation of Christ take place? There could only be one answer, as far as Brother Leonardo was concerned: the Extreme Sacrifice of God's greatest gift—one's own soul.

The reasoning was so straightforward that he wondered why it wasn't shared by every Christian. Was there a lonely creature, suffering, with no desire to go on living, who lacked the courage to perform that final, irreversible act? The act that would condemn that creature, and here the Scripture was very clear, to suffer eternal damnation for having taken unto himself a choice that belonged only in the hands of the Almighty? Then the task to help him or her fell to that creature's spiritual father, to the earthly interpreter of God's will; he took unto himself the burden of the sin.

Just as Christ died on the cross, sacrificing Himself for all mankind, it was Brother Leonardo's job to end the lives of those who wished to die but lacked the strength to kill themselves. In allowing those lives to leave this vale of tears, pushing them toward the Light, the diminutive Franciscan obtained two results, both of them of immense importance. He would stain himself with a grave sin, thus achieving the ultimate sacrifice of his own soul, and he'd also alleviate the irremediable suffering of their desperate souls. Simple. Perfectly simple.

As he listened to the young girl's complacent account of a sexual encounter in the school gym with two boys, Leonardo reflected for the millionth time on the interesting theological problem before him. Could helping someone reach the presence of God, if they lacked the courage to commit an unthinkable deed, actually be a sin? What would really become of his soul, once he passed on to a better world? This wasn't a thought he could report in confession, in part because his confessor, Brother Samuele, was something of a stickler in the application of the precepts, but he doubted there lived and breathed a man of the cloth so full of faith that he would not be surprised to learn of what he did for the benefit of the despairing souls in the neighborhood.

The monk, though, had faith. He was deeply convinced of the immensity of Divine Mercy. And also of the value of the intercession, on his behalf, with the Almighty, by those he'd saved from eternal damnation. They'd line up two by two and, in a heavenly chorus, implore the Lord to welcome him, too: their liberator. And the Lord Almighty would certainly grant their request, to great jubilation.

This, however, in many years from now, he hoped, and in accordance with the Lord's will. In the meantime, he still had a great many souls to save.

His mind went back to Giorgio Pisanelli. He was tired, weary, and sick, though it was only to Leonardo that he had confided the truth about the terrible disease that was devouring him. He was an ideal candidate for the particular kind of charity that Leonardo provided; in the afterlife he'd see his Carmen again, another of God's creatures that the diminutive friar had sent to meet her Maker, in order to spare her further atrocious suffering.

The parish priest of Santissima Annunziata had a principle to which he clung without exception: If the individual still had a reason to live, or even merely believed that he or she did, then the person in question could not leave this world. To force them to would be unjust.

Giorgio's case, therefore, constituted an intricate paradox: The only thing that preserved him from Leonardo's help was in fact his stubborn hunt for someone who, as it turned out, was actually Leonardo himself. As long as Giorgio kept hunting, investigating the lives of the poor angels to whom Leonardo had given wings, he'd go on having a reason to live; and that would mean that Giorgio was not yet ready.

Sighing in the girl's direction—she'd decided she'd gone too far just when she was getting to the good part—the monk decided that, while he waited for Giorgio to abandon his mission and thus become eligible for the mercy Leonardo could bring him, he'd work on other cases. He'd weave his usual web of visits, words, caresses, and admonitions, applying the variety of tools that he'd tested out over the years: gas, balconies, ropes, pills, and approaching trains. Always accompanied by a farewell note, written in various hands and using different phrases, always suited to the individual in question thanks to his in-depth knowledge, fruit of his role as confessor.

Just now, for instance, he was working on the case of a woman named Maria Musella: lonely and depressed, increasingly dependent on psychotropic drugs. He would go to see her, and he'd sedate her, and in her torpor he would administer a last, lethal dose of the pills that brought her peace.

Then, his heart light, he'd go have a nice lunch at Il Gobbo with his good friend Giorgio. Brother Teodoro had told him that Giorgio had come by the parish church just a few hours ago, while Leonardo was out looking for a pharmacy in another neighborhood—always best to be careful—where he could buy sleeping pills.

He wondered what Giorgio wanted, as he imposed an exemplary penance on the oversexed young girl. Maybe he wanted to tell him about some crucial discovery he'd made while investigating a suicide that had taken place five years ago.

Poor Giorgio. Leonardo would have been happy to help him, but of course he couldn't.

After all, he wasn't a murderer.

XXVII

By the time they reached the residence of Edoardo Borrelli, night was falling. Now that the sun had set, the air was much cooler; Aragona put on his jacket, but he didn't fasten any extra buttons on his shirt, leaving his carefully waxed and sunlamped chest uncovered.

In the lobby, they approached the private security guard who, after a brief conversation on the intercom, pointed them to an elevator without telling them the floor. And in fact, when they boarded the elevator they found only one button, the corresponding nameplate blank.

When the elevator opened, they were greeted by a stern-looking woman dressed in black, her hair pulled back in a bun. She might have been anywhere between fifty and seventy. She looked them up and down, her face expressionless, and, without holding her hand out, introduced herself: "I'm Carmela Peluso, secretary to the Cavalier Borrelli. We were informed you would be paying us a visit. You are Officers Romano and Aragona?"

It fell to Romano to reply: "Yes, *buonasera*. We're in something of a hurry, could you take us to Signor Borrelli?"

At first the woman didn't move; she just stood there staring at them. Aragona felt uneasy; her gaze made him uncomfortable. Then, without a word, Carmela Peluso moved off. As they trailed after her, the two officers observed the rooms that lined the hallway. Borrelli's home, no less than the woman who had greeted them, was somehow unsettling: First of all, the place was dark. There was only just enough light to see where they were stepping and to keep them from tripping over the thick wall-to-wall carpeting that swallowed the sound of their feet and gave them the feeling that they were moving through a muffling fog. The apartment was immense: Large, shadowy rooms appeared on their left and right. Aragona wondered what the place was like during the daytime; but, judging from the fact that no light filtered in from outside, perhaps the shutters were locked tight even then.

At the end of the hallway, the woman stopped at the foot of a flight of wooden stairs, as if making sure that the two men had followed her without losing their way, then began climbing them. Upstairs there was a sort of oversized living room. As at Eva's, there was an entire wall of glass that, again, enjoyed the same view, though the vista here was even broader. The city lights looked like diamonds scattered over black velvet, but the soundproofing made it seem as though they were looking at a scene projected onto the screen of a movie theater.

"Wait here," Peluso said tersely, and vanished into the darkness.

Romano and Aragona were left ill at ease; they were unable to pin down the feeling's origin at first, until Aragona, his voice low as if he were in church, said: "*Mamma mia*, it's like we're in one of those horror movies from the seventies."

Romano had to admit that his partner had accurately described what he was feeling. The place reminded him of a faithful reconstruction of a luxury apartment from forty years ago. The furniture, decorations, and carpets were a symphony of white and black, crystal and metal, with leather sofas and armchairs very low to the floor and coffee tables to match, walls in a wood veneer with recesses and shelves dimly lit by spotlights that illuminated abstract sculptures. But the thing that was most surprising, and which reinforced the surreal quality of the atmosphere, was the fact that every piece of furniture was perfectly preserved: It was as if no one had ever used that living room.

"I don't often have visitors. And I certainly never expected the first visitors in such a long time to be the police."

The deep, scratchy voice emerged from the darkness and made them both jump. Aragona even emitted a sort of shriek, which he tried to cover up by clearing his throat.

A wheelchair emerged from the shadows, silently, pushed by Peluso. In it sat an old man. His skin looked like tanned leather, and his sparse white hair hung lank and lifeless from the very top of his head. He was very skinny and must not have been tall, though it was Romano's impression that he'd been consumed by something from within. A cavernous coughing fit immediately confirmed that hypothesis.

The secretary solicitously handed the old man a handkerchief, which he pressed to his mouth. When the coughing stopped, the man began staring at them curiously. His eyes were out of place in the portrait of decay suggested by the rest of his face: They were lively and intelligent, with a hint of irony; they seemed like the eyes of a boy.

"And you're supposed to be in charge of the investigation? Aren't you a little low-level to be dealing with a case like this?"

Romano cleared his throat: "We got the call when the school alerted the police yesterday morning. We're not working alone, in any case; this investigation is being closely monitored by the higher-ups at police headquarters, and we report scrupulously to our commanding officers."

From behind Romano, Aragona broke in resentfully: "And after all, it's not like they had to send Spiderman to come ask you a couple of questions."

"Young man," Peluso retorted harshly, "just who do you think you're talking to?"

The man wearily waved a hand: "Don't bother, Carme'. I like it when someone has blood in his veins. Let's just hope they put the same energy into their work. I'm Edoardo Borrelli, as you've no doubt guessed."

Romano went on: "We've been to see your daughter: We know that she informed you."

The old man grimaced: "Yes, that fool's kept man came to tell me what had happened. The unbelievable thing is that it doesn't even seem to have been their fault. Dodo was on a field trip to a museum, isn't that right?"

"We weren't even certain that he'd been kidnapped until today's phone call. From the video footage in our possession it would appear that the child went willingly with a woman, but we can't identify her because she was wearing a hood. One of your grandson's classmates said that he thought she had blond hair. Does that suggest anything to you?"

"No. But I can assure you that my ten-year-old grandson has more brains than his mother, her kept man, and even that idiot of the boy's father all put together. My daughter has always had a formidable talent for choosing the wrong man."

He started coughing again. The secretary fiddled with a vial and a glass and gave him something to drink.

Romano waited a moment, then asked: "Do you see your grandson often?"

"Dodo is the finest and most important thing in my life. And if I were on my feet instead of confined for the past how-ever many years to this goddamned wheelchair, he'd be with me right now, I guarantee it. In my time, I knew all the people who mattered, and not only on this side of the law. It would have taken just one phone call, and you can rest assured that they would have brought him back to me. Along with the ears of the asshole who took him, on a silver tray."

The speech had been a short one, but delivered with breathtaking violence. Aragona observed Peluso's impassive face; it was evident that she was accustomed to these bursts of rage.

Romano went on: "Had you noticed anything strange or different about your grandson recently?"

"He's a child who keeps to himself, he doesn't talk much. When we see each other he sits near me and reads, or he plays with those superhero action figures. Sometimes he'll ask me to tell him stories about when I was young. He likes to imagine me up on my own two feet, since that's something he's never seen."

"And do you have any idea why someone might have taken him?"

"Why do you think? For my money, obviously. The same reason I'm surrounded by people who pretend to love me, pretend to be loyal to me, pretend to respect me. They know that he's my grandson, and they know that when they ask for the money, I'll produce it."

"You're hardly the only one who has money," Aragona said. "We understand that your son-in-law, Cerchia, isn't doing too badly. Isn't that right?"

Peluso hissed: "If you don't quit it with that tone of voice, I'll kick you out."

Aragona showed no sign of backing down: "Ah, then it's a family habit. Everyone wants to kick me out, but nobody wants to answer my questions; maybe what becomes of this child doesn't really matter that much to you all."

A sort of grinning leer appeared on Borrelli's face; it was more horrifying than the contemptuous sneer it had replaced.

"The young man's not wrong. He's got nerve, he knows what he wants, and he has no style to speak of. I like him. Back in the day, I'd have hired him. Yes, Dodo's father has money, that's true. But since I'm here, and it happened here, my guess is that I'm their target. I'm pretty prominent, my company has built plenty, and everyone knows that I have substantial resources. If they'd taken him up north, when Dodo went to stay with his father—which he does quite often because that idiot, luckily, really does love his boy—that would have been another matter entirely. But you'll see, these people are going to contact the mother, or else me directly."

Romano remained silent for a while, then said: "You don't seem all that upset, Cavalier. And yet your grandson has just been kidnapped, and nobody knows where he is or who has him; that can't be pleasant."

It hadn't been a question; merely an observation. Peluso reacted angrily: "How dare you doubt . . ."

Borrelli hushed her again: "Carme', I told you to keep out of this. You're an employee, and I pay you to do what I tell you to, not to weigh in on matters concerning my family."

The woman withdrew into the shadows as if she'd just been slapped in the face. The old man spoke to Romano: "You see, officer, I'm dying. I've been sick for many years, and my wealth and my connections have afforded me treatment that few others would have been able to obtain. That's the only reason I've held out this long. But now there's nothing more that can be done."

Peluso murmured an objection that Borrelli didn't even bother to try to stifle: "Carmela has been with me since she was a girl and she hasn't resigned herself . . . I know that Dodo is going to be treated with kid gloves because they know that I won't pay until I'm certain that he's safe and sound. That's why I'm not worried."

"But you also ought to know," Aragona retorted, "that whenever there's a kidnapping the magistrate orders all your assets frozen. And the district attorney's office has already taken steps to that effect."

Borrelli showed off his horrible leer again: "I might be able to find a little something lying around that isn't officially accounted for, officer. Don't disappoint me, you struck me as a smart boy."

Romano understood that he wasn't getting anything more out of him.

"All right, I think that's all. Please let us know immediately if you hear any news or if you think of any detail that could prove useful."

"At your orders."

Romano was about to say goodbye, when the old man added: "Officer, there's one thing I want you to know: The scum that have dared lay hands on my grandson have worse coming. They won't have time to enjoy the money. I've already taken steps to that effect, as your partner puts it."

They retraced their steps down the stairs and back along the hallway; before bidding them farewell, Peluso spoke to Romano: "Forgive him, officer. The disease is eating him alive and the doctors tell me the pain is atrocious. Still, he fights it. He might seem cynical, but he's not. He's a man who has suffered greatly."

"I understand, Signora. But we have to do our job. Did the child come to see you often?"

"There was a time when he was here practically every day; the Cavalier had a special little room set up and the apartment had become a sort of amusement park for him. The staff and I spent hours and hours. A woman had been hired just to look after him. Then his visits became less frequent, but two days never go by without him coming to see his grandfather. They have a special relationship, the two of them."

"I can imagine," Aragona said, "this is the kind of place that's perfect for a child; I'll bet he had the time of his life. Of course, the minute someone called his name, he toddled off cheerfully with his kidnappers."

Peluso didn't dignify him with so much as a glance.

"Find him as fast as you can. Because if the Cavalier finds them first, so much the worse for them. Good evening."

XXVIII

T he door suddenly swings open and slams against the
sheet metal wall. Dodo, who's fallen asleep wrapped in
the dirty blanket, jerks awake. He was dreaming of
being on a boat with Papà, who was asking him: Where do you
want me to take you this morning, my little king?

A person is thrown violently into the room. The child, his
eyes still stung by the light, can't make out the person's features. What he can see clearly is Stromboli: the enormous silhouette looming against the bare bulb, the voice echoing like
thunder: "You go, and look out, or I kill you! I come get you
in one minute!"

In the pitch darkness that follows the slamming of the door,
Dodo sees the figure on the floor shuddering; he can hear her
softly sobbing. He decides not to move, to wait under the blanket. Then he thinks he might recognize the voice murmuring
frightened words through her tears.

"Lena? Is that you?"

The figure rises from the floor and crawls toward the little
boy: "Dodo, Dodo, then you're all right! You're all right! I
thought that . . . that . . ."

Dodo emerges from the blanket and moves toward her,
crawling, like she did, across the floor.

"Keep your voice down. He can hear everything, and if he
hears anyone talking he gets mad and starts yelling. What did
he do to you? Do you know why he brought us here?"

Lena's sobbing, it takes her a while to calm down. In the

meantime she searches in the darkness for Dodo's features; she runs her fingers over his face. Dodo, too, seeks out her face, and he finds her tears; he dries them with a caress.

"He's just a bad man, sweetheart. A very bad man. I . . . I loved him, very much. We ran into each other on the street, he was nice to me . . . I don't why he's like this now. We have to be careful, Dodo, very careful."

"But Lena, why did he bring us here? What does he want from us?"

Lena sniffs loudly. She whispers, "Listen, Dodo: If we're good, if we do everything he tells us to, nothing will happen to us. He's only been here in Italy for a little while, and he wants to go back home: If he gets what he's asking for, you'll see, he'll let us go."

Dodo is afraid, very afraid; but it seems to him that Lena is even more afraid than he is. In his pocket he clutches the Batman action figure: Hero, you're a hero.

"Then we'll do what he wants, and we'll be free again. Don't be afraid, Lena: You're a woman, and we men know what we have to do."

In the darkness he can feel Lena's smile under his fingertips.

"My little one, you've gotten so big. I almost didn't recognize you at the museum, but you'll always be my little boy, like when you played with me at your grandfather's, do you remember?"

"Of course I remember. But I recognized you right away, even if you dyed your hair and became a blonde."

"He made me do it, you understand, Dodo. He made me. He told me: Go get the boy, we'll go for a drive, I'll take you to get an ice cream and then we'll take him back before the nun even notices; we'll go nearby, someplace I know. But instead he brought us here and put us in different shacks; if you only knew how dirty it is where he keeps me . . . And he does things to me . . . I can't even tell you, the things he does to me . . ."

Lena starts sobbing again, in despair. Dodo feels a twinge in his heart.

"But has he told you what he wants? What do we have to do so we can go home?"

The woman sits up; it takes considerable effort. She whispers: "Money, he just wants some money. As soon as he gets it, he'll let us go. But we can't make him think that we want to run away. Anyway, this place where he's keeping us is far away from everything. Even if we managed to get out of here, we wouldn't know which way to run."

Dodo has a vague memory of the trip in the car: Lena sitting in the back with him, talking to him sweetly, Stromboli driving slowly. It had taken them some time to get there, driving along roads he'd never seen before.

"Then what should we do?"

"We need to keep quiet and do what he tells us: eat, drink, everything. And then he wants your grandfather's telephone number, the private number. You know it, don't you?"

"Of course I know it. I talk to him every day. Even Mamma, if she needs to tell him something, asks me to call him, that way he'll answer. But why does he want to talk to him?"

"Maybe he wants to ask him for money. How is your grandfather? I haven't seen him since he . . . since I stopped working for him."

"He's sick, you know that. But he's strong, he's holding on."

Lena caresses his face: "And you're strong too, little one. So strong. And your grandfather would be proud of you, if he could see how brave you are."

"Listen, Lena: We can't be afraid. You'll see, someone will come get us, and it'll be my papà. My papà won't let anything stop him."

"Dodo, no one knows where we are, not even your father.

This is the second night we've been here. The longer we're here, the angrier he gets. Give me the number, I'm begging you."

Dodo thinks it over. He's seen it on so many TV shows and in cartoons, too: At times like these, the thing to do is stall.

"All right. But tell him that if he tries to hurt us he'll be sorry. Understood, Lena? He'd better not hurt us, otherwise my father will make him pay a heavy price."

Once she has the number, the woman crawls toward the door and knocks softly. Stromboli throws the door open again, slamming it against the sheet metal, and shouts: "Well? You are done? Woman, you have number?"

Lena nods, sobbing, and he grabs her and drags her out of the room.

Dodo pulls the Batman action figure out of his pocket. Batman, Batman, he murmurs. You see, poor Lena is a prisoner, too. Do you remember Lena, who lived with us before I started school, when I spent mornings with my grandfather? Lena, who used to tell me fairy tales, who played with me, who used to take me to the park. That's right, Lena, who we never saw again because once I started school they didn't need her anymore and my grandfather fired her. Stromboli has taken her, too.

He's a bad man, Stromboli. Just like Two-Face, or the Joker, or Bane. A terribly bad man. My papà is going to have to be very strong to defeat him.

But my papà will do it, you know, Batman. You know it, heroes stop at nothing. Heroes are the stubbornest, strongest people in the world; they have no weaknesses. That's why we have to hold out, Batman. Because even if someone isn't born a hero, he can become one. Heroes exist, Batman. Even if in the real world, even I know this, you don't see them flying from one building to another or zooming down the street.

I remember asking my papa about it once, because I'd

never seen them. And he told me: My little one, it's because in the real world, heroes don't seem like heroes. They have to hide.

Out in the world, Batman, there are a bunch of heroes, you know.

Lots of heroes.

XXIX

Heroes.
There are lots of different kinds of heroes, you know. There's not just one kind.

Heroes are courageous, they never get lost. They know what they're up against, they look their enemies in the face and take them on, fearlessly. Heroes never hesitate.

Because if they had doubts, fears, they wouldn't be heroes. In a black-and-white world, heroes know where to go.

You can recognize heroes right away.

They're the strong ones, capable of crushing evil in one fist and throwing it away.

They're the ones without fear, heroes are.

You've been lucky, Francesco Romano. When it comes to stakeouts, as everyone knows, it's all a matter of luck. This time there was even a parking place right behind a delivery van, which means you can keep an eye on the front entrance without being seen.

When they teach you police procedure, they never take luck into account, you think to yourself; but actually luck is everything. Not only in stakeouts, truth be told. In life, too, it's all a matter of luck.

Roll your car window up a bit. May is a dangerous month, at night the temperature can drop as much as twenty degrees and you can catch a cold before you even know you're sneezing. And you, after all, Francesco Romano, even though you're big and strong and muscular, even if you're capable of choking a man one-handed and sometimes you're even tempted to do so and you have to stop yourself and you do, you stop yourself just in the nick of time, you still catch colds at the drop of a hat. Do you remember how she used to wrap a scarf around your neck before you went out? Remember how she'd stand on tip-toes to kiss your reddened nose? Remember how she'd unwrap the chocolates and surprise you by popping them into your mouth, and then she'd read you the little slip of paper with the stupid romantic phrase and say, it's true, it's really true? You can remember plenty of other things, for that matter. You can remember everything.

You can even remember the letter she left on the table that night you came home and she wasn't there anymore. The letter that begins, "Dear Francesco," just like that, as if it were some stranger writing you, someone you barely know. Not Giorgia, your Gio, the girl that set the world on fire to get to know you back when you were at university, the same girl who couldn't stop crying tears of joy the day of your wedding, the same one who hopped around the house like a kangaroo for a solid hour the day you were promoted to the detective squad. Dear Francesco. It's just funny she didn't end the letter with "all my best."

That's no way to end a romance is it, Francesco Romano? Just because a poor hardworking man, in a moment of anger, raised his hand almost without knowing what he was doing. And what the hell, that was little more than a love tap, after all. It's not your fault, Francesco Romano, if she's so delicate that she got a black eye and a bruise on her cheek from nothing more than a love tap.

And you can't say that you're not a respectable person, Francesco Romano. An honest and upstanding man; it's no accident that you decided to be a policeman. Good men become policemen, don't they? Not criminals. Criminals, by definition, are bad men; they rob, they rape, they kill. And the policemen chase them, catch them; they don't do what those bad men do.

While you stare at the road that cuts through the night in silence, with your sleepless eyes wide open, illuminated by the streetlights, staring at dumpsters and parked cars, you think to yourself that no woman should leave an honest and upstanding man because once, just once, his hand got the better of him. A man, however honest and upstanding, can have some troubled times when they kick him out of his precinct just because some asshole criminal got under his skin. What were you supposed to do, Francesco Romano, should you have just sat there smiling when that two-bit criminal said to you, Hey superintendent, I'll get out of here before you do tonight, because I pay my lawyer more in an hour than you make in two months?

And in the meantime, she's left you, Francesco Romano. And here you are, sitting outside her mother's apartment building, spending your night in the car since you can't sleep at home anyway, that apartment is too fucking big for just one person, and noisy at night, so noisy you can't get a wink of sleep. So you might as well sit in your car, looking up at the apartment where that bitch of your mother-in-law lives; neither of you could ever stand the other. You can just guess how she's brainwashing her daughter now, you can almost hear her voice: You see, he's violent, he's a nut, I told you this is how it would end, I never even wanted you to marry him.

But that's not right, Giorgia my love. I'm the man for you, the only man for you, the same way you are and always will be the only woman for me. If only we'd had the child you wanted; if only for once fate had helped me instead of tripping me up. If we'd had a baby of our own, a boy, with your looks and your kindness, and my strength and my determination.

Your thoughts turn to the kidnapped child; and for that

matter, Giorgia always says that someone with your job never stops working. That poor innocent little boy; he had the money, and the beautiful homes, and the school for rich kids, and even so, some stupid asshole just took him and carried him off to who knows where, and no one stopped it.

I wish I could tell you all about it, Gio, my love. I wish I could talk to you, now, in our bed, after making love desperately, searching for some way to assuage the pain that I carry inside me, that never gives me peace. How I wish I could tell you about my day, and hear your delicate voice utter words of relief.

I'm strong; I am, you know. I'm a strong policeman, honest and competent.

A hero.

A hero who, without you, is weaker than a kidnapped child. At least he has someone who loves him, at least he can hope to come back to his old life.

Not you, Francesco Romano, you have no hope.

And no life to go back to.

It's a good thing there's a delivery van parked here in front. And that no one, hurrying past to get through the night, can see a man in a car watching a front entrance and crying.

Heroes.

Who, while everyone else is asleep, watch over us. Who scan the night in search of something that's just a little off, in search of wrongs to set right.

Who sometimes live in caves so no one can see them.

Or who live in our midst, in a luxurious penthouse, ready to throw on a special outfit at a moment's notice, or to take off in a souped-up car that looks like an ordinary automobile, but which actually flies, shoots, and can even travel underwater.

Heroes who know that evil can lurk anywhere, who can always duck into a phone booth, change clothes, and sally forth against the enemy in their brightly colored costumes: handsome, powerful, and invulnerable.

The night is the right place for heroes.

Marco Aragona walks unhurriedly, straight down the center of the sidewalk.

He left his car in the garage. The usual spectacular entrance: tires screeching, brakes slamming. The sleepy nighttime parking attendant's usual jerk into wakefulness, the usual resentful glare, the usual forced smile: *Buonanotte*, Dottore. He knows, that Moroccan asshole, that Marco's a cop. He knows that if he so much as thought of saying something, Corporal Marco Aragona would kick his ass sideways.

Striding smugly down the deserted street, Marco Aragona feels like the master of the night. The terror of all the two-bit sewer rats who populate this city, the rats who emerge from their holes only when darkness comes to shelter them. It wouldn't be hard to clean up this city, if there were a hundred Marco Aragonas, a special squad with license to come down heavy. That broom would sweep clean: So long, faggots, sluts, thieves, and illegals.

Marco thinks that all the mealymouthed optimism politicians, priests, and humanitarian associations spout is bound to be the ruin of the country. We ought to be *less* tolerant, he always says. A little spring-cleaning and then you'd see.

No fear of the night for Corporal Marco Aragona. And not much desire to sleep, as far as that goes. He takes the long way around, he feels like thinking. Hard day. The whole thing with the kidnapped boy really is brutal.

At first, he'd assumed this would be a good career opportunity: It's not like kidnappings come along every day. But then the idea of having to partner up with Hulk had almost convinced him to foist the thing off onto someone else. Working with that guy was like sitting on a crate of explosives, you never knew what might happen. And dealing with the little kid's family made him uneasy, too. Everyone's nerves balanced on a knife's edge, everyone ready to take offense or act all scandalized; and yet this was a kidnapping, not a palace ball. The quicker they got that straight, the better it would be, both for the investigation and for that poor little kid.

He stops before the front door of his home. Actually, it's not really a home at all. Aragona lives at the Hotel Mediterraneo, midway between police headquarters, where he'd been assigned when he first moved to the city, and Pizzofalcone's precinct house.

He's never told anyone at work that he lives here. He knows what they think of him: That he's there because of nepotism, that he doesn't need the 1,200 euros a month a policeman makes. A guy who could have snapped his fingers and had a job at any law office in the provincial town he came from, where his family might as well have been royalty with all the money they had. And all that gossip would be confirmed by the way he chooses to live; instead of renting a studio apartment, he lives in one of the finest hotels in the downtown area, where a room, breakfast included, costs more than his salary.

But Aragona has his reasons. He's served, flattered, fed magnificently, and they wash his sheets. He never has to tidy up after himself and there's even satellite TV, so he can watch the American cop shows he is so passionate about. And then it's all so secret agent to live in a hotel and drink dry martinis on the roof garden, the city stretched out at his feet, the traffic noise muffled by distance like faraway music.

Actually, there's also another reason. But to Mamma and Papà, who are only too happy to continue looking after their beloved son by sending a sizable wire transfer that the bank deposits punctually into his account every month, he hasn't mentioned it. The reason is Irina, the angel who, disguised as a waitress serving breakfast, brings him plates of scrambled eggs and bacon every morning.

He's never spoken to her. But sooner or later, as soon as the opportunity presents itself, he'll sweep off his blue-tinted eyeglasses and give her that famous look of his, as if he's only just noticed her. And, pretending to read the name tag that the girl wears pinned to her remarkable chest, only then will he say to her: Ciao, Irina. What are you doing for fun, after work?

Okay, he thinks, as he heads off to the elevator, his room key in hand, it's an immigrant's name. But not all immigrants are bastard sons of bitches like the one who's kidnapped the boy, right? You can't tar them all with the same brush.

We're heroes, fucking right, thinks Corporal Marco Aragona, trying out the look that he's planning to use on Irina in the elevator mirror.

Heroes aren't racists. And he certainly isn't one. Who could have ever said otherwise?

Heroes. Heroes with secret identities.

Because it's not necessarily the case that heroes seem like heroes.

Sometimes they seem like ordinary people, and they do it on purpose, so that no one will suspect they have special powers, so that none of the villains will suspect that at any moment they might find themselves face-to-face with the hero who'll throw them up against the wall, toss them into a cell.

Sometimes not even the people who live right alongside them know who they are, these heroes.

Perhaps they don't even notice them, they're so used to taking things for granted. Maybe even to those who love them, who've known them since they were small, maybe even to their own families, heroes don't seem like heroes.

Hidden behind their mundane alter egos, heroes can seem like something completely other than what they are.

Heroes, sometimes, are complete nobodies.

Alessandra Di Nardo, known to her friends as Alex, was sitting up straight, the way she'd been taught, watching TV. She didn't care much about whatever they were blabbering on about on the screen; she was listening with an eighth, or maybe even a tenth, of her attention. She was minding her own business.

She'd have gladly done without that ridiculous after-dinner ritual entirely. But it mattered to the general a great deal, her mother had explained to her, and if something mattered to the general, then no one else had the right to vote.

Alex lived with her parents. She could—she wanted to with all her heart—live on her own, in an apartment, however small, in any neighborhood in the city, ideally as far as possible from this one. But the one time, years ago, that she'd expressed that desire at dinner, breaking the silence imposed during meals because, as the general liked to say, you can only do one thing well at a time, so either you eat or you talk, the answer had been quick and decisive: Certainly, the general had said, when you get married.

That was the end of that, because Alex was never going to get married.

On the television, the guy that they always watched at that hour was talking; his voice was low and courtly, and he used the same tone on every topic, whether it was diets or politics or the economy. That night, the spotlight was on a famous murder, perhaps for the hundredth time. The scene of the crime was analyzed inch by inch, the psychologist sketched out a profile of the probable culprit, the magistrate outlined standard procedures, the criminologist laid out the evidence that had been overlooked by the dimwitted investigators who had taken on the case. Alex, with the tenth of her attention that she'd devoted to the show, realized how pointless all that talk really was, as if one crime were the same as another, as if it weren't true that each time, the weed of evil grew inside a soul in its own unique and twisted way.

She shot a glance over at the general; he had fallen asleep in his armchair, his mouth open and his head thrown back. He was getting old, she told herself with the usual incredible blend of tenderness, resentment, fear, and love that she felt for him. Her prison. The man whose opinion, to her, could be more damning than a verdict handed down by a court of law, seeing as they disagreed on everything.

Farther off to the side her mother had fallen asleep, too; her eyeglasses had slid down the sharp ridge of her nose. Alex knew that the minute she moved to get up, even if it was just to go to the bathroom, both of them would suddenly jump to attention like grasshoppers. Where are you going, sweetheart? her mamma would ask, in accordance with the general's silent command. Don't you like the show?

She decided that tomorrow, instead of coming home after work, she'd go to the shooting range. She only really felt like herself before a darkened hallway, a pair of soundproof earmuffs on, staring down the target with a bull's-eye on its chest. And when she had a regulation weapon in her hand, a gun that she'd modified all by herself. Six shots in a row, six bull's-eyes, and all around her, her fellow policemen looking at her in astonishment: a twenty-eight-year-old woman, slender and refined, with delicate features that made her look five years younger, who could shoot faster and more accurately than all the rest of them put together.

A passion for weapons was the only interest she shared with the general; the only thing that united a father and daughter who were otherwise opposites. He'd taken her to the gun range for the first time when she was ten. Her mamma's feeble protests—she had imagined her daughter partaking in more feminine pastimes—had proved as ineffectual as a spring breeze: For that matter, wasn't the general's wife the one who had been unable to bear him a son? And now what did she want, that he should resign himself to the idea that there would never be another Di Nardo in the army without even being able to share an innocent hobby like firearms with Alex?

Then she'd decided to join the police force, after boarding school. A decision that, deep down, though he gave no outward sign, the general had approved. What the old man didn't know was that it had been at boarding school, on a rainy night, that his blushing daughter had discovered her true nature with a particularly outgoing roommate.

Alex was never going to get married because Alex wasn't interested in men.

Alex liked women.

Unfortunately, she lacked the strength to be her own person, and for this, she hated herself. She hated herself because she had to go out at night to special clubs, because she had to wear a mask, because she had to pretend to be someone else in order to brush her fingers over soft flesh, to savor certain tastes.

She shifted uncomfortably in the armchair, tormented by a subtle quivering of the flesh. Nature. You can't fight nature, and she certainly didn't intend to. Still, it's hard to struggle against certain conditioned reactions, and the general was the father of all conditioned reactions. I wonder what you'd say about me, she thought, looking at the psychologist on TV with his green sweater, his checked shirt, and his tuft of white hair, if you were to analyze my profile. A good middle-class girl, shy and introverted, who's a crack shot and secretly sleeps with women.

For no real reason, her mind wandered to the Parascandolos, the burgled couple at the center of the investigation she was working with the Chinaman. A good guy, the Chinaman: practical, matter-of-fact, deductive. A first-class cop, and a reliable partner. Not one of those guys with wandering hands, like the ones she'd worked with at the station house she'd been expelled from for discharging her firearm. That was some story.

At Pizzofalcone, Alex got along with everyone. Pisanelli, Ottavia, even Romano, with his prickly personality: They were all her type. All bad apples like her, perhaps, but authentic. Even Aragona, rude as he was, was at least exactly what he appeared to be—and there were times when he was even likable. All of them were alone for one reason or another. Better to be alone, though, than to wind up hating each other like that couple who'd called in the burglary. Tomorrow, with the Chinaman, she'd go over to the Parascandolos' gym to take a look around. There was something not quite right about that burglary. The forensics chief had said so, too.

At the thought of Martone she felt a sudden ache in the pit of her stomach, a physical sensation so powerful that she was afraid it had actually made a sound, and that it would wake the general up, and that he'd look over at her with his usual probing glare. She was certain that the chief, with that beautiful ass lurking beneath her lab coat, was like her. And that, somehow—by smell, perhaps, or via some other signal unknown to others—Martone had identified her.

And as ridiculous as it might seem since she, Alex, had barely been able to speak, had made a fool of herself, she was certain that Martone had liked her. A lot.

Though maybe that was just an illusion. Maybe—no, almost certainly—her fate was to live all alone, caring for her supercentenarian parents, to quest, in the darkness, after the satisfactions of the flesh for the rest of her life.

That thought brought to the surface, from the fog of her subconscious, an image of the kidnapped boy. Who knows where they took you. Who knows how dearly you'll pay for the crime of being born someone's child. Just like me.

In response to her thoughts her cell phone vibrated in her lap, lighting up the dim shadows of the living room. On the display, she saw it was a text message from unknown number.

She typed in her passcode and read the text: "*Ciao*. I'm pretty sure I don't need to tell you who this is. I wanted you to have this number in case you ever felt like talking, or going out for a beer, or whatever. A kiss goodnight."

She turned her phone off right away, positive that the color of her face and the sound of the blood throbbing in her ears were as bright and loud as a fireworks display.

You're right, she thought. You don't have to tell me who you are.

In the dark, she grinned like a wolf.

That's the way heroes are, you know.

No one can say who they really are. But when the time is right, they come out, and they'll be one hundred percent themselves in their battle versus evil. They're there, and they'll always be there.

You can be sure of it.

XXX

She walks into the room and lets herself collapse onto the chair. The bare bulb casts a chilly light on the room's desolation.

"Give me a cigarette. This is definitely the hardest part, acting without being an actress."

He snickers: "Why, you were a star. I could hear you through the crack in the wall. It was a scene straight out of a major motion picture: I don't know how I kept from bursting out laughing."

"Eh, you could have given me a round of applause, too. Here's the old man's number, the private number; that way you don't have to go through her."

"Is it all that important, talking to him directly? There are things I don't understand about this job."

"And in fact you don't need to understand them. He told you that, didn't he? The less you understand, the less you know, the better. Just do the things you need to do, like he explained."

He shrugs: "As long as he pays us what he promised."

"And not just the money, remember. New IDs, too: passports and identity cards, for me and for you. They need to be Russian, nothing that can be traced back to our past."

"That's something I'm going to be sorry about, having to change our homeland. You have no idea what a pleasure it is when you come home at night, being able to speak in our own language instead of constantly having to struggle with these ridiculous words. I've always hated Italian."

This time she's the one who laughs: "And in fact you don't know how to speak it at all, not even after how many years? Ten years that you've lived here?"

"Eight. And I didn't spend them listening to lectures. I had to make a living hauling bricks and buckets of mortar. Back home, I went to school as long as I could afford to, and I wasn't a bad student either. But I just can't manage to learn this damn language."

"The important thing is that you manage to make that phone call. And the less you say, the less you improvise, the better."

"Yes, he explained that to me. I have a sheet of paper with what I'm supposed to say. At least for this next phone call. The one to the old man."

"Be careful: He's old and sick, but he's cunning as a fox. He'll try to deal with you, to bargain, to set traps. He expects us to demand money."

"I know, I know. All I need to do is read what's written on the sheet of paper, slowly and calmly. For now, he hasn't given us any other instructions; he'll call me afterward and give us new instructions as needed."

She snorts: "He doesn't trust us. Or at least he trusts us only to a certain extent. That's why he still hasn't told us where and how he's going to make the exchange, where the old man's supposed to bring the money, where we're supposed to take the child . . ."

He shoots a glance at the storeroom door: "The kid doesn't seem to suspect you at all. He went with you willingly, no whining, and even now he confided in you right away. Didn't it ever occur to him that we were in cahoots?"

"I raised him. I took care of him for three years while that slut of a mother of his was busy leading the high life. Then, when he started school, a kick in the ass and so long, Lena."

"Still, all these precautions strike me as a little excessive.

Dyeing your hair blond, for example: What good did that do, if you put a hood over your head? And all those twists and turns, all the detours we took on the drive here: He's a kid, he's not going to remember the way we went."

"You can never be too careful. And after all, he's a smart, observant kid, even if he seems to be living in his own little world, with his cartoons, his comic books, and his super-heroes. Don't underestimate him."

"The important thing is that everything turn out all right. He said that the whole thing will take four days, five at the most. Then we'll have the money, the IDs, and the plane tickets. And after that, South America."

"And when they question the boy, they're going to assume that you got rid of me somewhere."

He laughs: "Maybe I really will. That way I can keep all the money for myself."

She laughs, too: "There's just one small problem with that plan: You know neither Russian nor Spanish. You wouldn't even be able to get to the airport without me."

"Maybe that's why he picked us for the job. We have to do exactly what we're told."

"That's right. So let's keep doing it."

XXXI

Parascandolo's gym was in an unusual location.

The front entrance was in an alleyway just off a busy thoroughfare, not far from a stoplight, and it was a workout just threading one's way first across the river of slow-moving cars perennially streaming by, and then past the wall of motor scooters of all sizes and models parked sideways, blocking the narrow sidewalk. Di Nardo and Lojacono were especially unlucky because, in order to make their way down the five yards of narrow lane that led to the entrance, they had to wait for a group of Japanese tourists, walking single file and chirping and photographing as they went, to go by; the tourists were followed by two Junoesque matrons pushing baby carriages and complaining, in a dialect rife with elaborate insults, about the oriental foot traffic. The women's comments were incomprehensible to the lieutenant, but they did force a giggle out of Alex.

The young woman was in a good mood, Lojacono thought to himself. She hadn't burst into song or anything, that wasn't her style, but a couple of times he'd seen her smile faintly, as if something nice had occurred to her. And thank goodness, because the atmosphere in their communal office was turning grim. It had been three days since little Dodo had vanished, and now they were certain it was a kidnapping. Romano and Aragona were doing their best, but the child's life had furnished no clues. Ottavia and Pisanelli had energetically scoured the web and their networks of informants, but nothing useful had emerged. The deputy captain hoped to get something more from the director of a bank, a friend of his, who would be back from vacation that morning, but he wasn't holding out any great hope.

Lojacono was well aware that if you wanted to catch a criminal, the first few days after the crime were crucial, especially in a kidnapping; if you didn't come up with something then, it was unlikely that you'd ever solve the case, except through some stroke of dumb luck. Moreover, the hope that the victim was still alive added a sense of urgency and growing frustration to the investigation.

Since they couldn't do anything else to help, Lojacono and Di Nardo had gone back to working the Parascandolo burglary. While they waited for forensics to finish up the new tests promised by Martone, it was worth going for a little stroll to see just how the family business was doing.

The narrow street and the unassuming entrance stood in sharp contrast to the actual size of the gym's interior, which looked modern and well lit. A large room with a reception desk led to two hallways from which echoed an up-tempo beat clearly meant to get the customers moving. Two male body-builders were deep in animated conversation, and two very sweaty, older women, squeezed into workout clothes a couple sizes too small, were doing their best to attract their attention, though without success. Behind the counter sat a pretty young woman with a friendly manner. "Can I help you?" she asked.

Lojacono identified himself, saw the young woman's expression briefly darken, and asked to speak to Parascandolo.

"The dottore isn't in, but the signora is. Please, make yourselves comfortable, I'll get her right away."

Alex and Lojacono took a seat on a small sofa, and while they waited they took in the skirmishing of the four fitness fiends. The men were engaged in an emphatic discussion centered on the benefits of a new exercise machine designed to develop the dorsals, while the women talked loudly and cast sidelong glances that went unnoticed. Alex asked her partner whether, in his opinion, they had a duty to let the boys know that the ladies wanted to chat, which would at least quiet the latter's strident voices. Before Lojacono had a chance to reply, a very worried Susy Parascandolo entered the room.

The skimpy dress she'd been wearing during their first meeting had been replaced by a fluorescent bodysuit, whose color reminded Lojacono of the green highlighter that Marinella used to mark up her textbooks. The outfit was rounded out by a pair of shoes in the same color that added at least five inches to her height. Alex blinked rapidly, as if her eyes had been stung by a sudden flash of light.

The lieutenant got to his feet: "*Buongiorno*, Signora. Forgive us for showing up without an appointment."

Signora Parascandolo was on edge. She looked around, as if afraid that any minute someone else might show up.

"Not at all, Lieutenant, of course you're welcome any time. Did you find anything? Any news?"

"Nothing worth mentioning. We received a preliminary report from the forensic team, and perhaps if we had a little more information from you . . ."

"Fine. But not here: Please, let's go into my office."

She led them to a small room equipped with a desk facing two chairs, her sauntering gait showing off one of the parts of her body that had been the special subject of extensive cosmetic surgery. She closed the door carefully behind her and then sat down, gesturing to the two cops to make themselves comfortable.

"I'm very sorry to disturb you here at work," Lojacono said, "but we wanted to know a little something more about just what the burglars took. Have you had a chance to narrow that down?"

"What can I tell you, Lieutenant? As far as we can tell, they only took whatever was in the safe, and the safe is my husband's business, no one else's."

Alex broke in: "And he isn't here right now, is he?"

"No, he only comes here rarely. The gym is just an investment for him; I'm the one who runs it."

Alex persisted: "So what business is your husband in, if he doesn't come to the gym?"

Susy looked away and focused her eyes on the wall: "Well, my husband is . . . he's retired. He spends his time managing his family's estate. He's in business."

"What kind of business?"

The woman squirmed in her seat: "Listen, just business. He goes out, he comes back, he meets people: business. I don't know, and he doesn't tell me. And after all, excuse me, but what does that have to do with the burglary? It seems to me that you two are investigating my husband instead of the crime."

Lojacono raised both hands: "No, Signora. We're just trying to understand the motive for the theft, that's all. It's pretty unusual for burglars to take nothing but the contents of a safe. There were plenty of other valuables: silver, jewelry, even a wallet . . ."

Before the woman had a chance to respond, the door flew open and a young bodybuilder came in: "Sweetheart, listen, the sauna motor broke again . . . Oops, I'm sorry, I didn't know you . . ."

Susy's reaction to the young man's untimely entrance was spectacular: She jumped to her feet, blushed violently, then turned pale, pressing the palm of her hand onto the desktop, and so she remained, clearly embarrassed. Alex decided that, if you factored in her outfit, all the colors of the rainbow had just been displayed in about a second.

"Marvin, what . . . hey, don't people knock around here anymore? Where are your manners? Can't you see that I have visitors? Go away, we can talk about the sauna motor later!"

Lojacono was quick on his feet. He, too, stood up and held out his hand: "No, no, stay for a minute, please. We're the ones who should apologize for the intrusion, Signor . . ."

The man was still disoriented. His eyes begged Susy for help as he shook hands with the lieutenant, stammering out his own name. He was maybe twenty-five years old; the only clothing adorning his sculpted body was a pair of shorts and a tank top that showed off his bronzed, waxed torso.

Di Nardo was reminded of Aragona's chest, though the two men had nothing else in common. Unlike their colleague, the above-mentioned Marvin might as well have been an ad for the benefits of fitness: his twitching, well-defined muscles, decorated with numerous tattoos; the blond hair that framed a face with perfect features. If I liked men at all, Alex thought to herself, I'd already have fainted. His eyes, on the other hand, vacuous and inexpressive, betrayed the workings of a sluggish brain. Marvin, or whatever his real name was, was clearly an idiot.

Susy finally managed to open her mouth: "Forgive me, Lieutenant, he's just an employee of ours who . . . in any case, it's nothing he and I can't talk about later."

"No, Signora, I insist," Lojacono reassured her. "We're the ones who are intruding. What's your name, Marvin? Your real name, I mean." ·

"Oh . . . Mario Vincenzo Esposito, Lieutenant. At your service."

Lojacono glanced meaningfully at the tattoos on the man's forearm; he'd seen so many of them in his time.

"Have you been working here long?"

Once again, Parascandolo tried to break in: "I don't see what that has to do with . . ."

Lojacono cut her off, his tone serious: "Signora, what seems to be the problem? Is there some reason you'd prefer I not speak with Signor Esposito?"

The woman quickly took a step back, and let herself fall into her chair. Alex noticed her complexion changing color again, flashing quickly from fuchsia to ash-gray.

"No, no, what problem? Go right ahead."

"Thanks. Now then, Esposito, I'm Lojacono and my partner is Di Nardo, from the Pizzofalcone precinct house. We're here because, as you may know, your employer's apartment was burglarized. But tell me a little more about yourself: How long have you worked here in the gym, and what is it that you do?"

The chilly, formal tone confused Marvin, who did his best to lock eyes with Susy, though unsuccessfully.

"I'm the Pilates instructor and I help out with equipment maintenance. I've worked here for six months, more or less, but I'm on the books as an intern. I mean, my job isn't exactly on the up and up."

"You're working under the counter, then," Alex said. "And where did you work before?"

Esposito suddenly seemed terribly interested in the desktop. "Here and there. I picked up odd jobs."

Lojacono cut him off: "Esposito, the minute we get back to the precinct house, five minutes on the computer will tell us everything we want to know. So why don't you make our job easier for us; thanks."

"All right, okay, I was in prison. It was a stupid mistake and I paid the price. Why, don't you think a guy can take the straight and narrow, after making a mistake? Am I marked for life so that whenever something bad happens, it has to be me?"

The vehemence of the young man's reaction didn't surprise Lojacono: "No one's saying that. We're just asking a few questions, trying to figure more about this burglary that's so . . . out of the ordinary. That's all. And just what were you in for, if I might ask?"

The question prompted an awkward silence. Alex made an effort to keep from laughing.

The man looked up: "Burglarizing an apartment."

On the way back to the station house, Di Nardo couldn't stop chuckling at the scene they'd both just witnessed: "I mean, can you believe it? That guy walks in and calls the old lady 'sweetheart' while we're sitting there. Then he has to confess that he's fresh out of prison, where he was locked up for exactly the type of crime we're there to investigate. If that's not unlucky . . . Not even Donald Duck could be so hapless! Fantastic!"

Lojacono was focused on driving. He'd never learn to navigate the streets by car in that city: You had to be born there, or else just be completely crazy, like Aragona.

"Yes, that was bad luck for him. But the fact that he has a criminal record doesn't mean anything. I think his relationship with our girl Susy is more interesting. That woman is exactly the kind who's unwilling to resign herself to the passage of time."

"Sure, a little fresh flesh and she feels all young again . . . Truth be told, having seen her husband, I'm not sure I can blame her. By the way, I'd look into his actual line of work. The wife seemed a little too vague on the subject. The more I think about it, the more positive I am that there's something fishy there."

As he was trying to avoid being simultaneously hit head-on and rear-ended, the lieutenant agreed: "Yes, that's true. And it's also true that if the lady were directly involved, it would explain a great many things—for instance her failure to turn on the alarm system."

"And the fact that they didn't bother to take the silver. It's likely that the thief knew what was in the safe, and that . . ."

". . . and that whatever was in the safe came from her husband's actual line of work. In other words, the noose tightens. Among other things, any woman who dares to wear a bodysuit like that one must necessarily have the mind of a criminal."

Alex laughed: "Good work, Loja'. Now we know that Aragona isn't Pizzofalcone's only stand-up comedian."

XXXII

Giorgio Pisanelli had by now figured out that, at least in terms of its outward manifestations, the tumor's progression wasn't linear. At least not in his case. And that, he thought, was really very lucky.

He would have expected, as the disease progressed, that every day would be worse than the one before but better than the one that followed. Instead, there were times when all the symptoms disappeared, like an unwelcome guest who realizes that he's intruding. And at times like that, a new euphoria swelled in his heart, which on that day was already intoxicated by the sweet air of spring with its promise of summer.

Once he'd finished his round of phone calls and learned all he could about the Borrelli family's finances, Giorgio decided to pay a call on his friend, the director of a local branch of a major bank. There were things that couldn't be shared over the phone, and the understanding between the two of them was that not only would the source of the information never be revealed, but that the information itself would only be described in the vaguest of terms—as mere hints.

Pisanelli was a much-loved figure in the neighborhood. He was never reluctant to lend a hand when needed, and he was honest and upright: The thin line that separated understanding and collusion was to him inviolable. This earned him the respect of the many small-time criminals that infested the district, and even a few of their big-time counterparts. And so when crime attacked the most defenseless members of the community—children, for example, or the elderly—there were many who were suddenly willing and able to help.

As usual, Giorgio and his friend arranged to meet at a café with outdoor tables not far from the branch where the latter worked: better to be careful, and to avoid meeting in either's office. They sat talking for half an hour, discussing the state of the economy, the recession's effect on business, and the fall of real estate prices. Reading between the lines, Giorgio learned all there was to know about Dodo's family, things that couldn't be read in any file available on his computer. Now the deputy captain really did have something to report at the meeting scheduled in the communal office in half an hour.

He decided to use the free time to check in from afar on Signora Maria Musella, the woman he had identified as a potential victim for "the Dead-End Killer" which was the name he had given to the murderer he was trying to track down. At that hour, the woman would be at home making lunch, having just reemerged from the haze induced by the psychotropic drugs she took to help her sleep: The pharmacist had walked him through the dosage and effects of the medication, and his explanation had given Giorgio a schedule of the woman's waking and sleeping hours. A shudder of anguish had forked through Giorgio as he recognized the details of a lengthy phase in the last months of Carmen's life.

After setting himself up in the front entrance of the building across the way from the woman's own, he looked at his watch; the investigation into the disappearance of the little boy had turned the entire investigative squad's routine inside out, and he hadn't had a chance to swing back by the parish of Santissima Annunziata for his usual chat with Leonardo. He wanted to tell him all about the new path his investigation was taking, about the woman he was following and his line of reasoning: Talking to the friar helped him organize his thoughts; it always helped. And Leonardo had texted him; they'd have to skip their usual lunch at Il Gobbo, too. Maybe it was for the best, he thought to himself; he'd be able to savor all the more the monk's surprise at learning that Giorgio had seen someone pay this woman, who was completely alone in the world, a visit. And that the odds were strong that this visitor was the long sought-after murderer.

Because Giorgio was certain that Maria Musella was going to be the next victim, and that he, Deputy Captain Pisanelli, was going to catch the killer of the depressed red-handed.

Then, and only then, could he give in to his illness. And look forward to the moment when he'd be able to kiss Carmen again.

Brother Leonardo was in a hurry, his short legs pumping up and down as he climbed the hill toward Maria Musella's place. He was terribly behind schedule.

It's no easy matter, he would have said, if he could. You have to wait for just the right moment, when the time is ripe for the transition.

The angel-to-be must be weary, empty of all desire, not merely anguished and dismayed; those are momentary, transitory states of mind, which can be preludes to a recovery, a renewed attachment to life and the world. The angel-to-be must be in such a state that later, everyone will say: There, it happened, I'd been expecting it, I knew it, it was clear she couldn't go on any longer.

Sometimes, and in fact this had happened at least three times that he could remember, the body wasn't even found right away. Those were cases in which he congratulated himself for having clearly identified not only someone who was lonely, but also someone who had been separated out from the community. The suicide was thus abandoning a life that had long ago abandoned him or her.

Letting a person live so long in such conditions was the real crime, Leonardo thought to himself. Letting a heart that had been deserted go on beating, allowing the flesh to act as ballast, holding down a soul ready to rejoin the Heavenly Father who had created it.

By now, Signora Musella no longer even went to church. The pills she took resulted in an all-but-endless state of partial unconsciousness, and the few hours of lucidity afforded her were nothing more than further steps toward the abyss. Still, Leonardo wanted to speak to her, to understand whether her mental state was caused by her dependence on the medication, or by a genuine, deep-seated loss of her will to live: He needed to dispel that last doubt before proceeding.

Otherwise, he was well prepared. He knew how many pills were necessary to induce a deep sleep, followed by death, without causing convulsions and atrocious pain the subject would feel even if she were unconscious. He knew what room it would be best to do it in, depending on the time of day, to avoid arousing suspicions. He knew and could perfectly imitate the woman's handwriting, so he'd be able to write a suicide note that would leave no doubts about the victim's intentions.

The only thing missing was complete certainty that she was ready. One last visit, before the decisive one.

He needed to hurry if he was going to get there before lunch, otherwise he'd find her asleep again. As he walked he greeted the faithful, who smiled at the sight of the little monk hurrying to bring comfort to those in need.

Which was, in fact, exactly what Leonardo cared about most.

While he stood waiting, happy that he wasn't experiencing the same acute need to urinate that had plagued him the last time, Giorgio reflected on the instinct that had led him here: He couldn't have explained just why he was so certain that it was Musella who was the designated victim. He had read once that intuition is nothing more than the rapid application of accumulated knowledge; that the brain, on a subconscious level, compares and contrasts, associates and separates, until in the end it chooses, in a flash, the best hypothesis among many. If that was true, he thought, then it was the years and years of investigation, years of mistakes, years of butting my head against brick walls that have afforded me this certainty. You, murderer, are going to strike again and you're going to strike here, right at the front entrance across the street, in the apartment on the third floor. I'll see you go in, climb the stairs, knock. Through the window, I'll see Maria Musella drag her feet over to the door.

And after that, I'll come upstairs, too, and I'll see your face.

Just as he felt the adrenaline rushing through his veins, as he rejoiced in the complete harmony of mind, body, and heart, as he savored the taste of a hunt nearing its conclusion, he felt his left pocket vibrate. Palma's voice, tense and worried, informed him that the meeting had been moved up: He needed Pisanelli to return immediately to the precinct house.

It doesn't matter, the deputy captain murmured to the third-floor window. It's just a matter of time.

And he headed off.

At the very same instant, from the opposite direction, Brother Leonardo's minuscule, exhausted silhouette heaved into view.

XXXIII

Lojacono had promised Marinella that he'd take her to Letizia's for lunch, and he was worried that the interview at the Parascandolos' gym, which had gone longer than he'd expected, would interfere with that plan. Having to forgo a pleasure in order to give precedence to his work would be nothing new.

His daughter was more understanding than her mother, who could pout for days because he'd had to cancel, but that was precisely why he hated to disappoint her. And so, taking advantage of the fact that Palma had left them free until after lunch, when there would be a briefing session on the Borrelli case, he'd dashed over to the trattoria, where the girl was waiting for him outside the entrance.

Letizia's restaurant had been the first he'd set foot in in that strange new city, and in nearly two years he hadn't found a place where you could eat any better.

He clearly remembered the rainy night when his loneliness had pushed him out into the streets like a wolf. He'd been at his lowest then, marginalized at the precinct house of San Gaetano, where he'd been reassigned; he'd had no friends, or even acquaintances, and no desire to strike up conversations or put food in his fridge. Letizia's neon sign was the only one glowing on that stormy night, and he'd walked in through the front door more in search of haven than of food.

He'd been hit over the head by the celestial aroma of the ragù, which had immediately made him aware of a gurgling emptiness in his stomach. He'd sat down at the one unoccupied table, the one by the front door, a table that would in time become his alone, and he'd eaten in a way he'd never have believed himself capable of: head down, wet hair dripping onto the tablecloth, not stopping until he felt ready to pop.

Since that night, at least three or four times a week, he'd become one of the trattoria's regulars. It took him a long time to figure out that the place was quite fashionable. To eat dinner there, reservations were required, and there was always a long waiting list. But, though he didn't know it, Lojacono had an in; the little table by the door was always waiting for him.

And that was because Letizia, the restaurant's owner, chef, singer, and emcee, had a crush on him.

To be clear, it wasn't as if she were looking for a man; nor, attractive as she was, did she lack for suitors. She was just over forty, the age at which a woman attains the fullness of perfection and finally becomes aware of her own beauty. A buxom brunette with an infectious laugh, outgoing and welcoming but never intrusive, she was the restaurant's second most popular attraction, after the cooking, which she saw to herself in hours of happy hard work before the restaurant opened. After that, she left everything in the skilled hands of her two sous chefs, who saw to the construction of the individual dishes while she looked after the main dining room.

The men watched her move gently from one table to the other, dazed before the subtle swaying of her form and substance; the women didn't see her as a rival, sensing the absence of all coquetry in her frank cordiality. And everyone was captivated by the charms of the traditional dishes, rigorously interpreted according to old recipes and original ingredients, and by the serenades that she could conjure from the strings of her guitar when, at end of the evening, she'd take a break and become just another of the many guests.

Emotionally she was, or seemed to be, impervious. It was

known that she was a widow, but she was reluctant to speak of the past and she'd had no children; but no one knew of any relationships or boyfriends, though it seemed impossible, to the sharp-tongued neighborhood gossips, that such a sensual woman should allow no one to share her bed. Advances were received with a laugh and a pat on the cheek, but she made no dates. So it had been for the ten years of the trattoria's steady rise, until the night that the door had swung open and the pouring rain had pushed in Giuseppe Lojacono of Montallegro, in the province of Agrigento, known to his friends as Peppuccio.

Letizia couldn't have said what he had triggered in her. The sensation had been a physical one, like a levee breaking or a landslide. The fact remained that from that moment on, the Chinaman's almond-shaped eyes, his high cheekbones, and his shiny, black, perpetually tousled hair, had taken their place at the center of her fantasies, reawakening erotic feelings she'd assumed were forever dormant.

Instinctively, she'd approached him, and, instinctively, he'd confided in her. For months, she'd been the only person Lojacono talked to about his hometown, his family, his work, and the city, which seemed hostile and savage to him, a place where he was imprisoned in the open air. She'd listened to him then and still listened to him now, absorbing and then guarding him from his malaise.

More than anything else, Peppuccio—as she'd called him from the moment she'd learned what pet name his mother had used—had talked to her about his daughter. Evening after evening, she'd reconstructed, from his weary words, the girl's features, her traits and idiosyncrasies, imagining her as if she were there, in the restaurant; and in the support she gave a man she made a point of thinking of as a new friend—she lacked the courage to admit to herself the feelings she was developing—there beat the heart of the mother that circumstance alone had kept her from becoming.

When, little more than a month earlier, wearing an enigmatic expression, Lojacono had entered the restaurant saying that there was a person he wanted to introduce her to, Letizia's heart had leapt as if she'd been waiting for that moment all her life. She'd hit it off instantly with Marinella. The teenager—who was in transition, somewhere between the girl she'd been so recently been and the splendid, luminous woman she was about to become, so similar to her father and yet so different—had appealed to her from the start. And the girl had liked her, seeing in her both a friend and a mother she didn't have to regard as a rival because she sensed, though obscurely and imprecisely, that her father, though he liked her very much, felt toward her none of the more tumultuous emotions that women recognize instantly. The feelings she had, in fact, instantly detected in the embarrassed glance that Lojacono had turned toward Piras the evening of Marinella's arrival.

Marinella had thus become Letizia's secret ally. Between a ragù and a Neapolitan *pastiera*—she devoured the dishes that Letizia set before her with a teen's typical hunger—she'd spend hours chatting with her, the two women excluding Lojacono from the conversation even as they made him its subject, all in his presence and to his vast amusement; he liked watching his daughter enjoying herself. They'd become friends, Marinella and Letizia, and now that the girl had learned how to get around town on her own, she'd even go and see Letizia alone if Lojacono was busy with work.

And so, when she and her father walked into the restaurant, pushed along by a gentle, early afternoon breeze, everyone was contented and cheerful: Letizia, who had the finest bucatini alla carbonara, which Marinella had requested ahead of time, waiting for them; the girl, who couldn't wait to tell her, as soon as her father left the table, about the outcome of her exploratory expedition in search of the Whistling College Boy;

Lojacono, who was anxious to rid himself for a couple of hours of all thoughts of the kidnapped child.

The restaurant was brightly lit, and for once there weren't many customers: At lunchtime the place wasn't as crowded. Marinella hugged and kissed Letizia, who replied: "There's my girl. How is everything? Have you decided to get rid of this boring old grizzly bear of a father and come live with me? That way at night we can both get all dolled up and go pick up some men."

Lojacono made a face: "Say, have you forgotten that we're Sicilians? A hundred years of movies, stock phrases, and novels haven't taught you a thing? If I see her with a man I'll break her legs in three or four places, that way she'll be in casts, and in traction, and I can rest assured she won't be able to leave home for a while."

Marinella laughed: "You know, you have no idea what can be done, even when you're immobilized. A girlfriend of mine from school, in Palermo, told me about one time when she fell off her scooter and broke her leg, and had it in a cast: one night when her parents were out, her boyfriend came to see her and . . ."

Lojacono opened his mouth in feigned horror and took a swing at her, missing entirely. The three of them laughed, and the policeman thought, in a flash of insight, that he hadn't felt so light and happy in a long time.

The waiter brought three enormous bowls of piping hot bucatini, and just as Lojacono was sticking his fork into the pasta, his cell phone, which was resting on the tabletop, rang.

On the display, Laura Piras's name was blinking.

XXXIV

H ello?"
"..."
"Hello? Hello, who's calling?"
"Borrelli? Edoardo Borrelli?
"Yes, that's me. Are you the one who has my grandson?"
"You no talk. You listen."
"No, you listen to me, you son of a bitch. I'm going to kill you, you understand that? I'm going to kill you, and I'm going to watch you die slowly, you goddamn bastard, you . . ."
Silence.
"Hello? Hello?"
"You calm down? If you talk again, I hang up and I no phone back no more."
"I . . . yes, I understand. How is my grandson?"
"He fine."
"Listen, you bastard, if you so much as dare to touch him . . ."
Silence.
"Hello?"
"This last phone call. You shut up. Minute you talk, I not call back. You understand?"
"Yes. My grandson . . ."
"He fine, I told you. Now you listen to me."
"Can I talk to my grandson?"
"No now. Listen me."
"Yes. Yes, all right."
"If you want to see your grandson alive again, without any

harm being done to him, you have to procure five million euros in cash. In one day's time, you will receive a further cumin . . . communication that will tell you where to bring the money. The communication will not be by tephel . . . telephone, so there's no point trying to munit . . . monitor the lines. If something goes wrong, if we see even one policeman go by, even by chance, you'll never see your grandson again. Understood?"

"Goddamn son of a bitch, you're a dead man! You're a dead man, you understand? You're a dead man walking, I'll track you down, I know people that you . . ."

"One day. Five million. You last time hearing my voice."

"I'll find you, you bastard! I'll . . ."

Silence.

XXXV

The recording ended with a loud burst of static; profound silence followed in its wake. Everyone was looking at something else as if they wanted to avoid meeting their colleagues' eyes, as if keeping the horror to themselves might erase the fact of it.

Piras was the first one to break the spell: "He read the message this time, too. He even stumbled over a few words."

Aragona was drumming his fingers on the desktop: "He's from the East. A piece of shit from Eastern Europe: a Slav, a Russian, who the hell knows. But he's from the East."

Palma loosened his tie; the bright afternoon sunlight beat down, raising the temperature.

"The fact that he's reading, though, means there's someone who's writing. The situation is more complicated than it seems."

"Five million euros," Ottavia said; she was still staring at the monitor. "That's quite a sum to put together in cash, and in one day."

Alex, who was looking out the window, murmured: "If he asked for it, it means that he knows the old man can get it. And he asked him, not the parents; he knows that Borrelli is the one to talk to."

Lojacono agreed, his tone decisive: "Yes. These people know that the old man has immense resources, that much is clear. Unfortunately, that wouldn't seem to do much to narrow the field. Giorgio said so right away: The whole city knows that Borrelli is a very rich man."

"I've already ordered everyone's assets frozen," Laura retorted. "The banks have locked down personal and corporate checking accounts. Between Dodo's father and grandfather, we found six or seven companies: They're a couple of octopuses."

Romano, who had until then been sitting in silence, said: "Talking to the old man, I got the idea that even though he's stuck in a wheelchair, and even if he's been out of the game for a long time, he still has a few cards up his sleeve. In other words, what he shouted at the kidnapper doesn't strike me as an empty threat: Borrelli is a tough nut."

Palma nodded: "The kidnappers don't have much time, they need to firm this deal up quickly, otherwise it's going to get harder and harder just to keep the child hidden. Headquarters is working the city's outlying areas and they're reaching out to their network of informants; this has all been kept under the radar to keep from attracting the attention of the local media. They can't have taken the child far."

Aragona snorted: "It's not like we have much time either. The only reason the newspapers don't know anything is that it's in the nuns' best interest not to let word get out, but sooner or later somebody's going to wonder what became of that kid."

Laura, despite herself, had to admit that Aragona was right: "Yes, that's true. And I'm sorry to say it, but either we find something concrete, and fast, or else the case will be handed over to the special investigations branch, especially if it this becomes a matter of public knowledge."

Rage surged through Romano: "It seems to me that we're doing everything that needs to be done. I doubt the others have a magic wand."

Piras cut him off: "No one's saying that, Romano. In fact, I'd say that both the two of you and the rest of the squad are rising to the challenge very well. But in cases like this, success can hinge on an hour more or less, and having additional people on the job could prove invaluable."

Everyone turned to look at Palma, expecting a vigorous defense of his team's work. Instead, the commissario responded in a disconsolate voice: "The first priority, in cases like this, is the safety of the kidnap victim. As the dottoressa said, we're doing our best and we'll continue to do so; but we need results, otherwise the trail can go cold. If the special investigative teams can do better, we're certainly not going to fight any territorial battles when a child's life is at stake."

From the far end of the room, where he was sitting peacefully, Pisanelli's calm voice rang out: "I'd love to see, boss, just how the special investigations branch is going to lay its hands on certain information. Because sometimes the paths that lead to solid intelligence can be karstic, as the saying goes."

"So what the fuck is that supposed to mean, karstic?" Aragona murmured.

"Subterranean, son. Subterranean. Like an underground river. Let me preface this, Dottoressa, by pointing out that this is confidential information, though it could help us to direct our investigation. Since this is not intelligence concerning a crime, I'm going to avail myself of the right to keep the source anonymous. Agreed?"

Laura narrowed her eyes and, after a moment's thought, gave her reply.

"A slippery slope, Pisanelli. Be careful, and remember that you're a policeman. But given the situation . . . tell us what you found out."

Giorgio shuffled several sheets of paper into order and began: "Not all the people connected to Dodo have money, that much we know. The boy's father does; he's a hard-charging industrialist, the kind they have up north, a self-made man. But, apart from supplying scrap metal to a few customers, he isn't involved in any business in this area. No banking relationships. It makes sense to assume that, since the boy lives with his mother, the kidnappers don't know that

Cerchia is rich. But things change when we come to old Borrelli."

Aragona removed his glasses: "Well what do you think of that. Maybe it'll turn out that the old man is broke."

Pisanelli shook his head: "Actually, he's even wealthier than I had imagined. The point is that he only has as much as he needs on hand, plus the substantial income he draws from his real estate holdings. Temporary accounts; the money's in transit, in other words. From time to time, he empties his accounts, and my source had a one-word reply when I asked where the money went: out. In short, he sends everything out of the country. It seems to me, Dottoressa, that in Borrelli's case, freezing his assets, however quickly, can't have done much good."

Piras wasn't surprised: "We never really count on it. Go ahead."

"In that case, maybe, the kidnappers' demand makes a certain amount of sense after all. In Italy, putting together that big a sum in cash would take a long time; but if you had the money elsewhere, maybe not that far away . . ."

Romano stirred irritably: "How does that help us? Knowing who's going to pay the ransom and how doesn't get us an inch closer to the child; we're sitting here chatting about financial matters, while at this very moment . . ."

Pisanelli held up a hand: "Calm down. Calm down and stay cool. Getting angry isn't going to get us anywhere. This isn't the only information I obtained on my walk. I was telling you that not everyone in the family has money."

"Go on," Palma said.

"We know that Scarano, Eva Borrelli's boyfriend, is an artist. The truth is, he has a degree in architecture, but he paints."

Ottavia broke in: "Yes, I found that out online. Ten or so years ago he looked like he was on his way. He had a solo show in Rome, another in Naples, and one in Venice, not at the Biennale. But then he disappeared."

"That's right," Pisanelli confirmed. "He had some sort of nervous breakdown, and even after he recovered he was never able to get back to the levels he'd been working at before. Eva met him at the home of friends and fell in love with him when she was in the process of breaking up with the child's father, though the split wasn't yet official. She saw him again after the separation—though if you ask me they were in touch the whole time—and she let him move in."

Aragona snickered. "So he's living off her."

"You could say that, yes. It's just that Eva lives on what her father gives her—that is, basically the rent from a couple of apartments in both their names that were part of her inheritance from her mother. It's not like they have a lot of money; and yet Scarano blows through plenty of cash."

"Explain," Lojacono said.

"He plays cards. And with a bad crowd: a floating game run by professionals, in private homes. In short, Scarano gambles and loses. My source has seen a number of checks made out to dangerous individuals."

"And who pays his debts?"

"Old man Borrelli, and the funny thing is that he does it without letting the daughter know. Maybe he loves her more than he shows, or maybe he's just trying to prevent a scandal. She takes this Scarano with her everywhere, and everyone in the city's high-class social circles knows him as Eva Borrelli's boyfriend."

Romano was listening intently "Interesting. Here's someone who not only has no money, but who might desperately need some."

Pisanelli pulled out a new sheet of paper. "What's particularly interesting is the fact that Scarano recently went to the bank with Peluso, Borrelli's secretary. The woman delivered a lecture to the director in the presence of poor Manuel, who stood there, head down, like a dog who was used to being beaten: She said that the cavalier, now that he'd covered the last check, was going to stop meeting the family painter's needs, so to speak, and that from now on he'd have to get by on his own."

Piras was quickly jotting down notes on a sheet of paper. "So now we're starting to develop a profile. Scarano was familiar with the child's routines and schedules, knew all about Borrelli's personal resources, had his various phone numbers, and he also needed money. That seems sufficient to start doing a little digging on him, no?"

Pisanelli turned to another sheet of paper.

"Slow down, slow down, Dottoressa. There's a little something else. Scarano's not the only one to have secretly benefitted, shall we say, from Borrelli's money."

"Who else?

"Peluso. As far as I've been able to determine, the old man trusts her implicitly and, especially now that he can no longer walk, he relies on her to handle all administrative issues. The lady has complete power of attorney in all matters."

"So? In and of itself that doesn't mean anything."

"No, that's true. Only that for the past year or so, Peluso has started draining off a little cash here and there. It's been done very adroitly, over at the bank they almost overlooked it entirely, especially because the payouts were always mixed in with other transactions: payroll checks, utility bills, taxes, and so on. But to quote the comedian Totò, it's the sum that makes the total, and at a certain point the overall amount siphoned off became pretty sizable; the director asked the woman for an explanation."

"And what did she say?"

"She gave him a glare that would freeze ice . . ."

"Yes, I can just see her," Aragona piled on enthusiastically, "the spitting image of Frau Blücher in *Young Frankenstein*."

Piras looked daggers at him.

"The dottoressa here isn't kidding around either," the young officer said in a stage whisper, "when it comes to glares that would freeze ice."

". . . and she told him," Pisanelli continued, "you know, sir, it's up to me where we do our banking. Do we understand each other? At that point he raised his hands in the air and walked away."

"But shouldn't he have reported her?" Piras asked. "And wait, where is this money going?"

"No, Dottoressa, he couldn't file a criminal complaint because every transaction was executed through a legally issued power of attorney; there was nothing to object to. Peluso signed the orders, and she had every right to do so. The money went to a checking account in a branch office in Salerno, where Peluso is originally from. Substantial sums, on the order of a couple hundred thousand euros a year. After their discussion, though, the transfers stopped, and Borrelli's companies worked a great deal less with that bank. In other words, the signora found other channels."

Pisanelli fell silent; he relaxed in his chair, visibly satisfied.

Ottavia coughed and took the floor: "I've done a little research of my own. Carmela Peluso, born in Serre, province of Salerno, in 1951, has been working for Borrelli since 1973, when she was still just a girl. She's served in a number of roles, from secretary at one of Borrelli's companies to the old man's right-hand woman and special legal representative, that last position for at least the past ten years. She has always shown an absolute devotion to her boss, and she's acted as a buffer between father and daughter since his wife died, more or less to protect him from a new source of grief. She doesn't much like children, and when little Dodo, before starting school, used to spend his days at his grandfather's house, the old man had to hire a number of nannies and babysitters to look after

206 · MAURIZIO DE GIOVANNI

the boy because she wasn't cut out for it. She's extremely reserved, but recently she confessed her concerns about the old man's health: She's afraid she might be cut out of the will when he dies, since she doesn't rely much on his daughter's gratitude; she's described Eva as a selfish bitch."

Everyone turned to look at her in surprise. Palma was the first to find his tongue: "You found that on the Internet, too?"

Ottavia laughed: "No, of course not. That is, there's her personal information and a few pictures. But the signora did give in to the temptations of new technology and set up a Facebook profile so she could track down a couple of old girl-friends from her hometown. It isn't hard to get around privacy restrictions, you know."

Aragona put his glasses back on: "So the old witch has set aside a nice fat payout at the old cripple's expense. Interesting. But what does that have to do with the boy? I like Scarano bet-ter: the unsuccessful painter and unrepentant gambler who can't cover his debts. Those people will cut your throat if you try to stiff them, and fear is always an excellent motive."

Palma scratched his head: "I don't know. It's also true that one last payout would mean the lady was set for the foresee-able future."

Piras stood up: "My congratulations, I don't think that any other investigative team could have come close. Guys, you've earned yourselves another day; I'll talk to the chief of police. Keep your guard up, and in particular keep an eye on any com-munications between the kidnappers and old Borrelli. I don't want any ransom being paid."

Lojacono went over to Pisanelli: "Giorgio, I wanted to compliment you: You manage to find out more by going for a walk and buying someone a cup of coffee than would ten undercover agents infiltrating Cosa Nostra—and trust me, I've seen them work. I'm truly impressed."

"Don't mention it, Loja'. This is my neighborhood, my city: I know them well, and if you were back home, you'd do the same."

"No, I don't think so. People trust you, and they're right to do so: you wouldn't have revealed the name of your friend under torture, and he knows it, and that's why he'll talk to you. You really are something."

Pisanelli slapped him on the back: "We're all really something, we Bastards of Pizzofalcone. We should trademark the nickname. It's been years since I've had so much fun coming in to the office. Though I'd love it if we could get this kid out of the kidnappers' clutches."

"You're right, it's such a nasty story that the burglary that Di Nardo and I are investigating looks like a joke in comparison. You should have seen the wife of the victim in the gym this morning; we caught her with a tattooed idiot who, by the way, actually did time for burglary. Now we need to do a little cross-referencing, but we think that this half-baked burglary might actually have been concocted up by the signora with her young lover's help."

Pisanelli suddenly looked interested: "Excuse me, but what's the name of the guy who got robbed? You said he owns a gym?"

"Parascandolo is the name. He has a gym right down the hill from . . ."

". . . from Corso Vittorio Emanuele, right. Tore. Tore Parascandolo, you mean. A guy with a face like a bulldog and a voice like a little girl's. And his wife is all silicone and plastic surgery."

"How do you know?"

"I know because everyone in this city knows Tore the Bulldog. He's notorious."

"Why?"

"He's a loan shark, Loja'. A huge bastard of a loan shark. And the gym is his cover. We've been after him for a lifetime, but he's clever. We've never been able to pin anything on him."

XXXVI

Once the meeting was over, as soon as Piras had left, Palma signaled to Romano and Aragona to follow him into his office. He was reacting with unusual haste.

He closed his door and gestured for them to sit down.

"Well? What do you think of this new information? Do you have any ideas?"

"Boss," Romano replied, "can I tell you in complete frankness what I think? Even if I don't have the evidence to support it?"

"Certainly."

"It's clear that there's someone behind the kidnapper, or the kidnappers—some kind of inside man or client. Someone who is intimately acquainted with the intricate Borrelli family dynamics, who knows that the boy lives with his mother and her boyfriend, and that they don't keep a close eye on him."

Aragona broke in: "And it's clear that the people holding him prisoner are foreigners. All of them, not just the one who phoned."

Palma and Romano turned to look at him: "Why is that?"

"Otherwise they wouldn't have had someone with such a recognizable voice make the phone call. They'd have chosen an Italian, and that would have forced us to widen our investigation."

Romano was impressed in spite of himself. "There's a certain logic to that."

Palma agreed. "Yes, there is a certain logic."

Romano went on: "The research that Ottavia and Pisanelli have done points to two likely suspects, though I think one of them has a stronger motive than the other. Scarano really could be in deep trouble if it's true that Borrelli has turned off the tap. That might help explain why he agreed to give the old man the news: Maybe he was hoping to get in good with him by showing how conscientious he was."

Aragona broke in again: "I wouldn't underestimate the witch. Maybe she wanted to take revenge for all the years spent slaving away for him without him showing the slightest gratitude in return. I'll remind you that he treated her like crap even in front of us. Plus she didn't like the child, she wouldn't take care of him even when he was little. Not to mention the fact that she considers Eva . . . what did Ottavia say? . . . a selfish bitch. In other words, she strikes me as a good candidate, too."

"Yes, we can't rule her out," Romano admitted. "In any case, time is tight and we need to follow whatever slender thread presents itself. Continuing to investigate haphazardly, as we have been, would amount to searching for a needle in a haystack. And in any case, we've delved into the boy's daily life, and we know that he hasn't been in recent contact with anyone unusual. His life is fairly circumscribed, at school they run a pretty tight ship and, from the descriptions everyone gives of him, he's not the kind of kid to talk to strangers. They took him at the one possible moment, and Dodo knew the person with whom he left the museum."

"We've already said these things, and I agree that we need to focus on the inside man. Let's do this: We'll call them all together at the old man's place, since he can't get around, we tell them the way things stand, and we see how they react. Sometimes, when you throw a rock in the pond, something surfaces."

"It strikes me as a desperation move, boss," Romano said, trying to set aside his doubts. "But I can't think of anything else."

Aragona massaged his temples: "If we had more time to work, we could put them all under surveillance and wait for one of them to slip up. But given the way things are, I'm with you on the family meeting."

Palma stood up: "All right then. Make some phone calls and get a little rest. We'll head over there tonight."

Laura lingered in the courtyard and told her driver to wait for her. Then she went over to Guida, who was the guard on duty at the front door: "Would you do me a favor and call up to Lieutenant Lojacono?"

Guida snapped to attention, surprising Laura, and, after quickly punching in a number, handed her the receiver.

"I'm waiting for you out in the car," Piras said tersely. "Hurry up."

And she moved off.

A minute later, Guida saw Lojacono come downstairs, and decided to venture a knowing reference: "Lieutenant, the dottoressa drove the car around to the right, you'll find her there."

Lojacono stopped and looked at him with no expression. The officer, increasingly uneasy, snapped to attention and fixed his gaze on a point in space out in the courtyard. Then the Chinaman said: "Guida, when I need directions from you, I'll ask for them. More importantly: When I need your help in my personal life, which I imagine will be never, I'll give you written instructions. In the meanwhile, to put it very briefly, mind your own fucking business."

"Yessir, Lieutenant."

Laura opened the door for him and told him to get in. There was no driver.

"I told him to go get himself a cup of coffee. Weak, or he won't be able to get to sleep tonight. He's better behind the wheel than Aragona, but absolutely everyone who drives in this city, whatever the reason, seems crazy."

"Agreed; today I had to drive and I still feel shaken up. Well, what's up?"

Piras crossed her legs: "Why, now I need a specific reason to talk with you? Anyway, I wanted to hear your impression of this case, face-to-face, in private."

"Well, time is tight: They've been holding the boy for three days, though I don't think they're interested in hurting him. I'd focus on the family; what Ottavia and Pisanelli have found looks like good stuff to me."

Piras nodded.

"I admire the fact that Palma resisted the temptation to hand you the case; by doing that, he keeps morale high. Still, I wish it was you running the investigation; I would feel better about it."

"Don't worry, Romano is a tough nut, and even Aragona, you know, is much better than you'd think. He's rough and rude, but he pays attention, and he has good hunches. Plus, like you saw, we all talk things over together. That's the real strength of this precinct, the way we collaborate. And credit for that goes to Palma."

"Yes, I know. You're all doing excellent work. But work isn't the only thing there is."

Lojacono burst out laughing: "Wait, seriously? I can't believe I'm hearing this from you, with the reputation for being a workaholic. You're notorious for all but worshipping at the altar of the justice system, for having the penal code where your heart should be!"

Lojacono would long remember Piras's reaction, because it was so surprising. Instead of laughing in turn, the woman tightened her lips, her expression one of deep suffering, and started crying. No sobbing, no moaning: just tears streaming down her cheeks.

"Laura, excuse me . . . what did I say? It was just a joke, Laura . . ."

Lojacono wished he could just dig a hole and bury himself in it. The thought that he'd somehow triggered those tears made his gut ache.

"Is that what people say about me?" She said. "Yes, I can just imagine. And it's true. Or at least it was true, for you'd be surprised to know how long. It's so easy to throw your life away; you can't even imagine, Lieutenant Lojacono."

"Laura, I . . ."

"And by the time you realize what you've done, you're left empty-handed. Completely empty-handed."

"Listen, no one knows better than I do that it's possible to throw your life away. But then, maybe, your life comes back and brings you other opportunities. I . . . Laura, please, don't cry. I don't know how to talk to women when they're crying. I just can't do it."

Piras took her sunglasses out of her purse, put them on, and dried her cheeks with her hands; she reminded Lojacono of a little girl.

"Listen, I can't afford to waste time. Not anymore. I don't know how to flirt with a man I like, and I'm no good at sitting there patiently and waiting for him, either; I'm much better at pouring buckets of cold water onto the idiots who try to bag me just so they can add another notch to their bedposts."

Lojacono interrupted: "Excuse me, but what makes you think I don't like you? Look, ever since the very first time I saw you . . . Fuck, I'm too old for some things, too. And I don't want to say them to you here, in a car parked outside the precinct, while these lunatics go roaring past down the street like they're at some grand prix."

Piras sat motionless, looking at him. He couldn't see her

eyes, hidden as they were behind the dark lenses; but he did notice that tears were no longer streaming down her face.

In a harsh, low voice, her arms still crossed tightly, the woman said to him: "Be careful, Lojacono. Be very careful. Because if you try to break my heart I'll remember that I'm Sardinian and I'll cut your throat with a razor-sharp *pattada*. Consider yourself warned."

"Look, Dottoressa, I'm Sicilian. I'm used to the *lupara*, the sawed-off shotgun. But I don't think you're going to need one."

He brushed her lips in a rapid kiss and got out of the car, full of life.

XXXVII

Dodo poops in a plastic potty. A baby potty, with a handle on the side. There's a picture of Hello Kitty on it, so it's for girls.

At first, for several hours, he'd held it in. He'd peed in a corner, the minute day had dawned and there'd been a glimmer of light through the crack in the sheet metal, but he'd held the poop in. Then, when he couldn't stand it anymore, he'd used the potty. He thought it was kind of nice that it had the picture of Hello Kitty on it, even though he'd never really liked her.

Along with the potty, Stromboli had given him a roll of toilet paper. He didn't use much, for fear he wouldn't be given any more. Once he saw a TV show where a boy was held prisoner and there was no toilet paper and the thought terrified him: Of course you can poop on the floor or the ground, but how do you clean yourself afterward if you don't have any toilet paper?

Time passes slowly. Dodo tries to sleep, but at night, even with the blanket, he's a little cold, and every so often he wakes up with his teeth chattering. He has a sore throat; he didn't want to tell Lena because he didn't want her to worry. Poor Lena. Dodo heard Stromboli shouting in his language, and Lena answering: Maybe they're both from the same country, even though he remembers that Lena knows more than one language. She told him that when she went to school, she had to study Russian, and that she'd learned German from working in Hamburg for a year.

Sister Beatrice, in class, explained to them that these days *there is a great deal of violence against women. One of his class-mates, Bastiani, who's been held back so he's older, snickered in that annoying way of his and said that there are men who force women to have sex even though they don't want to.*

He's not really clear on what having sex means, but it seems like it's something pretty violent. He's afraid that it's what Stromboli does with Lena, and he doesn't want to give her even more to worry about, so he says nothing to her about his throat, the poop, and the cold hot pockets that by now he's used to eat-ing anyway.

Dodo tells himself that when his father, leading a squad of policemen with guns, comes to rescue him, he'll have to tell the truth and admit that Stromboli did give him food, a blanket, water, and even Coca-Cola, as well as the Hello Kitty potty. After all, he can't be all that bad, if he let him have all these things.

He's sleepy now, Dodo is. He feels hot but he's shivering. He covers himself up and fantasizes about saving Stromboli's life at the last second, when a policeman is about to shoot him in the head.

Perhaps Stromboli, Dodo thinks as he slips into a sleep made up of equal parts fever and exhaustion, has kids of his own at home. And maybe the money that he wants from his grandfather is just so he can feed those children.

His grandfather, Dodo thinks. Poor grandfather, old and sick. Maybe, now that he's been taken, Papà and Grandpa will finally make peace.

They're his heroes, Grandpa and Papà, Dodo thinks.

And he falls asleep, with his throat on fire.

XXXVIII

Old Borrelli's caretaker led Palma, Romano, and Aragona down the hallway and up the stairs, both of which were still immersed in shadows. But the shadows weren't muffled now: The place seemed to crackle with electricity.

Everyone was there in the living room. At the center, in his wheelchair, sat the patriarch, pale and expressionless; standing beside him was Peluso, rigid, erect, her gaze as fixed as that of a wax statue. Eva was sitting on one of the sofas, her face devastated by grief and lack of sleep, her fingers twisting a tear-soaked handkerchief; next to her sat Scarano, eyes downcast, one hand on her leg. Alberto Cerchia kept pacing back and forth in front of the large windows, ignoring the spectacular nighttime panorama.

The policemen understood that their arrival had interrupted a lively argument, which had left behind traces like those on a field in the aftermath of a battle.

Palma said: "We wanted to meet with you all together to report on the state of our investigation and the measures the magistrate has taken."

"Commissario," Eva asked in a trembling voice, "do you have any news? Who took my boy? It's been three days . . . I can't take it any more . . ."

Scarano put his arm around her shoulder. "What news do you expect them to come up with?" Cerchia roared. "They can't even find each other in this mess of a city; no wonder they can't find my son. All you know how to do is freeze our bank accounts: My partner called me from Bergamo and told me that we can't make payments anymore. That's what you know how to do. Instead of . . ."

Palma interrupted him firmly: "Dottor Cerchia, I invite you to refrain from exaggerating. I understand your state of mind, the state of mind you're all in, but certain measures are required by law. In fact, I wanted to remind you that while your assets have been frozen, you can, on a case-by-case basis, obtain the partial release of certain sums to make payments through banking channels. Moreover, all telephone lines, including cell phones, are subject to wiretapping and recording . . ."

Cerchia snapped yet again: "What are you trying to say? It's as if we were the criminals! You're all worthless!"

Romano gave him a surly look: "Cerchia, watch out. Talking that way to a police commissario could very easily constitute a criminal offense."

The man fell silent, though it took a visible effort; his face was twisted in fury. He too showed unmistakable signs—stubble; a wrinkled suit—of exhaustion; he clearly hadn't been sleeping much. Dodo's parents had been brought together again, but by grief and sorrow.

Old Borrelli spoke in a low voice: "Commissario, we understand. But if the reason you came here is to inform us of the restrictions you've imposed, which I'm sure we all expected, you could have spared yourself the trip."

"You're right, Cavalier. The truth is that we're here to work out our next moves with you all. A ransom has been requested, and the kidnapper told you that the details of the exchange wouldn't be communicated by phone. So we need to be sure that, as soon as the instructions reach you, you'll inform us at once."

Cerchia broke into a ghoulish laugh. Scarano said: "Excuse me, Commissario, but how are we supposed to pay the ransom if you've frozen our assets?"

Borrelli addressed him sarcastically: "Just what assets of yours could have been frozen, you idiot? I'm the one who froze your assets, so to speak, and you know it. Shut up and butt out of matters that don't concern you."

"Papà," Eva replied, "even at a time like this you can't show a little humanity? You can't even try? We've just finished flinging horrible accusations at each other . . ."

"You shut your mouth, too. It's your fault we're in this situation. You and your ridiculous choices, and your . . ."

Cerchia interrupted him: "But nothing's your fault, is it? Either you're in charge or you don't give a damn. That's the way it's always been: When you're not manipulating people like they're puppets on a string, you turn your back and let them make fools of themselves. Like your daughter, who dumped me so she could hook up with this worthless idiot."

Peluso got to her feet: "Well, what about you? What have you done except go back up north, forgetting all about your son except when you wire him some money or come down for a little visit every fifteen days? I don't think you're in any position to criticize."

"Oh, cut it out, you're just a glorified housekeeper. You shouldn't even be here with the real family right now."

"No, you cut it out, you idiot," Borrelli retorted. "In my home, I say who gets to talk. And after all, I'm the one that bastard demanded the money from, so I'm the one who gets to decide what to do."

"In fact," Scarano said, "the only thing that matters is getting Dodo. That poor child is in danger, who knows where, and we're just sitting here slinging mud at each other . . ."

"He's my son, you asshole!" Cerchia shouted. "My son, not yours! My son, my Dodo, and now he's being held by a couple of fucking gypsies, in this fucking city, in who knows what kind of fucking place . . ."

Eva burst into tears and stuck her fingers in her ears:

"Enough, that's enough! I can't stand listening to you shout anymore!"

Scarano spoke again, his voice calm, as if Cerchia hadn't just attacked him: "Commissario, we're all upset, as you can see. It's clear that we're in no condition to come up with a strategy on our own. Maybe we should listen to you."

Borrelli agreed: "Why, yes, let's listen. Let's hear what the commissario has to suggest."

Palma went on: "As I was saying, it's important that you get in touch with us if the kidnappers contact you in any way that we can't monitor."

Peluso asked: "Even if they were to use email or . . ."

"Even if they write you via Facebook," Aragona replied brusquely.

The woman blushed and shot a sideways glance at the old man, who hadn't noticed. Palma went on: "We have wiretaps on all your phone lines, so let me repeat, any phone call, incoming or outgoing, will be recorded: If they give you a number to call, we'll know it. I'm emphasizing this so you're not tempted to make some kind of deal on your own. The same applies to Internet traffic."

Peluso objected: "So you'll be sticking your noses into our business, investigating our professional and personal lives. And this is supposed to be a free country . . ."

Aragona looked her up and down: "So free that there are even people who will kidnap a child, or try to trip up the people trying to rescue him. A little too free, this country's turning out to be."

Eva said: "But if these . . . if these people were to get something to us, I don't know, a letter, a note . . ."

"That's exactly why we're here, Signora. We need to be sure you'll call us immediately. That way we can catch them and find Dodo."

Borrelli narrowed his eyes: "But what if they figure it out?

What if they sense you're on their trail and they do something to the boy? We'd run the risk of paying and not . . ."

Cerchia leapt to his feet, as if spring-loaded: "I'll give you back the money, don't you worry. As soon as our accounts are unfrozen you'll get every penny. Unfortunately, I haven't hidden my money offshore because I'm a stupid asshole who pays his Italian taxes. And these people, in a show of gratitude, freeze everything I own."

"Don't talk nonsense," Borrelli hissed. "No one's going to pay a thing, and if we were to, which, by the way, I've been told is no crime, someone would lend us the cash."

Romano broke in: "Cavalier, paying the ransom is dangerous. Once the kidnappers have the cash in hand, they might very well just decide to get rid of the child and . . ."

Eva moaned as if she'd just been stabbed. Cerchia went over to her and put a hand on her shoulder, drawing a venomous glare from Scarano.

"Don't you dare," Dodo's father said, jaw clenched. "Don't you even dare think it, goddamn you. I'm going to find my son, I'm going to rescue him, as soon as I can figure out where they're holding him. I'm not going to let them hurt him, I'll never allow that."

"We want to free him too." Romano replied, just as resolute and harsh. "And we're professionals. You need to remember that; you all need to remember that."

Palma reinforced Romano's words: "That's right. Stick to our instructions and let us know the instant anything new comes up. *Buonanotte.*"

Aragona got up from the sofa he'd been sprawled out on. "We'll leave you to your nice family reunion," he said. "We hope we find you all alive next time, seeing how much you love one another."

Before getting back in the car they all stopped to catch their breath. "My God," Palma said, "that's some atmosphere. You could slice through the air with a knife in there. Let's just hope they don't do anything stupid."

Romano was stunned: "It seems impossible to me that there could be so much resentment among people who once cared for one another. All of them feeding on their anger and hatred toward the others; none of them thinking about what's best for the child. I'm worried about the father, Cerchia: He really looked desperate to me. He hates the old man and Scarano so much that I don't know what he might be capable of doing."

Aragona's hands were in his pockets and he was rocking back and forth on his heels. "They all strike me as fairly worthless; the only smart one is Borrelli. The old man's going to pay the ransom, that's for sure, and I'm just as sure that he won't tell us he's done it. He's convinced he has the situation under control. We just have to hope that, given the state he's in, he puts his trust in the right people. Otherwise, so long, money and so long, kid."

Palma and Romano looked at him in disgust: "How on earth can you be so cynical?"

Aragona looked surprised. "Why, what did I say?"

Palma tried to bring things down a notch: "All right then. Let's assign an unmarked car to the area, just in case anyone comes along to deliver a message. Go get some sleep; tomorrow I want you in the office bright and early."

XXXIX

H is fever's very high. I went in without making any noise and I heard him snoring, so I touched his forehead."

"I believe it. That room is drafty as hell. It's terribly hot during the day, but at night the temperature drops sharply. Pass me the wine."

"Well, what were we supposed to do, get a hotel room? I didn't know any other places. This is where I always worked, since I first came to this city, until they shut the place down."

"We need to give him some antibiotics. I can get them."

"I'm worried. He needs to give me the instructions tomorrow. I might have to go somewhere and maybe the police will be there waiting for me."

"No, what are you saying? He can't run the risk of them catching you. Don't worry; if you're not safe, he's not safe."

"Eh, easy for you to say. After all, the guy who has to show up to get the money is me."

"That's bullshit, I'm in more danger than you are. Remember, the boy knows who I am. I'm going to have to disappear, change my name, cut my hair. And you can rest assured he won't leave you alone for more than a second. He can't run the risk of you running away with the loot."

"With the money we're going to earn on this job you'll be able to pay a plastic surgeon in Brazil to make you look just like Jennifer Lopez. Even though I like you the way are now, with blond hair."

"Don't be an asshole. This is no time to think about things like that. But listen, what do we do next? What's the schedule?"

"He'll call me on the cell phone he gave me, which I'm never supposed to use. He manages every last detail: He didn't even want to know where we are to avoid running the risk of giving himself away."

"And what's he going to tell you?"

"What you're supposed to write on the note, because you know the stupid language they speak around here, and then how and where I'm supposed to turn him over. Then he'll call me again to tell me where he's going to come pick up the boy and his share of the ransom."

"That makes it sound easy. When's he supposed to call?"

"It could be anytime. We just have to wait."

"Then let's wait. After all, you have a point; we can have a little fun while we're waiting. Give me some more wine."

XL

Ottavia had a dog.

To tell the truth, the dog belonged to Riccardo, she would never have gotten one on her own. In an apartment in the city a dog sheds and drools everywhere, and it's hard enough keeping an apartment clean in the first place. But one of the many doctors they'd consulted concerning their son's incurable condition had suggested that a pet might help sharpen his focus, and that was all it had taken to get her active, precise, punctual, tireless, and intolerable husband's attention. He'd immediately begun researching the matter on the Internet, at the library, in pet stores, to figure out the best breed.

The result was a calm and highly affectionate canine specimen, an oversized golden retriever who sat awaiting her return every night, anxious to slap his big old paws on her shoulders and run a quarter pound of rough dog tongue over her face. Dogs, it's said, choose a master for themselves from among the members of a family, and Sid—the name had been taken from a cartoon that Riccardo especially loved—hadn't hesitated. Even though she'd been the only one who opposed the dog's presence, even though Riccardo was supposed to be Sid's responsibility, and even though Gaetano took much better care of him, even as a puppy Sid had displayed an absolute, unconditional love for her. And Ottavia, after an obstinate initial silence, which had been followed by the occasional grudging pat on the head, had finally made up her mind to give in to Sid's advances.

One pleasant side effect was that it had become her job to

take the dog out before going to bed and sometimes, when she got back from the walk, she'd find her husband fast asleep, his glasses perched on his nose and his book lying on his chest. That meant she didn't have to invent some absurd excuse to put him off. Again.

May, she thought as she strolled along the finally empty street. May nights. One more reason to feel fresh air on her skin after a day spent shut up in the office, in the subway, in the pool where she took Riccardo for his swim lessons. Air certainly wasn't what you breathed in those in-between moments, while you ran from one place to another, surrounded by exhaust fumes, the acrid smell of the crowd.

But this was. This was the fresh air of a night in May.

Sid sniffed at a light pole and, after thinking it over for a moment, lifted his leg. The city didn't seem the same anymore at that time of night.

Ottavia wondered how Palma and Romano and Aragona's visit to old Borrelli's place had gone. Something about that whole story didn't add up. There was an element of disorder, a disturbance she couldn't identify and which annoyed her, a persistent irritation, a joint ache too minor to treat but still a source of discomfort.

Distractedly, she scratched Sid behind the ear and he swept the air happily with his tail. To leave the apartment she'd had to pry Riccardo off of her; he'd hung on to the sleeve of her jacket and refused to let go. He could be difficult, certain days more than others. Her thirteen-year-old son, locked in his world, didn't want to interact with her, didn't want to play with her, wasn't seeking her attention: He just wanted her to be there, and nothing more. Ottavia had to stay there, and he had to know she was there.

Like being in prison. No better and no worse.

What wasn't right about the whole Dodo Borrelli case? What kept bothering her?

She'd researched everyone involved in the case on the Internet. Everyone except for the kidnappers, obviously, she didn't know anything about them . . . But did she really know nothing about them?

Sid started sniffing in a circle, loudly, and she got her plastic bag and scooper ready. She hoped the boys had made some progress, over at the Borrellis'. And that the sensation that was tormenting her finally made up its mind to emerge, to reveal something to her.

She would have liked to go to the old man's place with them. In general, she would have liked to participate in on-the-ground investigations, in stakeouts, interrogations, confrontations. She'd have liked to rack up miles, in other words, rather than being relegated to the office. Instead, she felt like little more than a glorified old-fashioned secretary, whose only job was doing online research and prying into people's Facebook pages, as she'd done with Peluso.

More than anything else, though, she wanted to be sure she wasn't being given special consideration. She wouldn't have wanted anyone—wouldn't have wanted Palma—to think that her situation, that of a woman over forty with a seriously autistic son, was a hindrance to her work as a policewoman. But perhaps, after all, it was enough that the precinct hadn't been shut down after everything that had happened, and that major investigations were shared, so that everyone felt useful and busy.

Sid showed a regal indifference to a stray cat that stood on a low wall a few yards away, arching its back and raising its fur. Good boy, thought Ottavia: Don't talk to strangers.

Just what kind of a stranger was the commissario, to her? What did the new pleasure she felt in going to work in the morning mean? How could she, in her situation, be so reckless and foolish that she felt something quiver in her belly every time he came near her?

Sid, she asked in a low voice, in the night, you tell me what's going on. You're the only one who knows how I feel, I'm sure of it, because for the past month, as soon as I get home, you're right there next to me, you don't budge an inch, and at night when I watch TV, you watch *me*, as if I were a movie. Tell me what you're thinking, tell me whether I'm just acting like a teenager, whether I should just try to remember who I really am.

As if he'd heard the question, the dog turned his attention away from a piece of newspaper fluttering by in the breeze, fixed his intelligent brown eyes on Ottavia, and bumped her leg lightly with his nose. She patted him again and then whispered: While we're on the subject, do you happen to know what it is about this kidnapping that I keep turning over in my mind, that I can't quite seem to pin down? If so, help me out, because it's driving me crazy.

About fifty yards away, in a parked car with the lights off and the engine stopped, a man watched the woman walking her dog. She was putting on a spectacular show, he thought, the best he could ask for.

The man was Commissario Luigi Palma.

He'd gotten into the habit, when he left the office to head back to the studio apartment that was so perfect for a divorced, childless man, of letting the car go where it wanted; and the car always seemed to head over to a building that matched the address that appeared on the personnel folder of a certain deputy sergeant. Maybe his car just liked that quiet, tree-lined, residential street.

He told himself he was an idiot: Who was he trying to fool? The truth was that he couldn't stop thinking about that face, that supple figure, the line of that body that he could see every time she walked past his office door. And certain evenings, when mankind's miseries were thrown into particularly stark relief, like in the depressing human comedy he'd beheld at

Borrelli's home, he thought about her even more. He'd never run into her before, on these nighttime jaunts, and he wouldn't even have wanted to. It was enough for him to breathe the same air, to imagine her with her happy family, filled with love as she certainly was for her unfortunate son and for her husband with whom she shared so much. That night, however, he'd spotted her from a distance and he'd pulled over immediately. It had been an instinctive act, impossible to justify; in fact, completely unjustifiable. But after a day like the one he'd just had, his heart filled with mute sorrow for a child held prisoner who knew where and by who knew whom, he didn't want to go to bed with the sad spectacle of a family in complete disarray still before his eyes.

So she had a dog. He hadn't known that. A nice big blond dog, long-haired and soft, elegant. Just like Ottavia, in fact; she was also soft and elegant.

He watched as she leaned over to pet the animal. From a distance she actually seemed to be talking to it; Palma had had a dog of his own, when he was a boy, and when no one was around he'd always talked to him, though it had always made him feel a little stupid. From a distance, in the dark, he blew her a kiss.

He watched her go back toward the entrance of her apartment building, open it, and walk in, not in any hurry, the same way she left the office at night after smiling and telling him: *Buonasera*, boss, I'm going home, now you take care of yourself. She said that because more than once she'd been the first one in to work in the morning and found him fast asleep on his office couch, having stayed up too late the night before working on files to want to go back to that tiny apartment that always struck him as so depressing.

He waited a few more minutes. The May night was enveloping the street in an exotic perfume, and it almost seemed to him that the sweetness in the air was blurring his vision.

But no, it was a veil of tears and sadness.

XLI

D*arkness.*
In the middle of the night, there's darkness.
It doesn't last long, fortunately. Perhaps five minutes,
time enough for some heavy breathing and a little terror, as you
look down into the abyss.

It doesn't last long but it can leave its mark if it draws itself
out just a little bit further, if it manages to reach its fingers out
through the loneliness.

The darkness.

You're cold, as you struggle along in your dream.

You see the road leading up into the mountains. You're on your
papà's shoulders; Mamma holds your hand so you have to lean
over to one side because your papà is tall, but your mamma isn't.

You're cold and you'd like to stop, you'd like everything to stop
in this moment of the dream, when the three of you are together,
when the rest of the world isn't there because this is your last vaca-
tion; you know that in the dream, but you can't say it.

You can hear them fight, at night, from your little room. You
hear the accusations you don't understand but that you'll remem-
ber, word for word, explaining to yourself one reason at a time,
year after year, why it ended.

You trudge along with your throat on fire, your sweaty fingers
clutching the action figure to take from it the courage that you
don't possess yourself. In your dream, they're chasing after you—
you, your mamma, and your giant. The ones chasing you are

Stromboli, roaring words you can't understand; Manuel, his eyes red with fury; Sister Angela, with her voice like broken glass; Carmela, gray as death; even your grandfather, who's installed a motor on his wheelchair. They're chasing you and they're going to catch up with you at the top of the incline, unless all three of you run.

Too bad about the throat and the climb. Too bad you can't run any faster.

Too bad about all this darkness.

Darkness.

The moment in the night when all hopes vanish, chased away by the sorrow of what is to come.

The moment in the night when rest is shattered into a thousand fragments of nostalgia, which reassemble themselves into a shroud in the fragile expectation of dawn.

The darkness.

A little agitated sleep, and then right away the dream. The town square in Krivi Vir, two policemen behind you. Panting, weary. A large bundle in your hands: It weighs so much you can barely carry it.

You turn the corner, and instead of low houses and a shop here and there, you see the forest right away. You're happy, you know the forest, the forest is your friend.

You hear steps behind you; then they stop. They lack the courage to venture in among the trees. Perhaps you're safe.

Only suddenly it's night. The middle of the night. And the bundle in your hands is heavy, and it's hot. Hotter and hotter.

Darkness.

You can't see a thing, damn it. You trip over a root and you almost drop what you took, but you hold onto it and find your footing. The leaves brush against your face, cold as a witch's fingers. Your feet sink into the peat, you can feel the dampness soaking into you, you're wet with dew and sweat.

The sound of your name reaches you, the hoarse voice of the law. And your panting breath, broken by fear and running.

Darkness. You can't see a thing, fuck. And the bundle is heavy, and it's hot, hotter and hotter in your hands, and it's even moving. What is it? You can't remember what you stole, because they're after you.

You emerge into a clearing and you still can't see anything, but that's the way it is in dreams. Perhaps it's the clearing where the cave is. You know the cave. You went there when you were a boy with your friends. Maybe it's the cave. Maybe you're going to make it.

You go in and you find yourself standing in line at the construction site, begging for work. But everyone is dead, gray, standing in tattered clothing, eyes white, gnashing their black teeth like in one of those zombie movies that make you turn off the television set, big and strong though you are.

Now the bundle is too hot, you can't hold it any longer, you let it fall among the dead, no one turns around.

Behind you, far behind you but coming up fast, are the two policemen of Krivi Vir. They've followed you all this way, in the darkness, in the middle of the night.

Now the bundle falls open and it's the child's head, scalding hot from his fever, worms wiggling out of his ears and nose, just like years and years ago when you hid a hog's head and could only come back for it three days later. But the child is looking at you, worms and all, and he calls your name, and the policemen hear him and they've seen you and here they come, and you no longer have the strength to run away.

You sit down, bathed in sweat and terror, screaming in the night.

And in the darkness.

Darkness.
It's a good thing it doesn't last long, the darkness. Because if

it lasted any longer you'd lose your mind, so deep is the well it can throw you down.

It's lucky it only lasts a couple of seconds, the darkness. Because it has so many of those ghosts in it that each of them could drag you away for good, leave you to stroll in the mad land where hanged men dance from tree limbs and talons reach out of the earth and grab at your ankles.

It's lucky it only lasts a moment, the darkness. Because that's the moment that comes back every night, the moment that doesn't preserve sweet memories and doesn't encourage hopes, motionless as it is in a desert populated by regret for what you've done and the certainty of punishment.

Too bad for you if in that subtle instant of darkness you aren't asleep. Because then it will carry you off into its cursed fog, and never let you come back.

The darkness.

No sleep.

You wonder if you'll ever sleep again, even once it's over. Maybe you'll lie awake all night long for the rest of your life, eyes wide open in the shadows, chasing after the glimmer of a future.

You don't understand what's happening. It wasn't supposed to turn out like this.

It was supposed to be easy, fast, something you could forget in a hurry like a bump in the road, an unpleasant moment.

Unpleasant moments happen. They come along in everyone's life. And then they're over, and your memory discards them because your memory instinctually tries to preserve the heart, and so it erases everything that isn't right and opportune to remember. That was an unpleasant moment. There have been others, right? And you got through them; maybe it wasn't easy, but you got through.

As you hear your heart pounding—one-two, one-two, one-two; thump-thump, thump-thump, thump-thump—you tell yourself to cling to your hope for the future, you tell yourself that the night will end. Sooner or later.

You don't know what to do now. You can't call anymore. They said that the phones are tapped, that there's no way for you to talk to him, to them, without your voice being recorded; and an instant later they'd be at your front door, and that unpleasant moment would stretch on and on, until it swallowed up the rest of your life. No, you can't call anymore. And you gave them clear, precise, inviolable instructions, along with that phone and the phone card: to answer calls from your number, and only your number, to minimize the risk.

And you don't know where they are, you don't know where they're holding him. You don't know where they could have taken him, because you thought it was better not to know, to keep from giving yourself away.

You thought it wouldn't last long, that soon everything would be taken care of. The old man has so much money that he'd never even notice it was gone, the damn old man who ruined your life, who at first was the solution but soon turned into the problem.

That damn old man.

While the night surrounds you, wrapping dark fingers around your heart, clutching so hard it practically stops, you wonder what you'll do now that you can't call anymore. You hope they understand and that they wait, patiently; that they don't get anxious.

After all, the anxiety is all for you tonight.

Tonight, as you're lying here wide-eyed in the darkness, waiting for a dawn that may never come.

In the darkness.

XLII

M arco Aragona had slept really well.

Truthfully, it was only rarely that he didn't. Ever since he'd been a child, he was out like a light as soon as he laid his head on the pillow; and he slept beautifully until the alarm clock brought him back from the bliss of slumber.

Getting up was no burden. Why should it be?

He was doing the job he'd always dreamed of, he was working hard, he was fitting in well with a team of superheroes who were kicking the mistrust that had originally surrounded the restaffed precinct to the curb. He was one of the Bastards of Pizzofalcone: Doff your caps when you see us going by, you idiots. He'd worked alongside Lojacono, the guy who'd caught the Crocodile, that terrible serial killer; and at the end of the investigation they'd teamed up on, the Chinaman had told the commissario that much of the credit for cracking the case belonged to him, Corporal Marco Aragona. And now he was working a kidnapping with Francesco Romano, aka the Hulk, a human pressure cooker who was always a second from blowing his lid, a ticking time bomb. Who was better than him? Who was better than Marco Aragona?

After taking one quick last look at himself in the mirror, he left his room on the eleventh floor of the hotel. A well-groomed appearance was very important. Movies, TV shows, and novels were all very clear on this point: A policeman has to leave no doubt that he's a tough guy, otherwise the criminals will eat him for breakfast. A sporty blazer; an unbuttoned shirt so that everyone could see he liked the outdoors and physical exercise; the blue-tinted aviators that always obscured his actual expression—one's true feelings were an advantage one should never give away; his hair combed back in a pompadour, carefully arranged both to signal male vigor and to cover that fucking bald spot right at the top of his head—where his father, who had gone bald at forty, damn him, had started losing his hair; elevator shoes to give him that extra inch and a half that could prove decisive in a confrontation with a suspect, when you're eye to eye and the one who looks away first knows he's been beat.

As he walked down the hallway he passed the housekeeper who cleaned the rooms and flashed her his sunniest smile. He'd spent a lot of time practicing: a slight arching of the eyebrow to make it clear that this was no formal greeting and that the recipient enjoyed his special attention, if only for that fraction of a second; the upper lip lifted to reveal his bright white teeth; a tilt to the right to accentuate the cleft in his chin. Irresistible, he thought to himself.

Just look at that asshole, the young woman thought to herself, disgusted at the prospect of having to tidy up the mess in his room.

He headed for the stairs, which he'd climb with his stellar, athletic gait until he reached the roof garden, where he'd have breakfast. This was his moment, the brief interval that gave meaning to the rest of the day: He'd see Irina, the woman he was secretly in love with.

Well? You got a problem with that? he would have asked his audience, if he'd had one. Maybe a tough, pitiless policeman, a hero who fights crime from dawn till dusk, an investigator who, only because he's trying to keep a low profile, refrains from putting his colleagues to shame by showing off his investigative brilliance, maybe a guy like that, in other words, maybe a guy like him, can't have feelings, too? Have you forgotten, my faithful viewers, that in every novel and in every movie the merciless cop always has a weakness, a woman whose presence reveals that under that steely chest there beats a human heart?

Aragona had a crush. Was her name really Irina? He knew that that was the name written on the cunning little pin fastened just above her marvelous breasts because that angel had been sent down from heaven to serve breakfast to the guests on the roof terrace of the hotel that, by pure luck, he had chosen as his new home.

Today, Aragona said to himself, the gods had even heard his prayers and given him the gift of a beautiful day.

Of course even if it rained that was no tragedy; in that case, breakfast was served indoors and the guests still enjoyed a magnificent view: sky, sea, and volcano tempest-tossed by the fury of the elements. But nothing could be finer than the sparkling May air, light and sweet-smelling, and the still-gentle sunshine that showered warmth and light on the romantic expanse of rooftops stretching out below.

Unfortunately, though it was just a minor detail, Aragona hadn't yet been able to speak to Irina. His mouth dried up every time, and when he'd tried to ask her for a second cup of coffee, all that had come out of his lips was a horrible rasping stammer that he'd covered up with a fake cough.

As for smiling, though, he did smile at her. More importantly, she smiled at him, splitting open the clouds and brightening his morning with her spectacular blue eyes, with her hair, and with the fine, impalpable blonde fuzz that he could make out on the delicate, fair skin of her forearms.

Living at the Hotel Mediterraneo wasn't cheap, that was true. And the many advantages had to be weighed against the loss of certain freedoms, as well as the worried phone calls from his mother, who scolded him for living out of a suitcase. But to see Irina, who knew what he wanted before he asked for it, who whipped up a plate of scrambled eggs and bacon, his standard morning fare, was more than a good enough reason for him to stay. His investigator's intuition had wisely led him to observe that the young lady wore no wedding ring, and that her lithe body—which was none too tall, luckily for Aragona—showed no signs of the lumps and bumps of cellulite. He therefore hoped that she had no boyfriend, though he felt sure she must have suitors, and in great numbers.

Seated at his small table, chosen specially because it was kissed by the rays of his friend the sun, Marco watched the girl dance among pitchers of soy milk and tureens of natural yogurt, as she kept the bounteous buffet properly stocked. It was early and, aside from him, the only guests were a couple of ruddy Germans busy shoveling down food in an indecent manner, and a large northern Italian woman with two horrible boys who were trying to kill each other with their forks.

Irina looked at him and he put on an expression that suggested he was engrossed in thought—the one he liked best because it seemed to speak of some secret sorrow—and, to complete the effect, gazed off at the distant horizon. Sensitive soul that she most assuredly was, she'd wonder about the cause of his subtle suffering, and she'd immediately set out to offer some remedy. Out of the corner of his eye, he saw her approach; his pulse quickened. He pretended not to notice her presence until she spoke, in the low, warm voice that so excited him. "Coffee?" she asked.

It was the only word she'd ever spoken to him. And every morning he replied: "Double corto espresso in a large mug, thank you."

The longest sentence he could think of concerning a cup of coffee.

She smiled at him, as she did every morning, and as she did every morning, she went off to fulfill his wishes. At least as far as the coffee went.

Who knew where Irina came from. Who knew if that was her real name or just a nickname. And who knew where she lived, if when her shift was over she had other jobs, if she had to walk through neighborhoods where she risked being robbed or raped. Whether she needed the protection of super-hero.

If I could only speak to her, thought Aragona. If I could only manage to say two fucking words to her other than "double corto espresso in a large mug."

Irina continued to flit between the three occupied tables, serving sweet pastries and *caffelattes*, smiling at everyone but, Marco felt sure, at no one as much as at him.

He knew it, he could sense it: Irina liked him, the same as he liked her. It was just a matter of time. They were destined to be together.

One of the bratty little boys got up and, hopping on one foot like a lame pigeon, went over to the waitress: "Will you bring me another pastry?"

"Certainly."

The little brat wasn't done: "Hey, will you tell me where you're from?"

Aragona saw her tilt her head to one side. The sun played over her hair, kicking up a cloud of gold dust.

The girl patted the little kid's cheek and said: "Montenegro. I come from Montenegro, but I've been here for a long time."

That must be a wonderful place, Montenegro, Marco thought to himself, as he took in this new, fundamental piece of information with fascination. Creatures of her sort could only come from an earthly paradise.

"So, does that mean you're a gypsy?" the boy asked, and Marco would gladly have tossed him headfirst over the railing of the roof garden.

Irina laughed, and her laughter was like a cascade of stars.

"No, I'm not a gypsy. I'm just a south Slav."

At last the child's mother realized how much of an all-around pain in the ass her son was being and, lifting her snout from the dish of butter, jam, and honey she was rooting around in, called him back to the table. Irina went back to the counter to get Aragona's coffee, but before she did, to his immense surprise, she turned around and shot him a look.

Marco's heart stopped: Why had she looked at him? What was she trying to tell him, with that look?

Perhaps she meant for him to understand something. Perhaps the short conversation with the pestiferous child had been designed for his use and consumption, to tell him something about her.

He sighed, enchanted, lost in a reverie.

In the meantime, however, something had wormed its way into his brain, forcing him to think of the kidnapped child. Was it because of the little boy who had asked the indiscreet questions? No. It had been something else, like a dark outline moving beneath the surface of a pond, rapid but unmistakable.

What was it? What had jogged his mind?

Smiling at the wonderful Irina, who was bringing him a double corto espresso in a large mug, the light illuminating her from behind, Corporal Marco Aragona began, deep in his subconscious, his working day.

XLIII

W ell? Anything yet?"

"No."

"The boy still has a fever, though I think it's come down a little. I gave him the antibiotics."

"It'll pass. That's certainly not our fault."

"Yes, but he told us that nothing was to happen to him . . ."

"He also said that he'd call twelve hours ago."

"Something must have come up."

"Something that's lasted twelve hours."

"Do you think something could have happened?"

"I don't want to talk about it. He'll call. Let's just wait."

"What does that mean, you don't want to talk about it? What could have happened?"

"Nothing. He'll call."

"No, now you're going to tell me why you're worried! I threw my old life away to do this job with you. Nothing can go wrong!"

"Stay calm. I told you he'll call."

"You've been sitting here since dawn, drinking and staring at that fucking cell phone on the table, you look terrible, and you're telling me to stay calm?"

"Fucking hell, he'll call! I said that we need to wait, and we'll wait! Do you want to ruin everything just because a stupid phone call's a little late?"

"What if . . . Let's say they figured it out, that someone found everything out. Let's say the police . . ."

"Shut up, you slut! The police haven't figured anything out, no one's going to figure anything out, and everything's going to turn out perfectly, according to plan!"

"Then why isn't he calling?"

"He'll call. You'll see, he'll call. You said it yourself, no? Something must have come up."

"And you answered: Something that's lasted twelve hours?"

"Okay then, what do you want to do? What do you think we should do?"

"Have we come to this point? Do we need to come up with a Plan B?"

"I didn't say that."

"Oh, yes, you did."

"He'll call. We . . . we have the kid. He'll have to call."

"Or else the police will show up and throw us in prison. And we'll never get out again. Do you know what they do to people like us who kidnap a child? It's what they're most afraid of, to them we're all gypsies . . ."

"Shut up. I told you, he'll call."

"Even in prison, they don't leave people like us alone. They'll throw us into solitary, they'll . . ."

"Fuck, that's enough! That's enough! Dammit, shut up! You got me into this mess, and now you're telling me that instead of going to South America to live like a king I'm going to wind up in prison! What did we do wrong? We followed his instructions to the letter, we've been perfect. So he'll respect the agreement, won't he?"

"Listen, raising your voice to me isn't going to solve anything. And when I offered you the job, you accepted immediately, I didn't put a gun to your head, so don't blame me. We need to start thinking about what to do if things don't work out. Getting drunk and angry won't do any good."

"He'll call. He'll call. It's just a matter of waiting."

"And thinking. Thinking fast."

"He'll call. We have the kid, don't forget."

"Exactly. Which is the serious thing, the dangerous thing. Remember that he knows who I am, he knows my name."

"Shut up. We have to wait, I told you. He'll call."

"You wait. I'll think."

XLIV

The phone call came first thing in the morning, unexpectedly, like everything one anxiously awaits.

Alex was reading the file on Mario Vincenzo Esposito, also known as Marvin, the heavily tattooed Pilates instructor and Signora Susy Parascandolo's presumed boy toy. A story just like a thousand others she'd seen in her time. He'd quit school in fifth grade, been arrested for shoplifting here and there, had snatched his first purse at age fourteen, been put in a group home, had been set free and then again arrested, a brief but intense stay in a reform school, a little drug dealing, and then his first grown-up crime: a burglary in an apartment in a well-to-do neighborhood.

The heist had been reasonably well organized: They'd lowered themselves from the second highest floor, the only one without bars on the windows, and they'd gotten in through a balcony. Too bad that in the building across the street a retired magistrate with insomnia was looking out his bathroom window, sneaking a cigarette without his wife's knowledge.

Three years later, after a few mistaken summonses and time off for good behavior, here was Marvin back out on the street, determined to stick to the straight and narrow. At least as much as possible.

The cell phone vibrated on the desk just as she was closing the file. Alex had saved the number under the name "Forensics," in a pathetic attempt to keep the relationship professional, but her heart, unaware of that admirable intention, leapt into her mouth.

She waited for the third ring, at once hoping and fearing that this would turn out to be a wrong number. Pisanelli was about to go out; Ottavia, deep in thought as always, was typing furiously at her keyboard; Aragona and Lojacono were talking in low voices about the kidnapping. She decided to go out into the hall to answer.

"Hello?"

"*Ciao*. Is this a bad time?"

"No, no, not at all. I'm at the station house, but I stepped out of the office."

Idiot, she thought. I'm an idiot. What the hell does she care, that I left the office? And after all, why should I leave the office to take a work call? She also realized that she'd addressed a chief administrator with the informal "*tu*" without asking permission.

She tried to make up for it: "Forgive me, Dottoressa, ma'am, I used the informal '*tu*' without thinking . . ."

Martone laughed. God, she had a beautiful laugh.

"Come on, of course you should be informal with me. And I'm glad that you left the office to talk."

There, she'd noticed, of course she had. Doing her best to make up lost ground, Alex assumed a flawlessly correct tone: "So tell me."

"Yes, I'll tell you, and then perhaps you can report to Lojacono, all right? Now then, as I'd mentioned before, I ordered a second, more thorough, inspection of the Parascandolo apartment. And we hit pay dirt. In certain rooms, especially the bathroom and bedroom, we found both partial and complete fingerprints that belong neither to the couple nor to the housekeeper. And the fantastic thing is that we actually have these fingerprints on file. They belong to an ex-con, who answers to the name of . . ."

"Esposito, Mario Vincenzo, born in the city on March 16, 1987, convicted of burglary in 2009, out of jail since February of last year."

Martone seemed disappointed: "You already know? How did you find out?"

"Let's just say we figured it out by chance. So his finger-prints are actually there? You're saying that Esposito left traces of his presence everywhere but on the safe he broke into?"

"So it would seem, at first glance. But the prints we found are from before the burglary. Esposito is a somewhat, shall we say, intimate . . . guest of the house."

"Which means?"

"Some of the prints are on the headboard of the bed; bilat-eral, by the way. We can therefore safely assume that our ex-con, before going into the bathroom, grabbed the top part of the couple's bed with both hands. And pretty forcefully, too, judging from how strongly the fingerprints were impressed onto the wood."

Di Nardo thought it over while she responded to a wave from Romano, who was just coming back in.

"Yes, in fact we suspect he's Susy Parascandolo's lover."

Rosaria snickered: "Well, he could also be *his* lover, judging from the probable position."

The explicit reference to a homosexual relationship struck Alex, who felt her stomach do a somersault.

"No, no, we're pretty sure that the relationship is with the woman."

Martone laughed again. "I was kidding, Di Nardo. I was only kidding. Anyway, now you have your evidence. Esposito can't deny that he was there, and with his priors it won't take you long to pin it on him."

"Yes, though we still need to figure out what role the woman played: Did he drag her into it or did she organize the burglary herself, with the young man's help."

"Certainly."

That was the end of the conversation. Alex wondered whether she should say a formal goodbye or go with a more casual one and, weighing her options, said nothing. Rosaria too fell silent.

At last, in a low voice, the chief administrator said: "You got my text yesterday, didn't you?"

Alex's mouth went immediately dry.

"Yes. I got it."

"But you didn't answer."

She needed to let her know how ridiculously happy that message had made her. She needed to tell her that she'd spent the rest of that night staring at the ceiling, fantasizing about the spectacular body she'd guessed at under the lab coat.

"No. But I . . . I was very happy. Very."

Again, silence. Then: "I know who you are, Di Nardo. I understood it the minute our eyes locked. And you know who I am. Am I right?"

Alex would have given her whole paycheck for a glass of water. Ottavia, who was walking down the hall on her way to the bathroom, gave her a puzzled look. Everything okay? she mouthed. The young woman gave her a thumbs-up, but couldn't keep herself from blushing.

"That's true. Yes, that's true, that's how it is. But I . . . I don't talk about it, you know. It's something I keep to myself."

Had she lost her mind? Here she was, confessing to a stranger, on the phone, something she wouldn't have told any-one else on earth, not even under torture.

Martone replied with a kind of veiled sweetness: "I know. I understand. I don't advertise it either. It can be tough, some-times. But certain sensations, certain glances, are rare things, you know. Very rare. And it's not right to let them slip away. That's all. That's why I texted you that message."

Alex felt relieved.

"Thanks. Thanks for the text, and for this phone call. For everything."

"You're not getting off that easy, you know, Officer Di Nardo. You owe me a pizza, at the very least. I'll call you some night."

"Yes. Some night. But it's my treat. I'd better keep you happy, you're a chief administrator, after all."

"I'm sure you'll find some way of keeping me happy. Kisses, see you soon."

XLV

T hat morning, before leaving home, Giorgio Pisanelli had had a long conversation with Carmen. He did it all the time, but always taking proper precautions. He'd turn on the stereo and put on one of the symphonies by Mozart or Tchaikovsky that she'd so loved to make sure his neighbors wouldn't assume that loneliness had finally driven him crazy. Then he'd open the door to the bedroom, where he liked to imagine that she sat listening to him, and speak to his wife as if she were still alive. Of course he didn't raise his voice to make sure she heard him, and he didn't go in every five minutes to make sure she was resting easy, as he almost always had in the last few months of her life; he spoke in an undertone. There had to be some advantages to being in the afterlife.

He had told her about Signora Maria Musella, and of how he had picked her out of all the other potential future victims. You'd be surprised, my love, to know how many people there are in the neighborhood who make use of psychotropic drugs. They're the opposite of the tranquilizers you used to take to keep from suffering, do you remember? Oh, lord, not exactly the opposite, because these, too, in the end, put you to sleep. In fact, Signora Musella sleeps a lot, and most of the time she's in no danger.

This, he had told her, has been my crucial insight: I have to try to prevent another murder; to try to figure out where the killer's going to strike next. It's pointless to try to prove that those faked suicides are actually homicides; I've had to give up on that. Because you know, my love, whoever he is, he's really good, he's sly as a fox. He won't give himself away, he never uses the same method twice. He's good.

How can I be so sure that these are actually murders, you ask? I've explained that to you a thousand times, my love: I just know. These are people who lack the strength to live, but who haven't yet made up their minds to die. Not like you, when you couldn't stand it for one day, when you couldn't take the pain. Not like you.

And so, since everyone condescends to me and thinks that I'm just a senile old man, I focused on a potential victim, and I identified the individual who was, among all those who live close to the largest pharmacy in the neighborhood, the most dependent on drugs. I had to start somewhere.

Blowing Carmen a kiss, he'd left and gone by the office to see what was new. Palma, Romano, and Aragona had briefed him on their meeting with the Borrelli family the night before. A sad story: There are misfortunes that ought to bring people together, unite them before a shared sorrow, but often it's the reverse that happens. Even Carmen's death had created a chasm between him and his son Lorenzo. Though they still spoke on the phone every three days, the calls had become as automatic and perfunctory as the punching of a time clock; they were feeble moments of contact between two people who shared nothing but a sweet memory.

He'd chatted a bit with the Chinaman about Tore the Bulldog, the loan shark. An interesting character, Tore, in his way a modern entrepreneur, who'd expanded his tried and true tactics beyond the neighborhood's narrow confines. He organized full-fledged joint ventures with his colleagues from outside of the city, pooled operations, and cross-invested. Deputy Captain Pisanelli had explained to Lojacono that they'd been investigating Parascandolo for years, but the very fact that most of his earnings came from illegal lending done in other regions of the country had allowed him to get away with it. The fact that I'm supplying certain entrepreneurs, the Bulldog had explained in his high-pitched voice to a magistrate during a deposition, doesn't mean I know to whom they endorse their checks. And so all the clients of loan sharks on this side of the Alps wound up anonymously listed on Tore's accounts, while his victims turned up who knew where, and the cooperating banks looked the other way.

Giorgio Pisanelli liked Lojacono. And generally speaking, he liked the new atmosphere in the precinct since the restaffing. There was a healthy desire to get theirs back, the pleasure of being back in the thick of things, and Palma was putting everyone to use according to his or her skills and personality; even Aragona, who had at first seemed unserviceable.

He had the impression that the wrinkles furrowing his forehead were relaxing a little at the thought of the young man. There was some good in Aragona, he was sure of it. Though you did have to look hard for it.

He left the office, in the intoxicating May air that seemed as full of sparkling bubbles as a bottle of prosecco. He was determined and hopeful as he hadn't been in quite a while. He'd been working on the mystery of the suicides for years, but for the first time he felt he was getting close to the solution.

Not even a hundred yards from Musella's home, Giorgio Pisanelli ran into a good friend.

And the solution vanished into that air, deceitful and fragile as the scent of flowers in the spring.

Brother Leonardo was hurrying up a hill for the second time in two days. He was in a rush, and he'd be very irritated if he had to change his plans.

Signora Maria, who was all set to meet her fortunate fate—becoming, ahead of her time, and by Leonardo's hand, an angel of the Lord—would have to be removed from the ranks of his beneficiaries. So much effort, hours and hours of talking and reasoning in the cool air of the parish church, heavy with incense, careful study of the dosages of various drugs—all of it would go up in smoke. His friend Giorgio's stubborn obstinacy was threatening to become really annoying.

And yet, he said to himself, taking heart, he ought to be pleased, because he really had dodged a bullet. If his friend the policeman had seen him enter Musella's home and then emerge, and if the woman had then been found dead from an overdose, beside her a suicide note—a note that by the way he still had in the pocket of his habit—it would have been difficult to come up with a convincing explanation. Not impossible, but difficult.

The Lord, however had decided to help him by delaying Giorgio's arrival, or perhaps by moving up his by a couple of minutes, ensuring that they met just a hundred yards or so from Musella's apartment—further evidence of the sacred nature of his mission. His friend, delighted, had dragged him into a café, bought him an espresso, and proceeded to tell him his improbable but accurate theory. And just how accurate that theory was, no one could know better than Leonardo.

The little friar had put on his usual compassionate expression, demonstrating for the policeman's benefit an affectionate empathy for the latter's torment. It really was too bad, because it was nice to see the man cheerful and confident that he was right, sure that he'd finally understood it all, in the cheerful air of that May morning. He was almost tempted to go ahead and administer the contents of the vial he had with him to his beloved Signora Maria all the same.

But he, Brother Leonardo Calisi, parish priest of the church of the Santissima Annunziata and abbot of the adjoining monastery, had a sacred task to carry out, and he couldn't disregard it just to make a friend, however dear, happy. And so, wishing Giorgio all the best and expressing his hope that his friend's grim predictions would turn out not to be true, he'd headed off.

And now? If the Lord, in His infinite wisdom, had decided to give dear Maria a new lease on a pointless life, then He was certainly trying to tell Leonardo something. But what? That very evening the friar had retired to the cloister to pray, sniffing at the fresh smell of flowers opening up to a new life and to spring, and as always God had illuminated him, communicating His will to Leonardo. The task now assigned to him concerned Emilio D'Anna, a faithful member of the parish and a retired schoolteacher, hit hard by the loss of his wife and the indifference of his children, who could barely stand to talk to him and even refused to take his phone calls.

Yes, the Lord had answered his prayer. And at His suggestion poor D'Anna would begin, with the right guidance, to ask: What meaning does my life have? Why force me to suffer through long years of loneliness and silence, just because my heart stubbornly refuses to stop beating?

There was no doubt about it: Leonardo needed to pay more frequent visits to poor Emilio. And it was to see him that the pious monk went—his little legs pumping, his habit pulled up ever so slightly to keep from tripping—the following afternoon.

Delighting in the cool May air, to the greater glory of God.

XLVI

D odo has a fever again, and he's thinking about his mother.

Usually he thinks about his papà, but now that his throat is screaming in agony and his body is wracked with shivers, he wishes he had Mamma lying beside him in his little bed.

That's what Mamma does. When she sees that he's not well, or that he's feeling sad, she lies down next to him and strokes his hair; now and then she puts her lips on his forehead, a gesture that's midway between a kiss and a way of checking on his temperature.

She sees without being told that something's wrong, because he'd never tell her. Going to Mamma with a complaint is something little kids do, children who'll never grow up; but she notices right away, all it takes is a glance, and then she lies down next to Dodo and strokes his hair. She doesn't talk to him, she doesn't tell him stories like Papà does, stories that make you open your eyes wide and hold your breath, but now that his life is a painful waking dream, now that he's wrapped in a filthy blanket, in a warehouse that stinks of his own poop and hot pockets, what he wishes he could feel is his mother's hand running through his hair.

A little bit he thinks and a little bit he dreams, Dodo. He seems to remember Lena waking him up and giving him a pill with a drink of water. Just then, he'd thought she was Mamma, but it was Lena. He was confused by her blond hair, who knows why she dyed it, his pretty nanny from when he was little and *used to go stay at his grandfather's. He liked her better the way she was, but everyone knows that that's what women do; every so often they like to change.*

His papà told him that that's why Mamma lives with Manuel now, and not with him anymore. She told him that she wanted a change.

Dodo doesn't like Manuel. Dodo's not like those children of divorced couples who hate their parents' new partners on principle, and claim they've been mistreated even though they haven't been just to get an extra present or two and another pat on the head. Some of his classmates do it because they know that the other parent is happy when they say that Mamma's new boyfriend or Papà's new girlfriend is bad.

Manuel doesn't treat him badly. But he doesn't treat him well, either. At first, Mamma hoped the two of them would become friends, but then she realized that wasn't possible and she just settled for them not fighting; so many of her girlfriends had new boyfriends who fought with their children. So they started to put up with each other, Dodo and Manuel, and on certain evenings, when Mamma is home, they've gotten into the habit of curling up in front of the television, all three of them, even though it's not that fun, because nobody really has anything to say. So then he goes into his bedroom and plays with his action figures or reads comic books.

Sometimes, if Mamma can't do it, it's Manuel who goes to pick Dodo up at school. The nuns know him, and even if they don't like him because he isn't married to Mamma and that makes Jesus cry, they say hello to him all the same. In the car, on the way home, the two of them never speak. Each minds his own business.

Not Mamma. Mamma loves Dodo, and Dodo loves her back. Of course, she's a woman, which means there are certain things you can't talk to her about; and she's always studying him, trying to figure out how he feels, what he's thinking. Even when he goes to stay with Papà, either here or on vacation up north, she asks a whole bunch of questions to understand how Papà lives, how much money he has, whether he has a girlfriend. Papà, on the other hand, doesn't want to know anything about Mamma's life and never asks a single question. He's a man.

Now, Dodo thinks again in his waking dream, Mamma's the one who should be here. She'd be the one, lying next to him, warming him up with the heat of her own body, to make him smell that special, unique smell, that Mamma smell. Maybe she'd hum that sweet song that she's been singing to him since he was tiny, a lullaby he's never heard anywhere else.

Maybe she'd make him a cup of hot milk with honey, that burns his mouth a little but it's good and it makes his throat hurt less. Dodo's always had a problem with sore throats: Mamma says that's his weak spot.

He wonders how his mamma is. Who can say how worried she must be, how she's suffering without him.

When I'm home again, Dodo thinks to himself, for a couple of days I'll ask her not to make me go to school and not to go to her club. I'll ask her if she'll tell Manuel to stay somewhere else, in one of those places where he goes to play cards, and to give him a little extra money, so he can have fun and not come back.

I'll ask her to stay home alone with me for a while, curled up together in my bed, with hot milk and honey and her song, and her Mamma smell in my nostrils.

With her next to me, I don't feel hot or cold, Dodo thinks. With her next to me, the temperature's always just right.

You know, Batman, I'll whisper this in your ear and you keep it to yourself as a secret: When I go home, I want to be a little baby again. When I get home I want to hold tight my mamma.

That's what Dodo thinks, as he lies stretched out on the floor wrapped in the filthy blanket, in the stench of his excrement and of the stale food. That's what he thinks.

And he falls asleep.

XLVII

Manuel was looking at Eva, who was nodding off in an armchair. She seemed like another person, someone different from the woman he was accustomed to living with, whose bursts of anger and sudden mood swings he'd grown so used to.

She was much more like her father than she was willing to admit in the long tirades during which she cursed his personality, his harsh nature, his lack of generosity, before suddenly attacking Manuel for his inability to earn. In general, while he tolerated the cascade of insults as if they were a summer thunderstorm, knowing that it was sure to pass eventually, however intense, he also thought that his girlfriend wasn't being fair to her old and sickly parent.

Yes, he was a bastard and a son of a bitch who refused to loosen the purse strings of his immense fortune, as if he could take the money with him all the way to hell, which was where he would certainly wind up sooner or later, in fact, sooner rather than later, given his health. And he never missed an opportunity to point out what a useless fellow Manuel was, a gigolo that his daughter had taken in like a stray dog, to her own detriment as usual. Through that old witch Peluso he'd also turned off the taps, as if he had no idea that the scum who held his gambling debts weren't kidding around, and would before long leave him lying in some alley or other spitting blood. He, of all people, a man with a sensitive soul and an aversion to violence.

All this was true.

But it was also true that, for now, thanks to the old man's money, he'd been able to avoid entirely the trouble of working for a living, a vulgar, tawdry consideration that his elevated soul couldn't bear contemplating. Equally true was that thanks to all that wealth, built up over a lifetime of being miserly and dishonest, he, Manuel Scarano, an artist, had been able to cultivate his own interests without having to worry about how to make ends meet, something that he'd watched his own parents do over the course of their unhappy lives until they'd finally had the good taste to die, thus unburdening him of their awkward, sometimes embarrassing existence.

He only wished that Eva, his partner, the woman who was meant to share in his aspirations and support him, could understand that creative blocks happen, and that a temporary sluggishness in the market for his paintings was more than understandable, especially given the unscrupulous dealers and whorish critics. But things would get back on track soon enough, and then he'd be revered and acclaimed all over the world. After all, he'd had a solo show in Venice, like all the greats.

But Eva, who was now sleeping openmouthed, her face still red from crying—*mamma mia*, though, so much crying, it's been three days and she hasn't done anything else—failed to understand the needs and the infinite nuances of the soul of an artist. She didn't even understand that it had been for her, in an attempt to liberate her from her father's control, that he'd first started playing cards. So he could get rich quick and slap that old bastard in the face with the full measure of his disgust. Okay, so things hadn't gone quite as hoped, and now he also had the not insignificant problem of having to steer clear of dark and deserted streets: But no one had had the last word yet. Great souls, thought Manuel, are unfailingly optimistic.

Suffering ages you, thought Manuel, as he watched Eva toss

and moan in her sleep. She looked like a *dolente*, one of those women who, until the sixties, worked as paid mourners at funerals. But to Manuel, such sorrow was incomprehensible. He'd never much cared for the snot-nosed brat, who had anyway spent most of his time locked in his room with those damn action figures of his. Manuel had often wondered whether the boy might not be retarded, the way he dulled his senses playing war and combat games.

Perhaps it was a simply that he resembled his father, that obtuse and violent gorilla who had been on the verge of attacking him just the other night. It was obvious why Eva had dumped him the minute she'd met a sensitive soul like him.

Eva, Eva. I'm sorry to see you suffer, Manuel said to himself, but every cloud has a silver lining. Who knows, perhaps this will mark the beginning of a brand-new life in which we can think about ourselves and no one else. Grief ends eventually, Eva, and it leaves scars that you can learn to live with. And on the way, perhaps, it will give the old man his coup de grâce, finally leaving the two of us free to cultivate our love and my art.

Perhaps, my love, this grief will actually be a blessing. We can shed some dead weight: your father, that primate ex-husband of yours, the old witch, those goddamn criminals trying to track me down so they can get their money. And to help us forget, we'll go away, all alone, to some faraway island, like Paul Gauguin. I'll strike creative gold again and a few centuries from now, in the books they'll write about me, they'll tell the story of our lives, and they'll point out how this tragedy was the necessary preamble to my masterpieces.

A ray of sunshine came in through the window and struck Eva's closed eyes. The woman jerked upright.

"Dodo? Dodo? My God . . . how long did I sleep?"

Manuel did his best to calm her down: "Just a few minutes, sweetheart. Just a few minutes. I was here beside you the whole time. I'd have woken you if anything had happened."

Eva blinked and looked down at her hands. She seemed to be having some difficulty returning to the real world. Then she murmured: "I had a dream. But it was so realistic that I can't help believing it was something more. I was lying next to him, stroking his hair, the way I do when he has a fever or one of those sore throats he gets at the beginning of every season. I was singing him our song, the one that helps him get to sleep; I was just humming it, softly. And he had the smell he had when he was first born, a scent that only I can smell. Oh God, it was all so precise . . ."

She started crying, louder and louder, until her shoulders were shaking with sobs.

Here we go again with the same old lament, thought Manuel.

And with the appropriate pained smile, he walked over to take her in his arms.

XLVIII

They decided to wait for her at the entrance to the gym. Alex and Lojacono had talked it over, trying to determine whether it would be better to go formal and show up at home, at the scene of the crime, to talk to her in her husband's presence and see if she'd give herself away.

Then they'd agreed that it would be better to meet her alone and confront her with what they'd found out, so that she could choose whether to accept her guilt or else struggle to salvage the life she'd made for herself.

The first person to get to work at the gym was Marvin. He seemed tense. Something wasn't going according to plan, and the young man was aware by this point that he'd become a repeat offender, and that, since he'd conspired with one of the robbery victims, his sentence would be even heavier.

Assunta Parascandolo aka Susy came in half an hour later. Her anxiety was immediately apparent thanks to a pair of oversized sunglasses behind which she seemed to be trying to hide, and the aggressive way in which she berated the driver of a scooter that had come close to tearing off her car door—which she had thrown open without bothering to check her rearview mirror. Lojacono gestured to Di Nardo and they both got out of the unmarked car in which they'd been waiting for the woman.

They came up on either side of her before she could enter the building. She didn't seem surprised; her shoulders sagged as if someone had just hit her.

"*Buongiorno*, Signora. What do you say to a little chat with us? It might be better for us not to go into the office. It's in your own best interest; we're not trying to cause you any trouble."

The woman nodded and headed for a nearby café. Alex and the Chinaman followed her in and sat down at a table in a room off to the side.

Lojacono was the first to speak: "So: At your home the forensic squad has found numerous fingerprints belonging to Mario Vincenzo Esposito, the Pilates instructor we met yesterday at the gym. As you can imagine, that's some pretty significant evidence. But perhaps you have something to tell us, as far as that goes."

Alex was impressed by her partner's skillful handling of the information. He hadn't lied, he'd limited himself to the facts they had in hand, but he'd done so in a manner that sounded like: We know everything, that idiot boyfriend of yours left fingerprints everywhere when, with your knowledge, he broke into the safe; now, how do you want to play your cards—toss him under the bus or tell us the way things really went? Aragona was right: You could learn a great deal from partnering with the Chinaman.

Susy's expression remained indecipherable—assisted by the dark glasses and the stiffness of her features, which was thanks to extensive cosmetic surgery. Then it fell apart. Her lower lip started to tremble, and the tremor spread to the rest of her face in concentric circles; it looked like a pond into which someone had thrown a stone. She took off the sunglasses and slammed them down on the little table, shattering them.

"Asshole. What an asshole. You really have to be unlucky to go from a maniac to an asshole. It's no good, I just don't know how to pick men."

What she was feeling was rage, not sorrow. Pure rage. Di Nardo turned toward Lojacono and found him in the meditative stance he always assumed when he was intent on listening and reflecting: hands lying on his thighs, motionless, his face betraying no emotion, eyes narrowed into twin fissures. She imagined how that expression might induce in someone an urge to speak, if for no other reason than to shatter that stillness, to provoke a disturbance of some kind. She wondered if he did it intentionally or if it just came naturally.

Susy turned to Lojacono: "You can't have any idea, Lieutenant, what it means to be that man's wife. He chose me at twenty; my father, God rest his soul, owed him. He wasn't much more than a kid but he was already doing what he does now. He came to see us with a couple guys who worked as his debt collectors, men who were capable of killing without leaving a mark on you. My father had done what he could to keep the clothing store running, but things were going badly; he'd had to fire two shopgirls and I was going in to help out. I can still remember that morning. They showed up and he said to me, with that fucked-up little voice of his: Girlie, pull down the security blinds, I need to have a chat with your father. I looked him in the face, that dog face of his—you know that they call him Tore the Bulldog, right?—and I told him: Pull them down yourself, you asshole. One of his henchmen grabbed me by the arm but he stopped him. He looked me in the eye for a minute and then ordered his men, in dialect: *Iammuncenne, guagliu'.* And sure enough, they left. The next day, he came back alone, with a bouquet of flowers and all my father's IOUs."

The waiter came to the door of the little room, but Parascandolo waved him away with a brusque flip of her hand, hissing to him that no one else had better come in. She snickered bitterly: "There, you see, that's one of the advantages of being the wife of Tore the Bulldog. Almost everyone owes him something, and everyone's afraid of him. Because ever since the day he started, he's grown a little richer, a little more powerful and little bit more of a piece of shit—every day."

Alex shifted in her chair, uneasily; Lojacono didn't move a muscle.

The woman went on: "So I married him; what else could I do? Sure, I could have left town and moved to another city, in another country, but he would have found me; no one says no to Tore the Bulldog. He'd have taken it out on my old man, and on his shop. I married him. But I always hated him, from the very first day; and he hates me, too. Because he knows that I'm the only one, the only one, who's never knuckled under entirely. It's a war that's been going on for thirty years." She blew her nose and then went on: "I've grown old beside him. At least I managed to keep from having children. And to make up for it, I've sucked the blood out of the damn miser: clothing, jewelry . . . I've even allowed myself a few nips and tucks; I know it doesn't show but I'm telling you the truth, believe me."

Alex thought she detected a quiver at the left corner of Lojacono's mouth.

"Then I got him to buy me the gym. I've always loved exercise, aerobics, fitness, Pilates, spinning, the whole thing. He needed a business to use as a cover and he picked up this old movie theater without laying out a cent: The owner owed him I don't even remember how much. Taking advantage of certain friends he has up north, people in his same line of business, we fixed the place up."

Lojacono asked: "His same line of business, you say? What line of business is that?"

The woman stared at him, surprised: "Jesus, Lieutenant, do you really not know? I can't believe it, sorry, I guess I assumed you're sharper than you are."

Alex spelled it out: "We have to hear it from you, Signora. That's necessary."

Susy seemed to think it over: "Oh, yes, I imagine that at this point that's the way it has to be. My husband is a loan shark: He's a Shylock, and he's got half the city by the balls."

Lojacono spoke up: "But no one's ever managed to prove that."

Parascandolo gulped a mouthful of air: "Listen to me, Lieutenant, we need to make a deal. You're investigating a simple burglary, kid stuff. Can we agree to that?"

Lojacono didn't move a muscle.

Susy went on: "It's just that if the details emerged, Marvin would be in real trouble. And this time, he wouldn't forgive even me. That means that the only way I can save myself is this deal with you. Are you in or not?"

The lieutenant sat lost in thought; then he said: "I don't have the power to make deals. But go on. Let's speak hypothetically."

"Let's just say then, speaking hypothetically, that Marvin and I organized this burglary to coincide with a certain major payment in cash that that asshole the Bulldog was scheduled to receive, whereupon he'd send the postdated checks from his victims up north, as usual. Let's just say that I talked the Bulldog into taking me to Ischia for the weekend, and that Marvin did the job, though he forgot to wear gloves the way I told him to."

Alex complimented Lojacono mentally, admiring his instincts: He'd decided to confront the woman before she had a chance to confer with her boyfriend and find out that he *had* worn gloves after all, and that the fingerprints had nothing to do with the burglary, but, if anything, with Susy's own dubious virtue.

"Let's say that unfortunately, this time, instead of collecting cash, that piece of shit agreed to take a stack of postdated checks for twice the amount, checks that he can cash a few at a time, which means that we're stuck with a pile of scrap paper, instead of having the cash to make a new life for ourselves, the life we deserve, under new names. Now, what are Susy and Marvin supposed to do with ten million euros' worth of post-dated checks? Nothing. But what if, again, speaking hypothetically, those checks wound up being found by some policeman in, I don't know, some luggage locker down at the train station, a locker to which I just happen by incredible coincidence to be holding the key, and what if all those checks were endorsed by the Bulldog, who's a nut about security so he endorses them right away, not when he deposits them, out of fear that someone might steal them? And in that case, speaking hypothetically, like we were saying, the poor Bulldog would wind up being sent to the dog pound and staying there for the rest of his life, wouldn't he?"

The woman had taken care of every last detail.

"And what are we supposed to do about the burglary?" Alex said.

"What burglary? Nothing was taken, not a single thing. The suspects are unknown. And unknown they'll have to remain. But to make up for that fact, you now have a chance to get your hands on a loan shark who's been burning shops and breaking legs for forty years, and to put him away once and for all."

There was a long pause, during which Susy gestured to the waiter who was guarding the entrance to bring them some water. After she'd had a drink and wiped her lips, she went on: "Lieutenant, Marvin's a good boy. He's kind, he's good-hearted. He's made mistakes, but where he was born there are only two kinds of people: the ones who get caught and the ones who don't. But they all do the same things. He's young, he's cheerful, and he fucks like a Greek god. I have fun with him, and I used him to do this thing: I would have taken him away with me, if there had been money in the safe instead of just checks. But now the only chance we have of getting away alive is the one you can give us. Because if you don't say yes, if you decide to go ahead and prosecute the burglary, we'll both disappear inside of two days. They'll stick our feet in a tub of wet cement, take us out to sea, and drop us in, and they'll say we ran away together. That's how it works. And you'll be left with a handful of nothing, because you can't catch the Bulldog. Instead, if we do this, I'll liquidate the entire estate, and I'll get out. Overseas, you never know."

Alex was fascinated: "And if, again hypothetically, we were to accept the deal, what would become of Esposito?"

"Marvin? I don't know, maybe I'd leave him the gym, so he could become a small businessman and keep himself out of trouble. But Signorina—might you be interested in the item for yourself?"

XLIX

Marinella was walking up the street that ran from the big piazza up the hill. In an open area dominated by the façade of a church, she stopped to watch a construction site teeming with workers; they were building a subway station, though no one really seemed to know when it would be finished.

The fact that the city always seemed to be under construction was widely considered to be a defect, but she liked it. It was as if the city were some immense animal full of life that was continually changing its skin, rejuvenating itself before it could become old.

Renewal, change—those things were important, she thought to herself. She, for instance, could say that she'd already moved twice since she was born, that is, in not even sixteen years, since it was already clear to her, by now, that she would be coming to live in that strange, beautiful city. And for a long time, too, she hoped, because just a short while ago, going out earlier than usual to do a little shopping, she'd run into the mysterious whistler again, and he'd lost a bit of his mystery.

It had happened by pure chance.

Lojacono had left earlier than usual, after sitting silent and with his thoughts elsewhere all through breakfast, as he'd been doing regularly for the past few days. Marinella knew that state of mind her father got into very well; she'd see it whenever he was on the verge of cracking a case. Chains of thought and theories piled up inside him, occupying his mind and his heart, erasing the outside world. This time, though, that trance state had come along at just the right time; so he hadn't paused to wonder about her strange euphoria, the sudden joy that lit up her face for no apparent reason.

Once she was alone, Marinella dressed hastily, grabbing a pair of jeans, a T-shirt, and a jacket; she'd paused in front of the mirror to fix her hair and then, without makeup, she'd rushed out the door. Her intention had been to run a few errands and get the house shipshape in record time: She had a call to pay and didn't want to have to be in a hurry to get back home.

She was heading downstairs, taking the steps two at a time, when she'd run into the young man she liked so much. He was bent over behind a column tying his shoe, and she came very close to bowling him over.

"Hey, look out!"

Those were the first words either of them had spoken to the other.

"What, it's my fault if you tie your shoe where no one can see you?"

He'd stood up. God, he was tall.

"Nice accent you have. You're Sicilian, aren't you? I really like Sicilian accents."

Marinella felt a wave of anger begin to mount inside her. She'd been caught off guard by an encounter she hadn't been expecting at that early hour. She had no makeup on, she wasn't nicely dressed, she was wearing a pair of tennis shoes that made her feel even shorter than usual, and now there he was calling her out for her accent.

Her reply had been harsh: "Yeah, so what? I'm Sicilian, you have a problem with that?"

He'd stepped back, as if she'd shoved him: "But I just told you how much I like Sicilian accents. Especially in girls.

Anyway, let me introduce myself, though I know I should have done it before, just to be neighborly: My name is Massimiliano Rossini, and I live . . ."

". . . on the sixth floor, in the opposite stairwell, I know."

The young man seemed disoriented, but amused as well: "Well, since you seem to know all about me, could I at least know your name?"

Marinella took a deep breath and tried to steady her nerves: "Sorry, you're right. I just connected your name to the label by the doorbell; a couple of days ago I borrowed some sugar from your mother, and actually, I need to replace it. I'm . . ."

". . . Marinella Lojacono, from the fifth floor. I've known that for at least ten days, to tell the truth; I asked the concierge after meeting you on the stairs that first time. The tip-off cost me five euros. You live with your father, don't you?"

He'd been curious about her, he'd asked around to find out who she was. Good. Very good.

"Yes, well, I'm staying with him for a while, though I live in Palermo . . . That is, I've lived in Palermo till now . . . I mean, technically, I live there, but . . ."

Massimiliano had burst out laughing. "You don't know much, but what you do know you're not sure of, eh? Just answer me this: Will you be here, let's say . . . next week? And if so, can I buy you a cup of coffee some afternoon?"

What now?

"I don't know . . . Maybe we can talk about it . . . If I'm here, certainly, but I don't know."

"Yes, but if we're going to talk about it I'll need a phone number. And I'll need to know when is good to call you."

"Okay, fair enough. But, listen . . . I'm not a girl who . . . I mean, the fact that I'm giving you my number doesn't mean that I'm the kind of girl who opens up to strangers. It's just that I don't know anyone here, and it would be nice to know what's worth seeing: theaters, monuments, that kind of thing."

The boy's face lit up: "You almost knocked over the perfect person. If you want, I'd be glad to give you a little more information about me so you can stop worrying that I might be some lowlife: I'm a student at the university, a literature major, and I'm a journalist; still part-time, but I'm contributing to a big paper. What are you majoring in, here at Palermo?"

What am I majoring in? she thought to herself. I'm getting ready to start my junior year in high school, and I even skipped a year!

"Me? That's a long story. But I'm thinking about moving here, to live with my dad. He's alone, and he needs me. Now, if you'll excuse me, I really need to run. Give me your cell number, and I'll give you call, that way you'll have mine."

When a day starts like this, thought Marinella as she attacked the last stretch of the uphill climb, it's normal to be in a good mood. It's normal for everything to seem easy, solvable, organizable. It's normal to feel optimistic.

Letizia's trattoria was still closed, but Marinella knew her friend was inside, readying everything for the nightly assault of the locusts, as she jokingly referred to her beloved guests.

That was the great thing about Letizia. She was cheerful. Always in a good mood. And laughing. Not because she was stupid, anything but, because she was someone who had suffered, struggled, wept bitter tears. Certain smiles are like a college degree: Before you can show them off, you have to earn them. Marinella would have liked to see those smiles on her father's face again.

The woman welcomed her with a soft hug; her immaculate apron and her chef's cap flattered her like an evening gown.

They chatted for a while and the girl apologized for Lojacono's sudden flight the day before: "When it's about work, everything's super-urgent, nothing can be postponed. He's not rude, that's just the way he is."

"I know, I know. It used to happen, even before you got here. And then if the call is from that lady, the Sardinian magistrate, he's even happier to answer it. The night you first came here, they were here having dinner together with the rest of the team, but the two of them left together."

"I don't like her. She's a hard, selfish, silent woman."

"But he likes her, take it from me. He likes her a lot. I can tell that he likes her. Whereas, me . . . He likes me okay, he's always nice to me, but I don't appeal to him in that way. I'll confess that I've tried to make it clear to him just how happy I'd be to . . . talk to him, man to woman, but I'm afraid he just thinks of me as a friend. And nothing more."

This was exactly why Marinella had come. At last, Letizia had opened up to her, and that meant she was at last free to offer her own opinion: "No, you're wrong. If you ask me, he doesn't have the slightest idea that you might be thinking about him in those terms. Men are dimwits, they don't notice certain things until they bump their noses smack up against them."

Letizia laughed: "And just what do you know about men? Aren't you a little too young for certain things?"

"Maybe, but still: I'm a woman and don't you forget it. And I know my father better than anyone else does; I'm his daughter and I'm a little bit like him. I can assure you that, left to his own devices, it would never occur to him."

Letizia's face was suddenly worried: "You wouldn't think of telling him, I hope? Please, I'd never be able to look him in the face again."

This time it was Marinella who burst out laughing: "Are you kidding? The trick is to make him think of it, otherwise you'll scare him and he'll run off. It's a little bit like going fishing, no?"

"Nice picture you draw. But wait, why would you want to help me?"

"Well, we're friends, and you're such a good cook . . . and then, I told you, I don't like that Piras. We need to get busy, in part because I'd like to move here. I think my father needs me much more than my mother does. And just this morning I met a guy who . . ."

With a decisive gesture, the restaurateuse untied her apron: "I understand, we're not cooking today. Tell me everything, and start from the beginning."

And while the city outside wallowed in the dangerous May air, Letizia and Marinella lost themselves in conversation.

L

By now, Carmela Peluso was used to the directive: During the day, all windows were to be carefully and securely obscured by heavy curtains, to ensure that it was almost as dark indoors as it was outside at night. After years of stubbing toes on corners and hips on sharp edges, the caregiver, the housekeeper, and she herself had all memorized how the furniture was arranged, and they moved fluidly through the darkness like so many ghosts. But she loved daylight; every time she could go out she was happy.

Thinking back on her own life, she couldn't say exactly at which crossroads she'd chosen the wrong path, the path that had made her the woman she was now, the woman she saw in the mirror before her.

An old woman. A poor old woman with shriveled skin, her face a mask of wrinkles, her complexion ashen, her eyes lifeless. And yet there had been a time—still so vivid and present in her memory that it seemed like just yesterday—when she had been a cheerful girl, full of desires and whims, open to a life she imagined would be versatile and gratifying.

She'd hurled herself heart and soul into her job at the Borrelli company with all the vigor of her early twenties and the ambitious fantasies of that age. And she'd been good at her work, she'd climbed the corporate ladder until she became the cavalier's secretary. And his secretary she had remained, for the rest of her life.

There were times when it all seemed as if it had been a

nightmare: one of those terrible dreams where you don't have the strength to move an arm, to stretch out a hand, and you have to watch passively as everything happens around you, unable to do anything to stop the disasters befalling you.

She'd been Borrelli's lover, too. For years, now and again, he'd take her as if he were dictating a letter or telling her to take care of some routine task. And she'd gone along with dog-like devotion and self-destructive acceptance. Then, as now, she'd always kept to the shadows. No one imagined that that inconsequential young woman, well on her way to becoming an inconsequential old woman, was the plaything that the dread tycoon amused himself with during evenings spent on the top floor of the skyscraper that housed his offices.

No one knew about it, except for one person.

One day Borrelli's wife had called her on the phone and asked her to meet in a café by the waterfront. Carmela remembered the conversation clearly, a quick succession of sad observations. The woman had told her that she knew about the relationship but that she felt no rancor toward her, quite the opposite. She thanked Carmela for having relieved her of an enormous burden: being forced to go to bed with a man who loved no one but himself. If she had any regrets, they were for her, Carmela, because she knew that he would never give her anything more and yet would also never let her have her freedom. Edoardo only wanted what was convenient for him; he didn't give a damn about anyone else.

Carmela had come home in tears. That afternoon, for the first time, she'd glimpsed her own life, and her death as well.

The prediction had proved accurate. Her story had been so similar to that of many others that it wasn't even worth the telling. An existence made up of nights spent staring at the ceiling and fleeting assignations that lasted an hour, utterly devoid of tenderness. Carmela had been nothing but a simple object, a body with which to satisfy an equally simple physiological need.

So it remained until Borrelli's age and illness got the upper hand, depriving him of a virility that he'd always experienced as a burden, a need that limited his true ambition. Truth be told, money was, to him, just an accessory, a necessary evil. What Cavalier Edoardo Borrelli wanted above all else was power.

And it was possible to exercise power even if you were sick. In fact, for a long time, while he was proudly fighting, going from one hospital to another, checking into high-tech clinics, he'd kept on running his company; in fact, he'd branched out from construction into financial services.

Little by little, though, he'd been forced to delegate.

The woman who had been his secretary and his lover had now become the body he no longer possessed. Now it was she who went out and about, who negotiated with banks, politicians, other businessmen, and even with organized crime bosses. Nondescript, easy to overlook, and mousy as she was, she went unnoticed in any setting: an advantage in certain walks of life.

And yet Borrelli's attitude toward her had remained unchanged since the day he'd first assigned her a desk in the corner of a big room full of clerks, more than forty years previous; the same as when, two years later, he had ordered her to take off her clothes and wait for him on the sofa in his office. No kindness, no human attention. She was little more than a housekeeper, as that asshole ex-husband of Eva's had said in front of the policemen. He was right. He was an asshole, but he was right.

For some time now, though, the housekeeper had kept her eyes open. Taking advantage of the general powers of attorney that the old man had been forced to sign over to her so that she could take care of confidential tasks he could no longer perform, she'd started diverting funds here and there, rerouting the money into accounts set up in her name. She didn't do it for the money; by now, she'd given up on starting over from scratch, at her age. She wanted to punish him. To prove to herself and to him—he would only ever know it the instant before dying—that drab old Carmela, little more than a housekeeper, was the only one who had had the intelligence, cunning, and patience to rob him.

As she tidied up the papers on the desk, she thought back to when she'd asked the cavalier why he wanted the apartment so dark. The mirrors, he had replied; I don't want to be seen by the mirrors. As if he were afraid that the reflection of his own decrepit, malevolent image, nailed to a wheelchair, was a demon ready to swallow his soul.

The only moment she saw his lips curl into a smile was when his grandson came to see him. It was from the child that the cavalier got the only tenderness that he had ever had. And it seemed incredible, but Dodo liked sitting next to his grandfather and listening to his stories in that darkened apartment, with the stench of death heavy like the smell of stale cooking, as if he was Borrelli himself turned into a child, impatient to hear what had become of him in his previous life.

Now, though, fate had deprived him of that consolation, too, Carmela thought to herself. As if to restore order to an existence that was supposed to be devoid of all emotion, any gentleness.

But why should that child, whose only achievement had been to be born and carry his same name, have had a greater right to a pat on the head than she did? Why should the emotions have been set aside for him, emotions that she'd always assumed the old man was simply incapable of?

That was the one thing for which Carmela could never forgive Dodo; it was actually the reason that she'd always hated him, the reason she'd kept him at arm's length ever since he was just a baby, the reason she'd never even held him in her arms: The grandson had ignited in Borrelli an emotion that she'd never have guessed existed. Without lifting a finger, that child had proved that Edoardo wasn't incapable of love; he had just never loved Carmela.

She who had never left his side. Who had devoted herself to him more devoutly than could any man of the cloth to his god. Who even now couldn't imagine being able to live apart from him, though she hated him with all her heart.

Countless times, she'd fantasized about the old man on his deathbed, the agony of his last moments, when she would lean over him and whisper in his ear how bitter she was about the fact that he'd taken her life, especially since he'd been absolutely aware of what he was doing: a premeditated crime for which there could be no acquittal.

She fantasized that he might still possess a flicker of consciousness. It would be so wonderful to be able to throw back in his face everything he had done to her, and confess to him just what she had done to him.

Suffer, damn you. Suffer. Feel your heart sundered in two by the pain, feel the helplessness, your hands tied, the impotent anger. Suffer the way I suffered, when I threw my life at your feet so you could tromp on it.

Suffer.

LI

Romano drove from stakeout to stakeout, doing some cop version of the Stations of the Cross, checking to make sure that the unmarked cars placed in strategic positions outside the residences of Eva Borrelli, her father, and her ex-husband were ready to intercept anyone who attempted to contact Dodo's family in a manner other than by telephone.

The idea had been worked out with Palma and Aragona on the afternoon of the previous day, after the call came in warning the child's grandfather to get the money ready. They expected the criminals to get a piece of paper to the family containing written instructions, outlining when and how the exchange would take place; but Romano had his doubts about how effective those surveillance measures were likely to prove. He was certain that the kidnappers were connected to someone who knew the routines of the whole family to a T: They weren't likely to allow themselves to be caught so easily.

He wondered for the thousandth time who the inside man could be, and whether he was the gang's mastermind or just an accomplice. Maybe they should have delved deeper into the lives and friendships of the household help: Eva's housekeeper, the cavalier's caregiver and housekeeper. But that would mean putting everyone back in the running, even the nuns at the school: too vast a territory to be explored in such a short time.

He'd ask Pisanelli and Ottavia to do some digging of their own, the former making use of more traditional investigative techniques, the latter relying on new technologies. He had to admit that that lunatic Aragona wasn't all wrong: The Bastards of Pizzofalcone were one of those teams that no one would have bet on at the beginning of the season, but if you believed in them and you did, they would have paid off against ridiculous odds.

Where are you, little Dodo? he wondered. What corner of the world have they carried you off to, just so they can get the old man to pull out a few million euros he's stashed away who knows where? Who, out of all those you hug and even kiss, of those whose hand you hold when it's time to cross the street, who make your lunches and dinners, has betrayed you? Who will you have to thank for all this when, in the best possible outcome, you find yourself stretched out on an analyst's couch twenty years from now? If, that is, you survive. If, that is, your kidnappers don't mail you back to your family, one piece at a time, to try to pry the ransom out of them.

As he drove slowly along, he realized with a shiver just how much he wanted a child of his own, a son or a daughter to care for, to protect from the rest of the world. Except he wanted a child with Giorgia; he couldn't see himself becoming a father with another woman. In fact, he couldn't see himself doing anything at all with another woman. He was Giorgia's husband, and Giorgia was his wife.

A marriage, thought Romano, means something more than just staying together. A marriage is a commitment in the face of the world, a contract written, read, signed, and countersigned. A marriage can't be broken by opening a door and shutting it behind you, you can't annul it by writing some little fucking letter: Dear Francesco, I'm so sorry and blah blah blah, what a shame that blah blah blah, with fond thoughts blah blah blah.

Giorgia, he said, whispering into the cool spring air as it came streaming in through the open car window. Giorgia. What do you think you're doing? Do you really think you can

280 · MAURIZIO DE GIOVANNI

put an end to what's between us, just like that, with one fell stroke? Do you really think that we can just shake off eight years of marriage, and I can't even remember how many years of dating, as if it were the salt left on your skin after a swim in the sea?

Most important of all: Do you think that I'll sit here twiddling my thumbs, waiting to receive a letter from a lawyer?

I have a right to speak and to be listened to. I have that sacrosanct right. I need to tell you that the last thing that happens between us cannot be a slap in the face. Okay, I lost my temper. Okay, sometimes that happens, and okay, it's been happening more and more lately. But I'm not a criminal. I'm the one who catches criminals and throws them in jail. And sometimes I deal with people who beat women, or mistreat old people, and I become their worst enemy, which means I'm not one of them, don't you see that?

For instance, I'd like to be the first one to lay hands on whoever kidnapped this child. Whoever took him away from his father and mother, driving them out of their minds with grief; whoever might have hurt him, might still be hurting him now. Then you'd see my rage, I can assure you. You'd understand what it means to turn into a genuine fury.

If you could only hear me, my love, even just for a minute, I'd explain to you what I did and why it will never happen again. I'd prove to you that I'm not a violent man, but that the last few months have been hard: being tossed out of the place where I worked like a criminal, being sent to a precinct house where there were more crooks among the police than out in the street. But if you come back to me, if you help, I'll find my balance again. We could try again to have a baby, now that I want one, too, now that it's not the way it used to be.

Now that nothing is the way it used to be.

Romano was thinking about his wife so intensely that he thought he must be hallucinating when he saw her walking down the sidewalk on the opposite side of the street. In his surprise, he lacked the presence of mind to call out to her, to shout her name. He just sat there watching her walk, agile, confident, beautiful, a light skirt fluttering around her long legs, dark glasses, and a briefcase under one arm.

Behind him a bus honked its horn a couple of times; he realized he'd braked to a stop in the middle of the street. He raced all the way up to the piazza, went around the traffic circle, and came back. He had been afraid he wouldn't see her again, but there she was. Where was she going? Why did she have a briefcase under her arm?

She was going to see a lawyer.

She was going to see a lawyer to file for an official separation. What other reason could she have to be in that neighborhood, where there were only business complexes and office buildings? She must be there to make concrete the intentions she'd expressed in the letter. She wanted a legal separation without even discussing it with him, without even letting him know. But he had a right to express his point of view. She had to listen to him, fucking hell.

A red film descended over his eyes and he felt a surge of adrenaline coursing through the muscles of his arms and down into his hands. He clutched the steering wheel convulsively and angrily punched his fist into the car horn. A woman driving a compact car just ahead of him veered to one side and came dangerously close to running over a couple of pedestrians crossing the street.

He had to catch up with her. He had to stop her, force her to listen to him. Let her tell him to his face that it was all over, that she never wanted to see him again, that she didn't love him anymore.

He was no more than twenty yards away when he saw her walk up to a man in a jacket and tie who was sitting at an outdoor table, enjoying the fresh air and an espresso. He stood up and shook hands with her. You could see it plain as day on the face of the damn hyena, the infamous vulture: He was pleasantly surprised to find himself face-to-face with such a beautiful woman. He gestured for her to sit down, and she thanked him with a graceful nod. She smiled at him.

You're actually smiling at him. You're smiling at him, while you kill me. While you erase me from your life, making a clean break, wiping me away like an insect off your windshield.

He swerved up onto the sidewalk, two wheels off the road: A woman pushing a baby stroller jumped aside and almost fell over; a man keeled over the hood of his car, cursing.

Romano got out of the car, mechanically flipping down the sun visor so the police insignia could be seen. Seeing the look on his face, no one said a word; the man who had cursed actually held up one hand in a gesture of apology.

He ran full out the twenty yards separating him from Giorgia, his heart pounding in his ears, his face twisted in a mask of anger. His mind kept repeating like a mantra: a clean break, a clean break.

Giorgia saw him coming, and the smile vanished from her face like a lightbulb burning out. She saw him, and she recognized the fever and the fog that clouded his thoughts. She saw him, and thought of running; she looked around in desperation.

He recognized the terror in her eyes, and that only stoked his fury further. He went over to the table; she was riveted to her chair, hands half-raised, ready to ward off blows.

The voice that emerged from Romano's mouth sounded like the roar of a wild beast: "A clean break, eh, Giorgia? A fucking clean break and you erase me from your life. You already have the documents, don't you. You had them made up in advance, didn't you?"

Romano grabbed the table and gave it a shake, overturning the man's empty coffee cup and his half-drunk glass of water; he was forced to jump backyards to protect his trousers.

"Hey, what the . . ."

Romano didn't even turn around: "Shut up, you piece of shit. You and me can talk in a minute."

From behind Giorgia's dark glasses leaked a tear. And deep inside Romano, something cracked.

"Now you're crying? You're crying? Without even listening to me, without giving me a chance to . . ."

She turned and spoke to the man she'd been meeting, who'd taken a few steps back. All around them, everyone was watching them, curiosity and pity on their faces.

"Dottore, I apologize. This is . . . this *was* my husband." Then she turned to Francesco: "Dottor Masullo runs an accounting firm. And he was thinking about hiring me, if you hadn't once again found a way to ruin everything."

She stood up and walked away.

Leaving behind a marble statue of a policeman with a broken heart.

LII

Ask any cop.

He'll tell you that certain ideas are like a sharp rock under your beach towel, they keep you from sleeping, and you turn over and over again, trying to find it so you can get rid of it, but you can't.

He'll tell you that the idea sits there, right below the level of conscious thought, waving hello with its little hand and thumbing its nose at you, irritating and elusive.

He'll tell you that it's the idea's fault that his brow is furrowed as if he had a headache, that he seems to have his mind elsewhere when you speak to him.

Any cop will tell you that certain ideas, until they surface entirely, are like a toothache.

Ottavia looked as though she had a toothache. She was distracted, absent; every so often she seemed to think of something, and she'd break off a conversation without warning and go over to her computer and type something quickly, only to shake her head and stand up, angry.

Palma watched her and worried.

Actually, they were all worried. They knew that in the case of little Dodo they'd come to a critical juncture: If the kidnappers contacted them again, they could devise the moves necessary to catch them; otherwise the case would be handed over to the special investigative branch.

The commissario had heard that police headquarters was

considering reaching out to certain officers stationed in the north, who would come down especially to work on the case; experts who intervened only once the terms had been set for the payment of the ransom and the liberation of the hostage. No one liked the idea of jurisdiction being taken away from Pizzofalcone, no one was willing to give up easily, and that gave Palma a sense of just how much the Bastards, more and more each day, were becoming aware of themselves as an entity: no minor thing for people who until just recently had been thought of as scum. For him, too, the defeat would be difficult to accept; he couldn't stop thinking of the expression on the child's face, looking up at the video camera, as he walked off to meet his fate, hand in hand with his kidnapper.

In the bullpen, discussions were moving forward fitfully. Even Aragona was silent. He was looking out the window, where the sunshine shattered into a thousand sparks glinting off car bodies and the rooftops of the old buildings that sloped away downhill toward the sea; he seemed absorbed in an attempt to puzzle out a secret code. Alex and the Chinaman were out investigating the Parascandolo burglary, Romano was double checking the stakeouts on the Borrelli and Cerchia residences.

Pisanelli was perusing files. He was on edge and taciturn like the others. That night word had come in of another suicide: an elderly man who had told his neighbors more than once that he just couldn't face it anymore. He'd left a farewell message and then swallowed a bottleful of sleeping pills. Palma wondered why his deputy was so obsessed with those deaths; it was clear that the larger motive behind them all had something to do with the economic slowdown and the spread of loneliness, which was by now a social blight. Probably his fixation was a product of his personal history, and the fact that his wife, too, had committed suicide. He made a mental note to invite him to lunch and talk it through once they'd wrapped up the case of the kidnapped boy.

He was thinking that over when he heard a cry from Ottavia's desk: "That's what it was! I knew I'd think of it eventually. Boss, I know who took the boy. Believe me, I know."

It was the first time Ottavia had ever spoken to him using the informal "*tu,*" and that made an impression on Palma—even more than the news. Pisanelli and Aragona turned to look at their coworker. Francesco Romano came in at that very moment and joined the group; no one noticed his distraught expression.

Ottavia went on: "I couldn't stop wondering just who the woman Dodo left with could have been. I mean, I was wondering why he would have left with her without a word to anyone. I know, we've all wondered that, and we all concluded that he must have known her. But how did he know her? Romano and Aragona asked everyone, and they couldn't find anyone who was close enough to the child to lead him away like that, but who also even remotely matched the appearance of the woman on the video."

Palma nodded: "Go on."

"According to the police reports you gave me for transcription, the boy has a shy, reserved, timid personality. He doesn't make friends easily; he'd never go off with the first person to happen by. That means that the kidnapper must be a woman whom Dodo knows and trusts, but no longer sees."

"Well?" said Aragona. "Is she a ghost?"

Ottavia glared at him: "Do you remember the meeting with Dottoressa Piras? When we updated the information we had on all the people involved? Giorgio had uncovered a bunch of information on everyone, and I'd found something online about Peluso by digging into her Facebook page. I'd pointed out that she doesn't like children, and I'd reached that conclusion after finding out about a minor diplomatic incident caused by a sarcastic comment that she'd posted about a childhood friend who'd become a grandmother."

"Always delightful, the old witch," Aragona commented.

"There was an offended reply from the new grandmother, and Peluso had replied with an explanation of how she couldn't stand children and described with real distaste the period when little Dodo spent more time at his grandfather's home than his own. Peluso had complained about it so much that old man Borrelli had been forced to hire a couple of nannies and babysitters."

"And so?" Palma said.

"I mean, it's obvious, don't you all see? The only person who could have led Dodo away without making him think there was anything wrong would have been one of his babysitters. And since Eva never hired one, because she left the boy with her father, it could only have been one of the women who worked for the old man."

"Yes, but which one?" Romano asked. "He had so many."

"Of course, we'll have to get confirmation from Borrelli himself, but generally you keep changing nannies and babysitters until you find the one that's perfect. So, unless someone quit or ran away, the one we're looking for is the last one hired, who would also be the one freshest in Dodo's memory: Let's not forget that the boy spent time with his grandfather until he started school, and now he's almost ten, which means we're talking about five years ago. The last one would also be the one he remembered best, the one he'd trust most."

After Ottavia spoke, silence descended. Then Romano said: "I don't know. Is it possible that none of the Borrellis thought of it? It seems so obvious . . ."

"It may be obvious," she replied, "but none of us thought of it either. And after all, what do I know, maybe the woman moved away, or . . ."

Pisanelli broke in: "Or changed her hair color. We've always described her as blond based on the testimony of the other little boy, his classmate, what was his name . . ."

Romano spoke up immediately: "Datola, Christian Datola. She was wearing a hoodie but Christian saw a lock of blond hair emerge. He said she was a blonde."

"That's right, and so we always thought of her as a blonde, we and the family members. But let's say the babysitter was a brunette."

Palma was deep in thought: "Could be, it all adds up. Francesco, call the cavalier's house and ask if they remember what her name was, if they have any pictures, photocopied IDs, anything. Ottavia, you find out whether there were any hirings or firings at the Borrelli residence. I'm going to let headquarters know about this new lead. Let's get busy."

LIII

He isn't going to call."

"That's not necessarily true. He could call any minute . . ."

"He's not going to call, fuck! Don't you understand what's happening? He's not going to call, and we're wasting precious seconds, hours of time that in the end are going to screw us."

"Lena, calm down. If we give up now, no more money, no more fake IDs, no more South America. Nothing."

"You're a goddamned lunatic, I chose a lunatic. We're not talking about money, we're talking about them throwing us in prison and us never getting out!"

"Stop shouting, please. Don't shout; I can't hear myself think when you shout."

"It doesn't really matter, it's not like you're doing much thinking anyway. And I can't just leave you here, otherwise you'll get yourself caught, and then they'll catch up with me, too."

"We can't just leave. We have the kid."

"There, you see it. Took you long enough."

"I don't understand . . ."

"We have to get rid of the kid."

"What do you mean? Leave him here and just run away?"

"You see what an idiot you are? He saw your face, he can describe you in detail; and since you're big and tall, too, they'd have no trouble finding you. As for me, he even knows my name. It would take them five minutes to track us down."

"Then what can we do? You can't alter the facts, after all."

"There's a simple solution, and you know perfectly well what it is."

" . . ."

"We have to do it."

"You can't be serious. You're out of your mind. You can't really be thinking that."

"And we have to do it fast."

"Maybe he'll call right now."

"He's not going to call, and we both know it. It was a dream, a beautiful dream, but dreams are something people like you and me can't afford. Now we just need to defend ourselves, if we want to survive. The way we've always had to."

"Listen, let's just run away, plain and simple. Let's leave right away, now. We'll catch a ship, then we'll take another, and another after that, until we've shaken them."

"The only way that can happen is if they never know who we are. We don't have any choice in the matter."

"Please, don't say that . . ."

"We have to kill him."

LIV

Ask any cop.

It could be chain of associations, a muttered word heard out of context, a picture.

It could be like when you see a face you've already seen plenty of times before, you feel sure of it, but the fact that you see it in a different setting makes it impossible for you recognize it.

Or perhaps it's like a sound, one of those random sounds that worm a stupid song into your brain, and the song spins around in there all day long and you can't get rid of it, and you wonder to yourself: How the hell did I get this damn song stuck in my head?

Ask any cop, and he'll tell you that's how it works.

Ottavia's idea had been like an electric shock. Everyone was talking, phoning, running around. Even Guida, who had sensed the energy in the air, kept poking his head through the door into the communal office: one time with a tray of espressos, another time offering to run down to the archives if anyone needed him to check something. He wanted to help out: He felt for the boy in the video in every breath he took as a father.

Old man Borrelli hadn't hesitated in the least in his response to Romano's question: "It's Lena. It can't be anyone but her. She was with us for more than a year: a good-looking girl with red hair, that's why she didn't occur to me. She had this giant head of hair. Dodo was crazy about her."

"Of course we don't have any evidence, Cavalier. It's just a theory, but it's worth digging into. Do you have any idea where she lives? Or where she works?"

Borrelli burst into a fit of coughing; Romano waited for him to catch his breath.

"No. But I'm sure that Carmela kept her documents, she never throws anything away."

"Cavalier, if you could . . . you know, it might amount to nothing, but we have to move fast."

"In five minutes you'll have everything via fax. Keep me informed."

Borrelli had underestimated his secretary; three minutes later Guida walked into the room waving a sheet of paper.

The Xerox of the passport wasn't very clear, but it was possible to make out the face of a scared-looking young woman.

Palma read aloud: "Madlena Miroslava. Born June 12, 1971, in Krivi Vir, Serbia. Currently residing at Corso Novara 13. Come on, guys. I'll send a car straight to the address, you get busy on the phones with operators, employment officers, everyone you can think of. I want to know where she works and who she lives with. And if she dyed her hair blond."

LV

You're sick, I'm telling you. Sick in the head. Do you even realize what you're saying? You know what happens in prison to people who kill kids? Plus you're a foreigner and the boy is Italian . . . I don't even want to think about it."

"If you start thinking about what's going to happen to us behind bars, you're already screwed, it's as if you were already in prison. You just have to make sure they never catch us."

"But if they . . ."

"I don't want to hear another word! Say it one more time and I'm out of here, and you'll be left all alone with this mess on your hands."

"And . . . and if . . . God, I can't even bring myself to say it."

"Listen to me, Dragan. Listen to me. We have to make sure they never, never find him. Because as long as they can't find the body, there hasn't been a murder either, you see? That's the law. I saw it on TV. They just can't ever find him."

"But how can we make sure of that? We . . ."

"We'll cut him into pieces. And we'll bury him along the road, at night, in lots of different places."

"No. No, no, no. No! We'll take him with us. We'll take him away with us. If anyone asks, we'll just say he's our son."

"You're joking. He's ten years old, not three months. He'll talk, and then that'll be it."

"But how can you talk like that? You loved him. You

dressed him, you fed him, you spent a whole year with him. And he loves you, he . . ."

"That's an advantage, he trusts me. We'll put him to sleep first, he won't suffer."

"But don't you realize? He's a child, he has his whole life is ahead of him . . ."

"Listen, asshole: It's either his life or ours, can't you see that? We don't have a choice. When I left home, I left two of my own children behind, and I haven't heard from them since. Do you think they don't haunt my dreams? Do you think I don't wonder about them? If I abandoned *them*, I can certainly abandon him."

"That's not the same thing, fucking hell! You're talking about killing him! It's one thing for a stupid kidnapping to go wrong, it's a whole other thing to murder a little boy and cut him up into pieces!"

"We don't have any other options. We're just wasting time. If we stay here they'll find us, and then it'll be over. We just need to do it. Right now."

"No. We can run away and take him with us. We can escape, I have phone numbers, addresses. We can stay in Italy, maybe, until things have died down. And as for him, he's not going to talk because he's afraid. I can make sure he won't talk. I can take care of him."

"You don't even know how to take care of yourself, you're just a big ox. If you're not man enough to do this thing, I'll do it for you. And then we'll go."

"No, you won't do it either. We'll leave the phone here. And he'll come with us. Alive."

"I'm not going to let you ruin my life. I won't let you. Sooner or later, we'd give ourselves away, we'd make some mistake. Or else he'd talk to someone and they'd find us. Don't you understand? It's us or him. We have to kill him, cut him up into pieces, and hide until we can figure out a way to get out of the country."

"You aren't going to touch him. He's asleep right now. I'll wrap him in the blanket, I'll put him in the car, and we'll go."

"I'll kill him. I'll kill you, too, if you make me."

"No. No, you won't."

"Try and stop me."

LVI

Ask any cop.
It pokes you, like a thorn in the ass, like some mistake you can't seem to pick out in a photograph.

It's a forgotten chore, something urgent you've put off and keep on putting off.

It's the closet door hanging open, and you notice it from bed, when you're already under the blankets, and you know you won't get a wink of sleep until you get up and close it.

Go ahead and ask, ask any cop.

Reports started pouring in quickly: At first they all seemed promising; then it was nothing but dead ends. Guida came and went, shuttling between phone and fax, now with a broad smile under his bald dome, other times with a sad, sad face.

Yes, Madlena Miroslava had lived at Corso Novara, no. 13. No, she didn't live there anymore, and hadn't for five years. Yes, the concierge remembered her. No, she hadn't left a forwarding address. Yes, she must still be living in the city, because she had run into her on the street just a year or so ago. No, she hadn't told her where she was working now, in part because she, the concierge, liked to mind her own business. Yes, she'd signed up at the local employment office. No, she wasn't using their services anymore. Yes, she'd given her address. No, it was still the address listed on her passport. Yes, her phone number was listed. No, it appeared to have been out of service for months. Yes, she'd come to Italy ten years ago on one of the minibuses that ferried illegals over the border, the police informant working immigration had told the police team sent out to inquire. No, as far as the informant knew she hadn't returned home.

It wasn't that unusual for a foreigner to vanish into thin air: An under-the-table job implied a certain skill at covering one's tracks, even concealing one's place of residence. And so they were coming up empty-handed.

Romano's phone rang.

"*Buongiorno*, Dottore. This is Carmela Peluso, Cavalier Borrelli's secretary."

"*Buongiorno*, Signora. Go ahead."

"I heard from the cavalier that you're trying to track down Lena, the girl who worked here as a babysitter five years ago."

"That's right, in fact, thanks so much for the copy of the passport that you faxed us, it really is a piece of luck that you still . . ."

"Six months ago we received a phone call about her."

"You what? How . . ."

"It was a request for a reference."

"Ah, I see. And of course you don't remember . . ."

"Of course I *do* remember, perfectly. I have right here both the name and the address of the person who called. The young woman had said that she had worked here and the signora who called wanted us to confirm that. You should know that I make a habit of keeping notes on everything."

"An excellent habit. Please, tell me what you have. I'm ready to take it down."

"Lucilla Rossano, Via Giotto 22, in Vomero. The phone number is 081.241272222."

"I can't thank you enough, you've been. . ."

"It just occurred to me that, after all, the boy doesn't have anything to do with it."

"What?"

"Nothing. The cavalier is eager for news. Keep us posted. Have a good day."

Signora Lucilla Rossano was home, and she picked up on the third ring.

Once she was certain that she wasn't being audited, and after she'd been informed that she could be charged with obstruction of justice if she refused to cooperate, she willingly confirmed that Signorina Lena from time to time—that is, from time to time on a daily basis—had come to work at her home, earning six euros an hour, all in tips, of course; that Signorina Lena looked after Signora Lucilla Rossano's two children, because after all she had to go out and earn a living, that asshole ex-husband of hers, who was swimming in money but didn't pay his taxes and claimed to be penniless, hadn't been paying her alimony, hadn't been giving her a fucking red cent, sorry, eh, excuse my French, but when you've gotta say it you've gotta say it; that for the past week Signorina Lena hadn't shown up for work because she claimed she was sick, but Signora Lucilla Rossano, who was doing the best she could with her kids and her job, just assumed she'd found a better-paying job but that, since she was probably still on probation, she didn't have the nerve to tell her yet; and that now she had no idea of how to get by, with the two little demons that the asshole ex-husband had dumped on her, ruining her life.

In the end, after Romano threatened to send over a squad car to pick her up if she went off on one more tangent, Signora Lucilla Rossano answered him, in an offended tone, that as far as she knew, Signorina Lena didn't live alone; she lived with a man from back home, some guy named Dragan Petrović, who she claimed was just a roommate and not her boyfriend, at Via Torino, no. 15. They didn't have a telephone. She didn't know anything else but if they did happen to track her down, would they please ask her to get in touch by Saturday, because she,

Signora Lucilla Rossano, was supposed to meet a gentleman friend, and she needed someone to watch the two little monsters. Could they do her that favor? By the way, Signora, Romano asked her: What color hair did she have, this Signorina Lena? Ah, believe me, I told her the same thing. You looked so good with your original color, that nice dark red. Did you really have to dye your hair blond so you look just like a hooker?

The confirmation of Peluso's tip reinvigorated the investigation. Palma got on the phone and asked headquarters for two more squad cars, one to send to Via Torino 15 and the other to send to the station house, so that they could be ready if it proved necessary to move quickly on multiple fronts. Then he called Piras and brought her up to speed.

The magistrate wasn't on duty, but her calls were being forwarded to her cell phone, and he found her wide-awake and alert. She asked questions about every detail, made a note of the names she wanted to plug into the databases at the district attorney's office, and tried to focus on the situation at hand. "Palma," she said, "I don't believe that this Madlena Miroslava just woke up one day, after five years, dyed her hair, and made up her mind to kidnap a little boy she used to take care of. The more I think about it, the more I feel sure that the whole thing was orchestrated by someone in the family, the extended family, shall we say, and that this person was also responsible for writing the notes. We just have to figure out who that is. Now I've got to go, but I'll swing by to see you later."

When the commissario walked back into the bullpen, Romano was barking the address to the squad car, which was already rolling, while Pisanelli did his best to calm Eva down; the woman, informed by her father of Lena's possible involvement, had immediately called in. How could we have failed to think of it? she kept saying over and over again. The hair color, that's all it took to trick us.

Ottavia, in the meantime, was trying to find anything she could on Dragan Petrović, but she'd run up against the worst obstacle in online searches: too many hits.

"Dammit, this is like trying to find Mario Rossi, or John Smith. Does everyone in Serbia have the same name?"

The squad car radioed in, confirming that a certain Dragan Petrović did in fact live in a miserable attic apartment, dusty and drafty, at Via Torino, no. 15, and that the Dragan Petrović in question also had a roommate, a certain Lena, once a redhead and now a blonde, the object of the lustful concierge's frustrated courtship—or so the uniformed policeman had deduced from the dreamy voice in which said concierge had described her. Unfortunately, however, neither Petrović nor the woman was at home. They hadn't been seen in a week; they'd left with a large duffle bag saying they were going on vacation. As far as could be determined, they didn't possess an automobile.

Romano told the officer to ask the concierge if he knew anything else about the man. Where did he work? What did he do for a living?

He waited a few minutes, then the officer came back on and said: "He used to be a menial laborer with a full-time job at the Intrasit plant, that's how he was able to rent the apartment: The landlord only take tenants with steady jobs. Then last year Intrasit went out of business and he found a number of odd jobs—street vendor, construction worker—but basically, according to the concierge, he lives off his girlfriend, who cleans houses in the better part of town."

Romano passed the information on to Ottavia, who plugged it into her search engine.

"Here we go. There's a Petrović, D. in the list of those laid off by Intrasit and taking unemployment. We could do some digging over at the courts; maybe there's more information about him in the accounting ledgers of the receivership administrator."

Palma was disconsolate: "I doubt there's anything there; at the very most we'll get a copy of an ID. Let's send it over to Piras and start the request working, but I doubt it'll get us much. I wonder where the two of them could be hiding."

"Maybe they rented a car," Pisanelli said, "or borrowed one."

Aragona made a face: "I very much doubt they took the subway to kidnap a child."

That was when Romano piped up: "A couple of gypsies," he said. "A couple of piece of shit gypsies."

LVII

Ask any cop. Any cop you can think of.

He'll tell you that when the chain of associations finally clicks, it's like a fireworks display at midnight in the summer.

That it's absolute perfection, like squaring the circle.

That it's spectacular, because every tile in the mosaic is suddenly in just the right place; images match words and everything is explained; the mess disappears and suddenly nothing is ambiguous.

He'll you that it's like trying to put together a jigsaw puzzle. And the things that made no sense just a second ago now fit together perfectly.

He'll tell you, any cop will, that these are the moments that made him choose this damn profession in the first place, this job that is all miles, dust, blood, and humiliation, all dodged bullets and doors slammed in your face and being made to look like a fool.

He'll tell you that that fantastic, wonderful sensation is a shaft of light that shoots into the room and dispels the darkness.

Corporal Marco Aragona opened his mouth, shut it, and then reopened it. Then he took off his glasses, pausing mid-sweep, the gesture that had by now become his trademark—but only for an instant; then he set them down, his hand shaking, on the desktop.

Something singular was taking place in his mind, something

out of a scene in a sci-fi movie where, by some kind of techno-logical magic, a vast number of perfectly ordinary, innocuous objects suddenly assemble themselves into a deadly weapon at the hero's disposal.

No one even noticed the expression on his face until he emitted a kind of strangled shout in Romano's direction, inter-rupting Palma, who was speculating on where the kidnappers might be hiding.

"What did you just say?"

Everyone turned to look at him. Romano stared at him in surprise: "I don't understand what . . ."

Aragona had leapt to his feet.

"What you just said, say it again!"

"Aragona, what the hell . . ."

"What did you call them? What did you call that Miro-whatever, what's-her-name, and the guy who's with her, Dragović?"

Mechanically, Ottavia corrected him: "Madlena Miroslava and Dragan Petro . . ."

"Goddamn it, answer me!"

"I called them gypsies . . . Listen, Aragona, if there's anyone around here who's in no position to preach about that kind of thing it seems to me that . . ."

Aragona wasn't listening to him anymore. His mind was wandering back to the roof garden of the Hotel Mediterraneo, where a little pest of a boy had called an angel come down from heaven a gypsy, planting in Aragona's brain the seed of a hunch that had finally sprouted.

He noisily sucked in a mouthful of air: He'd forgotten to breathe. Then he seemed to freeze, his expression one of terri-ble, bottomless sorrow and, in a very low voice, he whispered: "He was the one who set the whole thing up. Oh my God, I can't believe it. And he even told us so: last night."

Corporal Marco Aragona's metamorphosis was such that

for one long moment no one had the courage to ask him what the hell he was talking about.

Then Romano stammered: "No . . . that can't be it, you must be wrong . . . It just can't be . . ."

Palma was about to shout at them both to explain what they were talking about when Lojacono and Di Nardo came rushing in with a stack of bank checks in their hands.

"Boss," the lieutenant said, "there's something you need to see. There's something you all need to see."

LVIII

The three of them went over. Not only Romano and Aragona; this time Palma insisted on being there, too.

He didn't do this often; in fact, ever since he'd become the chief of the precinct he'd made it a rule never to let his personal presence cast a shadow over whoever had been in charge of the investigation from the beginning. He'd come up through the ranks and he knew just how exhausting that profession could be: hour after hour spent on stakeouts, tailing suspects, interrogations, questions that went unanswered, dead ends, conflicting emotions, things that didn't add up, illusory solutions that went up in a puff of smoke like a cloud on a hot summer day.

That's why it had always struck him as unfair that precinct captains stole their men's thunder in order to soak up the final applause, the photo op, the interview. Palma preferred to hang back because he knew very well that behind every triumph there was always teamwork, and because he also knew that it wasn't a genuine success, that there was no real victory in bringing to light the rot that lurks in the souls of men.

This time, though, he'd impulsively grabbed his jacket and hurried out with his two men. He didn't want them to be alone; he wanted to protect them from the grief. He wanted to be there with them when they were forced to confront that awful, excruciating moment.

There was something surreal about the atmosphere that had settled over Pizzofalcone's communal office in the wake of

Aragona's hunch and the unbelievable corroboration Lojacono and Di Nardo had unexpectedly provided. Silence, horror, then a strange, disheartened melancholy, as if the darkness of the abyss where evil lurks had suddenly been enriched by a new, painful nuance.

Pisanelli had done his best: "Look, this isn't proof. A phrase, a misguided comment, for all we know uttered without thinking, certainly doesn't . . . I don't believe it. I just don't believe it. And then this other stuff, these checks . . . in and of themselves they don't mean a thing. Sometimes the banks just shut off the taps and then businessmen turn to these alternative forms of financing. I've seen things like this happen. No, I don't believe it. Of course you can speculate, but to go from speculation to saying that . . . You'll see, it'll turn out to be something else entirely."

Lojacono had nodded, tumbling the checks out onto the table: "Maybe you're right. In other words, this is a lot of money right here, quite a lot, but still it strikes me as unthinkable."

Ottavia was staring straight ahead, at nothing in particular: "No, no, listen to me. There has to be some other explanation. I can't believe it."

Aragona, who hadn't said a thing since he'd dropped the bomb, who had just been sitting there, eyes wide open, mumbling incomprehensible words as if praying, leapt to his feet: "Let's stop wasting time. We need to go get this bastard and make him tell us where the fuck they're keeping the kid. Don't you see that it all adds up? Do I have to draw you a map? I'm a damn fool, I should have figured it out right away."

Palma, too, could feel the frenzy mounting within, and he'd said: "Let's go. We need to check it out, so let's get going. Dottoressa Piras is coming here: Lojacono, you explain everything and tell her to wait for us. We'll report back."

Romano was already galloping down the stairs; he was still as pale as he'd been after his run-in with Giorgia.

On the way over, they hadn't spoken a word to one another. And anyway, what did they have to say? The only thing left was to get to the bottom of this thing, ask for an explanation of this series of coincidences.

The unmarked car was parked on the opposite side of the street with an unobstructed view of the building's entrance: The luminous vista out over the bay seemed even more enchanting on that bright May morning.

Palma greeted the officers on duty.

"Has anyone come in or left since the last report?"

"No, Dottore. No activity. They haven't even rolled up the blinds this morning."

"Good. Keep your eyes open."

They climbed the two flights of stairs in silence. But the building, far from traffic and surrounded by greenery, was so silent it seemed abandoned. From one of the apartment doors on the first landing came the short wail of a very young child; The sound pierced Palma's heart.

They rang the doorbell once, twice. They exchanged a worried glance. They knocked.

While Romano was asking the commissario whether it wasn't time to kick the door down, the door swung open.

And if they'd had any doubts, the face they saw now in front of them dispelled those doubts then and there.

In the dank, shadowy apartment, reeking of stale food and alcohol, a shambling, tottering silhouette stared at them for a long while, as if he didn't recognize them.

Then he turned on his heel without a word and went back inside.

The person that the three policemen were looking for was the man before them, Alberto Cerchia, Dodo's father.

LIX

What a mess, eh? Yeah. A real mess.

Forgive me if I receive you surrounded by shit. Then again, it strikes me as appropriate, because I've been in deep shit for a while now. For such a long time; you can't even imagine.

I'm tired. I'm going to pieces, really. You can see, I drink. I've always been a drinker when times were tough: I lose my senses, my mind gets free of its chains, and I start to fly somewhere else, far from problems that have no solution.

I was expecting you, yes. I guess I really should have come to you. But as long as there was hope that we might come out of this in one piece, it was my duty to wait, don't you think?

I'm not just responsible for myself, you know. I have a son. I have a little man who's going to grow up and when he does, he'll ask me to explain what I'm leaving him and why. It's not like I'm alone in the world. Do you have children of your own? You don't, do you? Then you couldn't understand.

The checks. Where did you find them? Unbelievable, the way things come around. They're for three million eight hundred thousand, those checks. And that's not all of them; there are others out there, in other people's hands. The signature is the same on them all, the signature that you read to your great surprise on the drafts: Cerchia SpA, Chief Administrator. In capital letters.

You talk about the economic crisis, what a nice big mouthful of a term: economic crisis. But you can't even begin to imagine what an economic crisis really is, since you all collect your miserable little salaries at the end of the month anyway; at worst you'll have to do without your usual week at the beach, or maybe you'll be forced to miss an installment on your mortgage. If it took the rest of your life, you wouldn't be able to understand what an economic crisis really means, for someone like me. If you count the salesmen I have more than five hundred employees here, and another three hundred in the other plant, outside of the country. I'm responsible for the livelihood of thousands of people. And I haven't gotten a good night's sleep in three years. I'm too busy searching for solutions I don't have.

Because it starts so slowly that you don't even notice it happening. People who owe you money drag out the payments, people you owe money to are asking for payments early; the price of raw materials goes up, but only a little, and the price of the product you sell has to drop if you want to keep selling, but only by a little. And the next thing you know, you need a line of credit. Just a small one.

Then the situation gets out of hand, but it takes months before you realize. Months. And by then it's too late. The bank officers, who used to line up outside your office, stop taking your calls. And after a while they start lining up outside your office again, but for a different reason.

Then there's them.

They don't try to collect their debts with notarized forms and certified letters, you know. They come and get you, and you're there one day, gone the next, because there's only one thing they can't afford: for word to get out that somebody got away with not paying.

Hunt them down, instead of hunting down good people. Wipe them off the face of the earth, and free us of the temptation to go to them. Because after the first time, you can't stop. It's worse than cocaine. Worse than alcohol. Worse than anything.

Hope. What screws you is hope. The damn hope that keeps making you think you can get out quick, that everything is going to get back on track, the way it was before.

My father-in-law was a loan shark his whole life. They call it finance; but it's the same thing. When I thought of this idea, I convinced myself that, in a way, I'd be seeing that justice was done, forcing them to give back their ill-gotten gains. A fucking Robin Hood, that's what I felt like. I thought to myself: It'll take me a couple of days and then I'll take care of everything. I couldn't see any other solutions. Do you think that if I'd had another way, any other way at all, to get out of the bind I was in, I would have gotten myself mixed up in this? No, I wouldn't have. I'd never have done this.

My father-in-law, you see, ruined my life.

Maybe I should say that my wife ruined it, even if I think it was really him. Because she's like him, she has the same horrible personality, the same bitchy attitudes, and she's also shallow and stupid. Marry a girl from home, the saying goes, your wives and your oxen should come from your own hometown; I should have listened to the proverb.

But she was pretty, and she was the daughter of a famous tycoon. It seemed like the right move on my way up the mountain. Instead, in order to try to keep up, to rise to her level, I just kept trying to grow, grow, grow, making investments, buying land. Growing, even when the right thing to do was stop. I should have known, but there he was, always bigger than me, always stronger, and we'd even given my son his name.

My son.

I love him, you know that? I love him more than anything else. I love him so much it kills me.

So why did I do this? I know that's what you're wondering, and from your petty perspectives as wage earners, it's incomprehensible. But I did it because it was the only way. Believe me, if I'd gone to him and told him, old man, listen to me, I'm flat on my ass, old man, help me, do you think he would have lifted a finger? Do you think that when that whore of a daughter of his brought her lover home and kicked me out of the house, sent me far away from my son, he stood up for me? No, he did not.

The old man only has one weakness. For my little boy.

He's my weakness, too, you know. Wasn't it for him that I was trying to get back on my feet? Isn't it him, his estate, his future that I was trying to rescue? I'm his hero, you know. His great hero. We always say to each other that I'm his giant, and he's my little king.

It seemed fair for him to pitch in. For him to do his part. It wouldn't last long, just a couple of days at the most. I got in touch with his old babysitter, a smart girl, smart and tough. I explained, I told her what I needed; there was a guy, a man from back home, who could help her. I promised her money, airplane tickets, new IDs, a new life. Aren't we all looking for that, for a new life? Don't we all want a chance to start over? Maybe that's what the economic crisis really means. A change. Not enough money, and the need for a change.

I told him, I told Dodo. I told him Lena would come by to pick him up, and that he should go with her. He was to tell no one, before or after, otherwise they'd get mad at me, at his papà. My little man knows how to keep a secret, you know. He's a smart boy. Then I promised him that right afterward I'd come get him. It was going to be a way to get him to come stay with me for good. No one would be able to separate us again after that.

I prepared for it. I planned it out. I knew our assets would be immediately frozen: It wouldn't seem strange that I was unable to pay the ransom. I also knew that when they froze our accounts, they wouldn't check into the size of them, so no one would notice that there was nothing in there to freeze, neither in my personal nor in my corporate accounts.

I decided that it wouldn't seem so strange if they demanded a ransom from the old man. He's still famous in this fucked-up city, fucked-up person that he is. I planned it out. I prepared for it.

I gave Lena a phone and a piece of paper with what needed to be said in the phone calls. I told her she shouldn't do the talking, that someone might recognize her voice; to pretend that she'd been kidnapped with Dodo, so he wouldn't be afraid. I think about him, you know, about my son. I'm his father, I have to think about him.

We came up with a schedule, Lena's guy and me. A big brainless beast of a man. I was supposed to call him at preestablished intervals to make sure everything was going according to plan.

I fucked up, though: The phone I gave Lena, the one I was calling them on, is in my company's name. So when you told me about the wiretaps I lost it.

You see, I'm not a fool. I know perfectly well that you don't have anything solid on me. Just a few postdated checks, a series of clues that, unless you catch Lena, you can't prove. It wouldn't have made any sense for me to spill everything. I'm not a fool.

It's just that, listen, I have a problem. A problem that I'm sure you can help me solve.

They're not answering their phone anymore. I'm a day behind according to the schedule we'd agreed on, and I called the minute I saw you arrive, from behind the shutter. I understood that it didn't make sense to worry about wiretaps anymore. I wanted to tell them to run away and just leave Dodo there so I could go and get him: I promised him I'd come.

But now they're not answering anymore, and I don't know why.

And I need to know where the fuck they're holding Dodo. Because just to be safe, I made sure they never told me: You never know, I might have blurted something out by mistake.

So, please, can you help me?

Can you take me to my little boy?

LX

F ast.
    They'd have to move fast, and get nothing wrong.
    This is sheer madness, thought Palma, for days all we've been doing is waiting around, waiting for a phone call or a message, and now we're in a frenzied race against time.

At first, the three policemen had stood there silently listening to Cerchia's confession, practically hypnotized by the man's flat, drunken tone of voice, wrecked as he was by lack of sleep, too much alcohol, and the ravages of guilt. It was a curious coincidence, the commissario had thought to himself, that the three of them, who were childless, had been the ones to witness the abyss of darkness that this father's soul had become.

Then they'd reacted differently. Romano had shaken himself out of his trance and, with a roar, had lunged at him, bellowing in blind rage and shaking Cerchia like a rag doll. The man hadn't even changed expression; he just kept weeping and telling them to bring him his son. Aragona and Palma had struggled to pry him out of Romano's hands.

Palma got on his cell phone and called Laura. He needed a cell phone locator, and he needed it as quickly as possible. It was no simple matter: The device was an expensive one and it was always either out of order or being used by the intelligence services.

Piras, who was at the precinct awaiting news, sprung into action: In less than fifteen minutes, an operator and the machine, a sort of portable computer, arrived aboard a light-blue van.

Palma, Romano, and Aragona climbed aboard, dragging

along a sack-like Alberto Cerchia; they ordered the driver to go as fast as possible, and had the squad car that had just pulled up go ahead of them, to clear the road. The operator had briefly explained that the location device could trace a phone only if it was being used, which meant that at one-minute intervals it was necessary to call the number they were looking for and let it ring.

Romano, his expression grim, told Cerchia that he'd better be praying that the kidnappers' cell phone battery wasn't dead.

Aragona made it his job to push the redial button so that the location device could do its work. Palma was constantly updating Piras, whose anxiety was spreading through the entire communal office.

They sailed through the city, sirens wailing, trailed by the resentful glances of pedestrians who had been forced out of the way. Downtown. The outskirts. A small town. Another one.

"Where the fuck are they?" Romano was asking through clenched teeth.

"Of course!" Aragona exclaimed. "Intrasit. The abandoned Intrasit plant. Isn't that where the asshole used to work?"

Palma was ever more impressed with how shrewd the young officer was demonstrating himself to be, and he told the driver to go even faster and to head for the industrial district. The operator confirmed that that was in fact the right area.

In time, Palma prayed, addressing a god he'd until then completely forgotten. Let us get there in time. He's so small, he's only ten years old. Let us get there in time. Dodo's face appeared before his eyes, in black and white, turned up to look at the security camera. Let us get there in time, Palma prayed.

Aragona kept on calling, but there was still no reply. The operator on the computer said: "We're there, it's right around here. Within four hundred yards."

In front of them was a sign, which had been damaged in a hailstorm of stones thrown by newly unemployed workers after they'd been laid off a year earlier: "Intrasit."

LXI

Piras, on the phone, was saying nothing.

Her face was white; the extreme stress had hardened her lovely features; her lips were pressed tight. At regular intervals she repeated: "Well? Well?"

The bullpen was immersed in a despairing silence. From time to time a jumble of sounds from the city below came in through the half-open window. A car horn, a siren. A song sung in a loud voice by who knew who.

Ottavia was weeping tearlessly. She was weeping for lost love, for damned souls, for blameless children. She was weeping for Dodo, she was weeping for herself.

Pisanelli had covered his face with his hands, as if he couldn't stand to look. Alex was standing, arms folded over her chest, eyes on the window; she was turning her back on it all, giving up.

Lojacono, his heart in his mouth, hadn't taken his eyes off Piras's face, hoping it would spread into a smile. He couldn't remember ever having wanted to see a smile so badly.

Behind him, just outside the door, Guida stood motionless; his eyelids refused to blink, his lips murmured an age-old prayer over and over.

Let him be safe. Only You can help him.

Guns drawn, they burst into the old factory that had been plundered by thieves and vandals, their eyes darting into shadowy corners.

Silence. A couple of cats took to their heels, abandoning the scraps of a torn paper bag containing some leftover food.

Romano was holding Cerchia by the arm. Aragona pushed the redial button one last time, and from some point inside a low building they heard a ringing in response.

They rushed into the building, abandoning all caution. Palma's heart was in his throat; anxiety swelled in his chest with every step. He and Aragona found themselves in a room that had once been an office.

A table, two chairs. An electric heater, a gas hot plate. A blanket, two dirty plates, utensils. At the center of the table, a cell phone was vibrating and ringing.

They stood there motionless, their guns in their hands, their arms hanging at their sides.

From the side opposite from where they'd entered came a scream. Palma would long remember, in sleepless nights, the irrevocable heartbreak that pierced him at the sound. There would be no more life, after that scream. No more hope.

A door opened out onto a good-sized storeroom with a sheet-metal wall, shrouded in darkness. A profound darkness, a bottomless darkness. Darkness.

Cerchia lay curled up on the floor; Romano stood a few feet away, ashen-faced.

Dodo's father was clutching a blanket and sobbing: He had something in his hand.

Palma took a step closer, just one step, because he knew he couldn't go any further into the abyss; he let his eyes get accustomed to the lack of light, and then he saw what it was.

An action figure.

A dirty superhero, with a torn cape.

Just a plastic action figure.

Batman. Batman.
I'm so sorry, Batman. I promised you I'd never leave you behind.

That we'd never be separated.

But I have to do it, because when my papà sees you, he'll understand.

He'll understand that I'm waiting for him, and he'll come looking for me, and he'll find me.

You can tell him so, Batman, you can explain it to him.

Say hi to him and give him a hug for me, tell him I love him more than the moon and the stars, that I'm counting on him. That I know he'll come get me, and that then we'll be together, forever.

Because he's the only one who's my giant.

And I'm his little king.

ACKNOWLEDGMENTS

The Bastards, as you know, are a team. No one comes first, and no one comes last. That's the way a team works; that's the way a team has to work.

And so there are three teams that the Bastards must thank for this story about them.

The first is the team that fights crime every day, in this strange, absurd, beautiful city. Dottoressa Simona Di Monte, magistrate; my friend Luigi Merolla, chief of police. And Fabiola Mancone, Valeria Moffa, Gigi Bonagura, and Stefano Napolitano, on the street and in the labs, in the offices and at the computers, fighting for all those who wish to live honest lives.

The second team is made up of those who work on the stories and the pages, pouring in their hearts and souls: Severino Cesari, Francesco Colombo, Valentina Pattavina, Paolo Repetti, and Paola Novarese, in my words and in each character much more than you'd ever imagine.

Last of all, the team that's closest to my heart: the Corpi Freddi. To invent this and other stories, as if they were true.

Even more than if they were true.

2